An Invitation to Die

Also by Tanushree Podder

A Closetful of Skeletons
Before You Breathe

An Invitation to Die

Tanushree Podder

HARPER
BLACK

First published in India by Harper Black 2021
An imprint of HarperCollins *Publishers*

HarperCollins *Publishers* India, Cyber City, Building 10-A, Gurugram,
Haryana – 122002, India
www.harpercollins.co.in

2 4 6 8 10 9 7 5 3 1

Typeset in 10.5/13 Adobe Caslon Pro at
Manipal Technologies Limited, Manipal

HarperCollins *Publishers*, Macken House, 39/40 Mayor Street Upper,
Dublin 1, D01 C9W8, Ireland

For Ajoy,
the rainbow in my sky

Prologue

'How can a van go missing? It's not a sock, a stray pen or a piece of jewellery to disappear without anyone noticing!' Violet's voice was shrill with annoyance. It was the morning after the party, and they were at the breakfast table. Having overslept, they faced each other across the table at 9 a.m. 'It couldn't have driven off by itself, could it? And why didn't you call the police when you realized it was nowhere to be found?'

'I assumed you had driven the van home,' Pia explained patiently. 'It was only after I reached home and didn't find it parked in the porch that I realized something was wrong. It was too late to wake you up or call the police. Besides, I was too exhausted to do anything.'

'Didn't you lock the van?' demanded the elderly lady, her eyes blazing. 'You are too careless for your own good.' Saying this, she shook a finger at her granddaughter for a moment, the arthritic pain forgotten. And then she winced as pain shot through her broken wrist.

Things had spiralled out of control when Pia had walked out after the rambunctious party the previous night. The van had disappeared from its parking spot.

'Unfortunately, I didn't. Ramsar is such a safe place that I never lock the van.' Pia hung her head sheepishly as she toyed with her breakfast. 'I am sorry, Gumma. It was careless of me.'

'Was it on handbrake or did you forget to put on the brake?' Violet shook a finger again and winced. It was a week since she'd fallen, but the wrist was yet to heal.

'Of course I didn't,' retorted the young girl. 'I haven't forgotten the basics of hill-driving.'

'I have been using that tin box for decades and never have I forgotten to lock the van. You use it for one day and look what happens,' Violet continued to vent her ire.

'Gumma, please stop shouting. Your blood pressure will shoot up. How many times do I have to say that I am sorry?'

'Well, don't just sit there and apologize. Call your young man and report the theft.'

'My young man?' Pia raised her left eyebrow enquiringly. 'Who's that now?'

'I meant Timothy Thapa, the police officer.'

'For God's sake, Tim's the assistant superintendent of police. He isn't my young man,' grumbled the granddaughter as she scrolled through the contact list on her phone. She dialled, but the number was busy.

'Go to the police station and meet him,' ordered Violet. 'It will do you good to take a walk.'

'You forget that I have a café to run. I can't be walking to the police station when I have work to do,' objected Pia, running out of patience. 'I will try his number a few minutes later.'

A little later, just as she was finishing her coffee, Pia's phone rang. Glancing at the caller's name, she picked up and said, 'Hi, Tim.'

Violet perked up her ears to catch the conversation. Whatever the police officer was saying seemed to stun the granddaughter.

'What are you saying, Tim?' Pia asked in a horrified voice. The girl's face had taken on an ashen hue. 'You found a dead body in my van? That's impossible!'

1

Rhododendron Cottage, retired Judge Jawahar Joshi's humble abode, was the favourite watering hole of the three men who were now seated around a table. The cottage was centrally located, which made it an ideal meeting point. It also had the largest lawn and the best-kept garden. The toppings, of course, were the judge and his wife, Geeta. Jawahar Joshi, aka JJ or Judge Sa'ab, was an affable man whose love for cards exceeded his love for an evening walk, and Geeta was the mother hen of the town, fanning out her wings to shelter hungry and weary souls.

The four bridge players, having finished one round of the card game, embarked on a discussion about Violet Williams and her family.

The bridge partners lived very close to the judge's cottage, on Oak Street, which led to a tiny temple perched atop a hill. The street boasted a potpourri of colonial bungalows with ornate wrought-iron gates and windowsills concealed behind a riot of shrubbery. They made a lovely picture. The street meandered in an unruly manner with houses lined on both sides. The one redeeming feature was the luxuriant flowering vines that hung over the fences and covered the exteriors, and also encircled the trees and lampposts, adding a riot of colours to the street.

'Violet's son is a rascal,' remarked Sunil Rawat, the widow's family physician, who had joined the card players after checking on the old lady. Rawat was a confirmed bachelor and the youngest in the group. 'He expressed no concern when I called to inform him of his mother's condition. The poor lady is suffering from osteoporosis and has broken her wrist. The least he could do is speak to her on the phone.'

Like in most small towns, the rumour mills of Ramsar constantly churned out gossip. Nothing was secret and everyone's life was an open book, to be read by the town's denizens.

Violet Williams, the Anglo-Indian widow of a British army officer, had settled in Ramsar after her husband's demise. After the country attained independence, most of the Anglo-Indians left the country, but Violet refused to go anywhere. Left alone after her only son, Derek, went away to Australia to study, she lived in the hope that he would return one day. That was not to be. He took up a job there, met an Australian girl at university and married her.

Derek's wife visited India once and hated the country, complaining about the dirt, noise and crowd. That was over twenty years ago, when Pia was three years old. Not just India, Adrianne found Violet quite tiresome and decided never to return to Ramsar. Hurt by her son's indifference, Violet refused to visit them in Melbourne. She now lived alone in a beautiful cottage surrounded by trees and a few good friends.

'What did he say when you informed him of Violet's condition?' asked Anil Uniyal, popping a piece of fried papad into his cavernous mouth.

A retired professor with a roving eye, Uniyal lived in a quaint bungalow across the street. Three years ago, the professor and his wife had given up their teaching jobs in Dehradun and arrived in Ramsar to live a relaxed life.

'As usual, he gave some stupid excuse for not being able to visit her,' replied Rawat. 'Either his boss does not grant him leave or he is unwell.'

'By opting to stay with her, Violet's granddaughter more than made up for the son's apathy.' The judge switched his attention to the cards lying on the table. 'Now that we are done with the discussion about Violet and her granddaughter, shall we get on with the game?' he asked.

'I will deal the cards,' saying which the professor picked up the cards and began shuffling them while the doctor continued the conversation.

'I don't think anyone expected Pia to come to Ramsar.'

'One thing is for sure—no one in Ramsar expected her to open a café here. I am glad she did, though. Pia makes the best coffee in a hundred-kilometre radius,' added the colonel, smacking his lips.

'I hope it is only the coffee that directs your feet to the café,' bantered the professor, distributing the cards.

'Shh! Are you planning to send me into the doghouse?' The colonel chuckled and glanced towards his wife, who was following the discussion.

Only twice in his life had Arjun H. Acharya, a retired colonel from the army, broken the rules. The first time was when he married a Muslim girl, defying family objections, and the second was when he went against his commanding officer's order and challenged a couple of militants single-handed. They expunged the second act from the records after he returned victorious, though grievously injured.

'Really, Arjun!' admonished Laila, the colonel's plump and pretty half. 'After thirty years of marriage…'

'Darling, let me confess. Much as I would love to flirt with a girl my daughter's age, I wouldn't risk my bones to do so.' Her husband chuckled. Winking at his wife, he said, 'Old bones don't heal well. You can ask the doc if you don't believe me.'

'Shut up!' Laila rolled her eyes. 'Do you think the girl is likely to stay here for a while? I am surprised she's been here so long. One would assume Ramsar's too dull a place for her.'

'According to Violet, her granddaughter was planning to stay for a year at least,' informed the doctor. 'I like the girl. She is chirpy and helpful. My patient's temper has improved after her arrival.' Violet was famous for speaking her mind without mincing words.

Ramsar was a haven for retirees. Dotted with red-roofed bungalows, rhododendrons, oaks and cedars, and endowed with an uninterrupted view of the magnificent mountains in the north, the town was picture-perfect. Life in the tiny town was laid-back and serene. The scenic beauty and bracing air were a big blessing. Most of the inhabitants had found like-minded friends and formed groups, which acted as a support system and diversion. Some, like the one at Rhodo Cottage, were engaged in pursuing social work. The judge doled out free legal advice, the professor taught the poor, the colonel contributed his mite to keeping crimes at bay, and the doctor attended a charitable clinic. Evenings were reserved for card games and socializing.

The discussion was gathering momentum when Tim sauntered in with his dog.

'Any guesses where I was this morning?' he announced, walking towards the kitchen. 'But first, let me find something for Dim. He's hungry.'

'In bed, I am sure,' responded his uncle, JJ. 'With Dim for company.'

'I wish he would find a better bedmate,' muttered Geeta, Tim's aunt. She had been badgering him to find a wife, much to the young man's annoyance. Footloose and fancy-free, that's how he liked to lead his life.

'He's a worthless fellow! I guess you will have to do the bride-hunting for your nephew.' The judge nudged his wife.

'I was at Pia's Peaberry this morning. It's a delightful place. I don't know why I hadn't thought of going there earlier!' Tim's disembodied voice floated from the kitchen as he rummaged through the refrigerator for titbits.

Just that morning, while walking his obese Labrador, the police officer had visited the café that had become the talk of the town. It had been a pleasant visit, with a cup of steaming cappuccino in the company of the charming young owner. They had chatted like old friends, and he found himself enchanted by the bubbly and beautiful girl.

'I am sure you found the owner more delightful than the fare,' quipped the judge.

'Did you say something?' Tim stuck his head out of the refrigerator.

'I just asked how was the coffee?' The judge chuckled.

'It was fantastic. The pancakes were delicious too.' Tim spooned a generous amount of chicken biryani on a plate and microwaved it for a few minutes before emerging from the kitchen. 'Pia is quite good at making both.'

'I am sure she is,' said Geeta. 'Didn't you find anything for your fat dog at the café? Now that you have found a place to hang out, I hope the two of you will not raid my refrigerator.'

'No such luck, dear aunt. You still occupy the position of numero uno chef of Ramsar. By the way, Dim is feeling ravenous. Do you have a chicken leg for him?' Tim asked.

'I don't stock chicken legs for your dog,' she retorted. 'All I can give him is bread.'

'Dim will be rather disappointed if you do that.' Her nephew grinned, throwing a half-eaten chicken leg at the dog. 'Can't you give him something he can enjoy?'

'Didn't you say that you had coffee and pancakes at Pia's café?' Geeta asked her nephew. 'So why are you raiding my refrigerator?'

'You can't grudge me a few bites of the leftover stuff. Don't forget I am your biggest admirer in town,' Tim informed her.

Rolling her eyes, his aunt walked to the kitchen, followed dutifully by the dog.

'Pia was telling me she was planning to stay here for at least a year or more,' Tim said, settling on the sofa. 'This is delicious,' he remarked, continuing to eat.

2

On Pinewood Street, a myopic woman parted her window curtains and peeped at the two arguing men who stood at the gate of Negi Mansion, the imposing building across the street. Her house was the last one on the eastern side of the street that veered to the left to join the wider Laburnum Street. From the distance, the arguing men appeared unrecognizable to the woman.

It was 2 in the afternoon and, having finished her lunch, she was lolling on the chair near the window of her bedroom when she heard the men quarrelling.

Well known as the nosiest woman in town, Laxmi Badola liked to be on top of things, pleasant as well as unpleasant. Arguments, estrangements, brawls were of special interest to her and, in the past forty-five years, she had made it her business to dig into the private lives of the locals. A widow and a busybody, she was the originator of gossip in Ramsar and nothing escaped her keen ears and watchful eyes.

Laxmi, who had come to Ramsar after marriage, knew everyone in town. Negi Mansion held an added attraction for her. At one time, she had nursed a soft corner for Major Ratan Negi, the suave and dashing officer who inherited the house from his father. The rambling house lay gathering cobwebs and dust as long as the man served in the army. The officer found the mansion a burden to maintain.

A confirmed bachelor with no hobbies, Negi found time hanging heavily on his hands after retiring from the army. He had no inclination to spend his life in the huge house, so he booked a modest apartment in Kathgodam, which was a four-hour drive from Ramsar. The apartment was close enough to spend a few days at Negi Mansion whenever the mood struck him. At the same time, Kathgodam was the railhead that offered a convenient connection to New Delhi.

His visits that used to take place once a month soon petered out to once in six months and then once every eight or nine months till the medical problems took over. The mansion, which was already in a state of disrepair, now wore a desolate air.

Unfortunately, the man was too fond of drink. Ratan Negi died of excessive drinking, his liver giving up on him. He died at the military hospital, unloved and alone.

With him dead, the sprawling mansion began crumbling like old bread. Like a doddering old man, it shivered through the frosty nights, waiting for a bright sun to arrive so the rays could warm its worn-out walls. With its bricks beginning to show under the peeling plaster, the garden overgrown with weeds, the gate creaking on rusted hinges, it was a creepy place. And one fine day, ten months after Ratan Negi's death, his widowed sister, Sita Gudyal, and her son, Umesh, came to live in the mansion.

Either they lacked the money to renovate the house, or they had no wish to spend any on repairs. The duo did up a few rooms for comfortable living and locked up the rest of the house.

Curiosity got the better of Laxmi. Carrying a bowl of thechwani, the woman had called upon the newcomers at the mansion. A strong smell of cigarettes hung inside the house. It permeated the worn curtains and upholstery, making her feel nauseous. The son was a chain-smoker, she learnt within the first five minutes of her visit.

Laxmi's overture was firmly rejected by the surly sister, who made it clear that she was not looking for company. The son, a shifty-eyed fellow, turned out to be equally rude.

'Thank you for bringing food, but my son doesn't enjoy Kumaoni cuisine,' said Sita, nevertheless accepting the bowls offered by Laxmi.

While the woman emptied the bowls in the kitchen, Laxmi looked around the sparsely furnished hall, which needed a coat of paint. It was a cold and forbidding place with grim memories. Involuntarily, the woman shivered.

'I am sure it is haunted,' she went on to tell people later. 'I could feel an eerie presence.'

The same evening, Laxmi's friends, who had gathered at her house for a session of gossip, nodded their heads with understanding. Ghosts never spared a house that lay uninhabited for a long time, they agreed. Over a period of time, all that the neighbours could glean was that the son worked as a sales officer for a company and travelled almost twenty days a month. The mother, emotionally unstable, spent much of her time cleaning the place.

Two years had passed since the mother and son arrived. In those two years, they made not a single friend nor visited anyone in the neighbourhood.

Cursing her short-sightedness, Laxmi Badola returned with a pair of spectacles, which she had placed on top of the refrigerator while working in the kitchen. Now, armed with her glasses, she looked at the duo, recognizing one of them as Umesh Gudyal, the ill-mannered nephew of Ratan Negi. As usual, he was smoking like a chimney.

As the woman stood peering from behind the window curtain, she noticed the other man waving his arms angrily at the mansion. Although the two were shouting at each other, she could hear only snatches of the conversation. Deciding to get to the bottom of the affair, she moved to the tiny kitchen garden, which was closer to the road. Once there, she crouched behind the lush hedge, unseen.

From her vantage position, she could hear the conversation more clearly. The wind carried the angry words of the two men, who were in an aggressive mood. It also blew away a part of the conversation. However, she had no difficulty in filling the gaps.

'I have an equal share in Uncle's property,' said the visitor standing at the gate of Negi Mansion.

'We will see about that,' replied Umesh Gudyal, towering over the stranger.

'I have written so many letters, but you have not replied to any of them.'

'I don't write letters.'

'I have sent you a few emails too. You have not responded to them either,' complained the man.

'Why should I waste my time checking emails that don't concern me?'

'So, you are bent on acting difficult, are you?' The man pointed his forefinger warningly.

'Take it whichever way you like,' said Umesh Gudyal in his usual churlish manner. 'I can't alter your opinion.'

Laxmi clicked her tongue disapprovingly. She didn't like the residents across her house. That isn't the way a person treats a visitor.

'I will sue you,' the stranger was shouting. 'I will not let you get away with this. My lawyer will get back to you.'

'Get lost!' Umesh Gudyal pushed the man away from the gate. He ground the cigarette stub under his feet. 'If I see you here again, you won't go back in one piece,' he threatened.

'And if I don't get my share in the property, you won't live to enjoy the luxury of this mansion.'

Alarmed at the violent turn their conversation was taking, Laxmi perked her ears, hoping to catch more.

'You are a bloody rogue. I will see you in court,' the man shouted as he walked away. He was short and slender with a thick mop of hair, unobtrusive enough to get lost in a crowd, Laxmi noted.

A sense of unease hit the woman as she stared at the two men.

Umesh continued to stand there, arms akimbo, watching him leave. As though sensing her presence, he narrowed his eyes and stared in her direction. Startled, she crouched lower behind the hedge. Once Umesh had disappeared inside Negi Mansion, Laxmi Badola scampered into her house.

That man is dangerous, she decided. Overwhelmed by an urge to share the incident with her friend, Laxmi threw a shawl over her shoulders and left the house through the back door. Minutes later, she was hurrying down the alley to her friend's house, her feet energized at the prospect of gossiping.

Over the last twenty months, the two women had often discussed the unfriendly Gudyals, wondering how Sita could spend the long spells of her son's absence without speaking to any of the neighbours. It was not natural, they concluded. The friends spent several hours speculating if the mansion was haunted by ghosts, and if Sita Gudyal practised witchcraft.

Urmila Thapliyal was delighted to see Laxmi at her doorstep. The day had been far too boring, with nothing much to perk her up. Her friend's arrival heralded a good gossip session. With too much time on their hands, the two widows nodded their heads frequently over hot and spicy news in town. And when there wasn't any spicy news, they invented some to make life more interesting.

Ramsar, with many of its men enrolling for the army, had a substantial number of widows. While there were old men with medals and tales of valour, there were also women shedding constant tears and narrating tales of loneliness and despair. Some widows accepted the inevitability of their husband's profession, while many wasted away in gloom. Urmila, with her sons in the army, lived life on her terms, and so did Laxmi.

The two women embraced each other warmly.

'You won't believe what happened just now,' the words tumbled out of Laxmi's mouth even before she entered the house. Breathless after the fast-paced walk, she halted meaningfully and waited for a reaction from her friend.

'Has there been an earthquake? It must have been a mild one, because I didn't feel the tremors.' Urmila's eyes twinkled with mirth. She was familiar with her friend's habit of exaggerating.

'You could call it that, but it wasn't a mild tremor. I felt the earth slipping away from under my feet.'

Laxmi loved creating suspense. She would not satisfy her friend's curiosity so easily. She held back the words that were threatening to suffocate her.

'Now, don't act pricey. What happened? Did someone get killed?'

'Someone is likely to get killed, and quite soon too.'

'I hate the way you work up my curiosity. Why can't you come to the point?'

'Well, I overheard that rogue Umesh Gudyal threatening a man.'

'Threatening? Why would he do that? And who was he threatening?'

'It was a stranger, someone I have never seen before, someone who wants a share of Ratan Negi's property.'

'Well, it doesn't surprise me. Umesh Gudyal has a violent temper, I have heard. Some time back, he bashed up a guy just because the man had urinated near Negi Mansion.' Urmila added her bit, 'What I find interesting is the way Ratan Negi's relatives keep crawling out of the woodwork. I saw none of them when he lay dying at the hospital.'

'Well, the visitor was saying something about going to court if Umesh Gudyal didn't hand over his share of the property.'

'What did Umesh have to say to that? I am sure he wouldn't hesitate to land a few blows on the guy.'

'He asked the man to get lost and threatened to break his limbs and kill him if ever he was seen in this town. Seeing the muscular and hefty Umesh staring menacingly at the short and unimpressive man, I was scared he would kill the guy,' Laxmi added her bit of spice to the story.

'Did he now?'

'Do you think I should tell the police about the conversation?'

'I don't see why you should. There has been no killing or breaking of limbs. It is just his way of ticking off the chap.'

'Umesh Gudyal meant every word. His tone was cold and menacing.' Laxmi shuddered delicately. 'Frankly, I am quite concerned.'

'Don't you worry, the two men will sort out their problems. Let me make you a nice cup of ginger tea to calm your nerves.'

Urmila waddled off to the kitchen, followed by Laxmi, who was worried about the uncouth behaviour of the Gudyals. According to her, Umesh was the most dangerous man in Ramsar.

3

While Laxmi and Urmila slurped their milky tea, a little distance away, at Elm Cottage on Ludlow Street, a group of four women chatted over tea and cakes. The women belonged to the tiny population of Anglo-Indians in Ramsar, who had resisted the call of foreign shores and chosen to live in the small hill town. Quaintly known as Firangi Colony, the place smelt of baking and roses, which grew in abundance in each cottage.

Most of the residents of the colony, where women outnumbered men, had worked in the Indian Railways, Indian Post and Telegraph, and defence services. Having retired from their careers, they now spent their twilight years in the serene town. Their needs were few and hobbies fewer. They were satisfied with good food, drinks and plenty of gossip.

There was a small but impressive church with a bell tower, the bell having long gone out of service. The cemetery behind the church, with its rows of flower beds and greenery, stood facing a mountain. It would be a nice place to rest one's body, felt the elderly residents of Firangi Colony.

The church was a place where they congregated more for social interaction than religious fervour. The preaching and sermons were incidental. The inhabitants were a jolly lot. They lived for the day, eating, drinking and enjoying a friendly game of cards or chess. Everybody knew everybody, including their birthdays and anniversaries. Every occasion was a reason to celebrate.

Most of the houses in the colony were quaint, some of them decrepit and crumbling. A few of them, which had changed hands in recent times, had gone through a renovation, upsetting the idyllic picture. They stuck out like sore thumbs, making the old residents cluck their tongues with disapproval. *Garish and incongruous* was the consensus. Happy in the company of their cats and dogs, their houses overflowing with antique furniture—grandfather clocks and rocking chairs—the residents lived in harmony.

Violet Williams was an important and active member of the community, the active part having been compromised a little in the past few months because of her tendency to break bones—her own, of course.

Presided by Violet, the four women indulged in thrice-a-week meetings. The group of septuagenarians, who lived near each other, swapped jokes, gossip and advice over a generous spread of tea, cookies and snacks. Often, they indulged in a game or two of canasta or mah-jong.

Each of the women had a distinctive style of dressing that reflected her personality. Mary was a quiet and mousy person, who preferred to dress in grey or brown tweeds; Nancy, tart as her pickles, fancied bright and lively colours and patterns and boasted a modern style of dressing. She was the fashion icon for the women of Firangi Colony. Her imaginatively designed and vividly embroidered dresses never failed to draw envious glances from the others. Claire, creative and intelligent, preferred comfort over style and stuck to practical clothes like trousers and pullovers in sedate tones. As for Violet, she loved flaunting her enviable collection of jewellery, matching them with cheerful floral dresses.

The four women, born before or at the cusp of Independence, talked fondly of the good old days, when there were parties and dances, moonlight and romance, banter and beaux, excitement and adventure.

Sharing the joys and sorrows of widowhood, plotting the downfall of unfriendly neighbours, planning fun events and celebrating every sliver of happiness that came their way formed a part of their get-togethers. Not that they wasted their time. The women lived on their tiny retirement incomes, adding to it by capitalizing on a hobby or skill.

Age had done little to rob them of vivacity or style. Mary's nimble fingers had knitted many a woollen scarf and cap, which adorned the shelves of Almora shops; Nancy's pickles and wines were a rage with the locals; Pia's café was a showcase of Violet's baked products; while Claire's short stories published in women's magazines brought her money and recognition. The four all-weather friends had stuck together through several storms.

Now, while enjoying their tea at Violet's bungalow, the women chattered about the way things were.

'These cupcakes are delicious. They are quite different from your usual ones,' commented Nancy, picking one from the tray on the elegant centre table. 'The tea is excellent, of course.'

Violet always laid a generous table, which the ladies enjoyed. They served as tasters for her innovative recipes. Her reputation as an excellent cook helped, of course. Besides, she was financially better off than her friends.

'It's the one with the ginger-lemon-almond combo,' said Violet, flicking the ash off her cigarette. Smoking was a habit shared by Pia and her grandmother, though they chided each other constantly about its ills. 'I have been experimenting with different combinations and flavours, like mint and lemon, chocolate and peanut, coconut and pineapple. Why don't you try them and let me know if they work for you?'

That morning, they were on a reminiscing trip. 'I was thirty-two when Tom bought the cottage,' recalled Mary, whose husband had worked as an engineer in the railways. 'It was meant to be a getaway during the summers, but I resented the idea. Ramsar at that time was a lonely, underdeveloped hinterland.'

'And now you love the place,' added Violet. 'I never resented nor regretted moving into this town. It is a lovely place. Besides, thanks to you, I have never felt lonely. Not even after Richard passed away and Derek deserted me.'

'I don't know how I would have survived if the three of you were not here for me,' remarked Claire. Losing her husband of forty-three years to cancer had left her broken for a while. Harry had been a jolly and flamboyant person, who had spent much of his life working with the post and telegraph department. It was the support of her friends that brought her out of depression and put her back on track once again.

'That's true!' remarked Nancy. 'Loneliness is a scourge. One can survive a disease, but not loneliness. I am glad to have you in my life. I don't think I could have survived without your support.'

'Speaking of loneliness, Violet, have you considered holding your granddaughter back?' asked Mary. The women were fond of Pia, who ran errands and entertained them with stories of her life in Australia. With their children having flown the coop, the women enjoyed the company of the young girl.

'I shall certainly miss Pia when she leaves. You are here for me, but having a young person at home is rejuvenating.' Violet sighed. Her eyes ran across the room and settled on the well-maintained garden beyond the French window. The house her husband had bought was beautifully landscaped with trees that gave shade and flowering plants. Climbing roses spilled over the wall near the gate, adding a splash of colour. 'The cottage is too big for a single soul.'

'Why don't you ask her to stay on?' suggested Claire. 'She might consider. Her café is doing well too.'

'I will do nothing of the sort,' retorted Violet. 'The girl has a life of her own. It was nice of her to come all the way to keep me company, but to expect that she will live with me forever is ridiculous.'

'What if she were to fall in love with a young man and marry him?'

'Here? In Ramsar?' Violet laughed. 'There is no young man worth considering.'

'What about Tim?'

'Tim Thapa? You mean the police officer?'

'Yes. He is a very handsome young man. I would have fallen in love with him if I were younger,' said Claire.

'It's an idea worth mulling over,' seconded Nancy. 'If the two were to fall in love and marry, you could look forward to dangling a few great-grandchildren on your knees.'

'Wishful thinking!' commented Violet. 'A very tempting thought, of course.'

Turning to her friends, she asked, 'So you think I should start matchmaking?'

'Why not?' echoed the women.

'There's nothing to lose,' said Mary, her dexterous fingers flying over the knitting needle. She was knitting the third pullover of the season and had to finish two more before the end of the month. 'We will have something to keep us busy.'

'I thought you have enough to do, and more,' teased Violet as she nibbled on a coconut-pineapple cupcake. 'Frankly, I would love to see her marry and settle down here. If wishes were horses…'

'There's nothing wrong with dreaming. They could come true,' retorted Claire. 'For all you know, Pia would be open to the idea.'

'Did I hear someone mention my name?' The subject of their discussion burst through the door at that moment.

Just then the grandfather clock in the dining room chimed the hour, and the women smiled conspiratorially at each other.

'What?' Pia's startling green eyes wore a mystified expression. Picking up an éclair from the plate, Pia walked up to Violet and put her hand on the old woman's shoulders. 'What are you young ladies conspiring about?'

'It's nothing. Claire is planning to write a book, and she wanted to seek our opinion on the plot.' Violet winked at her friends.

'Is it a romance or a thriller?'

'It's a romance.' Claire chuckled.

'Don't you want my opinion on the plot, Aunt Claire?' Pia stood behind her grandmother, enjoying the cold creamy filling of the éclair. 'I could tell you a thing or two about romance,' she added.

Claire cleared her throat and looked daggers at her friends. 'Well, it is about a girl from London, who takes a sabbatical in India.' She threw a pleading look at Violet, but the latter just picked up a piece of cake and began to eat it with great relish, pretending to be absorbed in the task.

'And then?' Pia threw a knowing look at them.

'... She falls in love with an Indian and lives happily ever after,' finished Violet, an amused smile playing on her face.

'Let me guess.' The granddaughter threw a stern look at Violet. 'The story is inspired by me. Isn't it?'

'Yes, of course,' the women chorused.

'Let me warn you ladies. If you are planning to play matchmakers, it won't work.'

Pia knew that the women, including her grandmother, were trying to fix her up with a young man. Six months back, her boyfriend had dumped her and she was now in an 'I hate all men' stage in life. She hadn't told her grandmother anything about the heartbreak, of course. The old woman had more on her platter than she could handle. She didn't need her granddaughter's heartache to add to it.

'Why are you here, at this time of the day?' Violet changed the subject. 'Is the café closed?'

'No, Meg is in charge at the moment,' replied Pia. Meg, short for Megha, was her assistant. The pert young girl had dreams of opening a coffee shop in Almora, so she was learning the tricks of the trade at Pia's café. She was proving to be an invaluable asset as well as a reliable confidante. 'I left my phone here and there are some urgent calls to be made, so I had to rush back.'

Two minutes later, after picking up the phone and warning the women against any attempts at matchmaking, Pia hurried out of the house.

'A whirlwind of a girl.' Mary sighed. 'I was one, once upon a time, and look at me now.'

'Whew! That was close.' Violet let her breath out in a whoosh. 'Now the damage is done. Pia won't let her guard down and trust us. I wish she hadn't stolen up on us.'

'Let's organize a surprise party for her birthday,' suggested Mary, ever the practical one. 'Didn't you say her birthday was on the twenty-first of this month?'

'That's a fabulous idea. We could invite Tim and some young people,' seconded Claire.

'I think it could work,' said Nancy, who had been quiet all this while. 'I could make some ginger wine for the party.' Her ginger wine was a big hit among the Ramsar and Almora folks.

'I guess we could try bringing the two together,' Violet agreed, a mischievous smile on her finely boned face. At seventy-one, she retained traces of the beautiful woman who once made men swoon. The deep-set grey eyes and a generous mouth were a testament. 'Let's get cracking on the guest list, menu and games. There is just a fortnight left to Pia's birthday.'

'Why don't you fetch a pen and paper?' suggested Claire. 'We could start making the list right now.'

The four women put their heads together as they discussed the details for the surprise party on the girl's birthday.

4

Even as Pia's grandmother and the three friends were planning a surprise party at Pia's Peaberry, the girl was standing before a difficult customer who couldn't decide between an espresso and a cappuccino. It was a routine dilemma for many Ramsarians, who were clueless about the different types of coffee. They loved to experiment but were unsure about the choice.

About six months back, when the girl arrived from Melbourne to spend time with her grandmother, no one imagined that the visit would extend beyond a week or two. Mrs Violet Williams, a charming and friendly septuagenarian, was surprised when her granddaughter declared she was taking a sabbatical and would stay on in Ramsar for a fairly long time. The surprise turned into shock when the girl expressed her desire to open a coffee shop after a couple of months in Ramsar.

Almost everyone in Ramsar had tasted the offerings at Pia's Peaberry. Everyone had something nice to say about the menu and its owner. For a no-horse town like Ramsar with nothing more than tea shops, a café that offered a range of coffee and baked stuff was a novel experience.

Pia's Peaberry soon turned into a rendezvous point for youngsters, who enjoyed the informal setting of what was popularly known as PP. For the older folk, the café offered a tryst with lost youth and a topic for conversation. The inviting ambience, the owner's friendliness, the charming decor and the tantalizing aroma of coffee brought in a steady flow of business.

'Ugh! This is horribly bitter,' saying this, the middle-aged man screwed up his eyes and pushed the cup towards her. 'Madam, you forgot to add milk and sugar.'

Meg rolled her eyes at Pia, who was trying to be patient.

'You asked for an espresso, sir,' she reminded the customer. 'Espresso is not sweet or milky. If you wish for me to add sugar and milk, I will do so of course. Next time, you may like to try out a caffè latte, which has both milk and sugar in it.'

'Thank you, I will. This espresso thing is quite horrible.'

Pia glanced impatiently at the quaint wristwatch that belonged to her grandmother. She was in a hurry. A busy evening awaited her at Bhandari Villa.

It was her first outdoor order, and she wanted to make sure nothing went wrong. The occasion was Rohan Bhandari's wedding reception. The Bhandaris were one of the richest families in Ramsar. They had requested Pia to set up a coffee counter at the venue. It was a novelty for the locals, and the Bhandaris were supposed to be the trendsetters in town. Rohan, who worked in the merchant navy, was the one who suggested that a coffee counter be set up for the invitees.

At first, Pia had been reluctant to accept the order. Setting up a counter for a large number of people required extra hands, and she had only one helper who doubled up as waitress and barista. Her granny, however, was convinced it would be a good idea to accept the challenge.

'You must think of diversifying. Besides, I don't see any competition for a barista in this town. The order will offer an opportunity to test your mettle. I will be there to help you with the stall,' Violet had said. Her three friends were equally vociferous about the idea. Pia should accept the challenge, they said.

'We will all pitch in,' declared the trio. In the end, the four women prevailed upon Pia to set up the counter.

As she faced the dithering customer, Pia wished she hadn't allowed Gumma and her friends to persuade her. The party was to begin at 7.30 p.m., so she had decided to close the café early and reach Bhandari Villa by 6. That would give her enough time to set up the stall and prepare everything well in time for the reception attendees.

Despite all attempts at shooing away customers, it was past 6 by the time the café could be closed.

Pia drew in a deep breath of the cool air as she drove towards Bhandari Villa. Her mind was not on Meg's incessant chatter as she swung her grandmother's old van into the street that led to their destination.

Laburnum Street was a prestigious address. A row of bungalows on the street ran till the edge of the precipice, with Bhandari Villa standing at the end of the road. The gorgeous view from the house proclaimed the value of the property.

Bhandari Villa was one of the most opulent houses in town. One could easily see the uncouth touch of wealth in the structure that stuck out like a sore thumb amid the quaint red-tile-roofed bungalows squatting all around it. Enclosed by high periphery walls, it was an ugly and ungainly house. It smacked of arrogance in a town where modesty was considered a virtue. Most Ramsarians were hard-working, God-fearing, honest souls, who steered clear of a flashy lifestyle. Few could afford it anyway.

Pia reversed the van carefully to park it across the house, a few metres from the edge of the road. The two girls had not visited this part of Ramsar before. They climbed out of the vehicle and stared at Misty Mountain looming majestically across the valley. A gust of chilly winds lashed at them as they stood admiring the scenery. Meg drew a deep breath and stretched herself, saying, 'Isn't this a beautiful spot?'

'Yes,' agreed Pia. 'Buying property here must cost a bomb.'

Curious, they peered down the precipice and saw a rivulet gurgling 40 feet below. Although lovely, the sheer drop alarmed Pia and she shivered involuntarily. Together, the two girls unloaded the cartons containing all their requirements for setting up the coffee stall and walked in through the massive gate.

The spacious lawn that fronted the villa had been converted into a makeshift fair for the evening. A flamboyant marquee covered much of the lawn, with flowers draping the pillars that supported it. The place was abuzz with activity. Several long tables covered in white satin had been placed on one side of the garden for the caterers to lay out the dinner. The extravagant use of colours and lights reflected the host's philosophy of adding more fairy lights when in doubt.

Loud music blared from a huge system placed on one side of the lawn. Pia wrinkled her nose in distaste. Some people would do anything for attention. A few more families like the Bhandaris and Ramsa could say goodbye to its charming, vintage atmosphere.

'Quite a set-up,' remarked Meg, struggling to catch up with Pia's long strides. 'With a flourishing business and one son in the merchant navy and the other a commercial pilot, I bet they have pots of money. Now, if I had that kind of dough—'

Pia cut her off with a shake of her head. 'Warn me if you are embarking on your start-up dream spiel, so I can tune out.'

She had heard Meg's dream business so many times that she could recite it verbatim.

'That's not polite, Pia,' protested the girl.

'Right now is not the time, Meg. We have a job at hand, which needs our complete attention.'

The younger brother of Rohan Bhandari led them towards a table in one corner of the marquee. 'I am Ravi,' he introduced himself. 'And I have been told to look after you. Will this do?' he asked solicitously. 'We can arrange for the table to be placed at any spot of your choice, if this one doesn't suit the purpose.'

'Thank you, Ravi. This is perfect,' Pia assured the anxious youngster who was responsible for overseeing the arrangements.

He flashed a grateful smile and said, 'Thank you. If you need anything, just let me know.'

The two girls went to work over their arrangements, laying the table attractively. Pia set down an antique pewter tankard and placed a bunch of red and yellow roses in it to make the table look brighter. She had brought cupcakes for those who might like a bite with their coffee.

By seven, they were ready for the guests. Pia had been told that a variety of coffees should be made available throughout the evening, although most guests, especially the gentlemen, were likely to settle for alcoholic drinks. It was a fact: Ramsarians loved their pint more than any brew in the world. And that applied across the board, to both men and women. Of course, concessions were occasionally made, and that was where coffee came into play.

The ever-helpful Ravi came by just as they finished the preparations.

'If you want to freshen up, I can show you the way to the guest room,' he offered.

'That would be nice.' Pia was glad he had offered to show them to the room. She needed a couple of minutes to touch up her face and hair.

'Come along then,' he said. Minutes later, he led them to a well-furnished room that stood at the end of a long corridor. 'Do you want me to wait or will you find your way out?'

'Thank you, Ravi,' said Pia. 'We can find our way out.'

A few minutes, a dash of lipstick and a touch of eyeshadow later, the two girls were back at the coffee counter. Meg stole a look at her employer, who looked gorgeous despite the busy day at PP. Over an emerald-green dress, highlighting the green in her eyes, Pia wore a smart denim apron with a quirky message. A touch of bronze on the eyes and subtle pink on the lips added colour to her complexion. Her long hair was swept up and twisted in a stylish bun. The few curls that had escaped the clips caressed her cheeks.

Sensing Meg's eyes on her, Pia complimented her assistant and said, 'You look hot.' Meg was looking smart in a trendy jumpsuit topped with a blazer.

Guests had begun to arrive already. The Bhandaris had invited almost everyone who mattered, socially or politically. The first to arrive were the ever-punctual colonel and his gang. Gumma and her friends arrived soon after, chattering like magpies. Soon the lawn was filled with exuberant Ramsarians looking forward to an exciting evening. Apart from the locals, there were guests from other cities as well. Rohan Bhandari, who worked as the third engineer on a ship, had invited six of his friends and colleagues. The boisterous lot had been housed in Hotel Misty Meadows.

Champagne bottles were opened, and the bubbly served. Tables groaned under their load of dishes, even as a team of cooks whipped up new offerings. Waiters moved between guests, serving drinks and snacks. Cameras flashed, photographs were taken, and the party swung into top gear. Loud music drowned the chatter and the clatter of cutlery. Everyone was in high spirits. The party was declared the event of the year.

Tim arrived with Nick, who like his father, Colonel Acharya, had joined the army. He was currently posted in Almora. Ignoring the champagne, the two of them walked towards Pia's coffee counter, drawn by the two pretty girls.

'Hi, this is Pia,' Tim introduced Pia to Nick. 'Pia, this is the brave Captain Nikhil Acharya, aka Nick.'

'Hi,' Pia responded. Pushing Meg forward, she introduced her to the two men, 'This is my friend, colleague and confidante Megha, aka Meg. She wants to be a barista one day.'

'Nice to meet you, Meg,' Nick stressed on the name. 'I didn't expect to run into two beautiful women at the party.'

'Flatterer!' said the girl, a dimpled smile breaking out on her face. 'I am surprised that you didn't make a beeline for the bar. Half the townsfolk are draped around it, as you can see.'

'We didn't want you to be disappointed with the lack of demand for coffee,' Nick said, his eyes crinkling in the corners as he smiled.

'You are absolutely wrong,' retorted Meg. 'For your information, our coffee is in demand. It is a hit with the women at least.'

'In that case, they must try out a cocktail of cappuccino and champagne,' the irrepressible young officer bantered, drawing a chuckle from Meg.

'Ideally, I would like some Irish coffee,' Tim said, interrupting their teasing. 'But that is not possible, so I will settle for anything you recommend.'

'Who says it is not possible?' Pia retorted. 'I can whip up my version of the drink, but I warn you not to complain.'

'Whatever you serve will be ambrosia to him.' Nick winked. 'The guy is completely smitten, as you can see.'

'What about you, smart alec?' Meg asked, directing a mocking look at the young man.

'I am game for Pia's Irish coffee.'

From a corner of the lawn, Violet stared at the four young people.

'They make a lovely couple, don't they?' Mary, noticing her friend's interest, said. 'All we have to do is invite Tim for the birthday party and throw them together. Sparks are already flying and you have to just fan them a bit.'

Stealing a look at the young couple, Tim's aunt had similar thoughts running through her mind.

It is time Tim got himself a wife, she ruminated as she walked up to the coffee counter.

'This is my aunt, the venerable judge's wife,' Tim introduced his aunt to the girls.

'Hello, Pia,' Geeta greeted the pretty girl. 'Since everyone, including my nephew, has been raving about your coffee, may I have a cup of caffè latte? I like it sweet and milky. Not for me the bitter espresso.'

'My aunt is a sweet person,' Tim ribbed, wrapping his arms around his aunt's shoulders. 'No bitter words, no bitter thoughts and no bitterness at all.'

'Ignore him,' commented Geeta. 'He likes to exaggerate my virtues. I have heard so much about your café. One of these days, I will drop in for a cup of coffee.'

'I will be delighted if you do,' replied Pia, handing her the caffè latte.

'In the meantime, why don't you come and spend an evening with us at Rhodo Cottage? You could meet your fans there.'

'Fans?'

'The judge and his friends have also been extolling your coffee. In fact, I would love to spend time with the two of you,' Geeta included Meg in the invitation. 'Are you free the coming Sunday?'

'Thanks for the invitation. I would love to visit you but it is almost 7.30 by the time I close the coffee shop,' Pia replied.

'That's not an issue. The bridge gang is usually at the cottage till late evening, so you are welcome to drop in after you close the shop.'

'You would be foolish to refuse the invitation,' Tim butted into the conversation. 'My aunt is a superlative cook.'

'I can't speak for Pia, but I am tempted to knock on your door,' Meg said, dimpling shyly.

'So am I,' said Pia.

'We will be there this Sunday,' the girls promised.

Geeta gave them a quick hug and walked away, smiling to herself. If she knew anything about her nephew and his friend, Geeta was sure that Tim and Nick would be present at Rhodo Cottage on Sunday evening. Nick was an inveterate flirt and he wouldn't miss the company of two attractive girls, and Tim was unmistakably smitten by Pia.

Pushing the glasses firmly up her aristocratic nose, Violet shook her head from a distance and smiled as she sensed Geeta's mind working in the same direction as hers. It was time to work on the details for Pia's birthday party and send out the invitations. Heading the list, of course, would be Tim and his family.

The DJ began belting out popular numbers and the party switched into top gear. By now, many of the guests were inebriated enough to drop their inhibitions and shake a leg.

With most of the guests raving about the food and drinks, the evening was an immense success. The Bhandari clan basked in the warmth of praises. Success for Pia came in the form of two catering orders.

It was past midnight by the time the party broke up. Most of the guests had left when Violet walked up to her granddaughter and asked if she needed help with winding up the counter.

'Why don't you leave with the others, Gumma? You must be exhausted. Meg and I will wrap up in a jiffy and leave this place.' Saying this, Pia led the lady towards the other women. 'I will drop Meg and reach home within the hour.'

Once everyone had left, the girls put their things together. The temperature had dipped and the two of them felt drained after the hectic day.

'What a day!' exclaimed Meg. 'I am dying to hit the sack.'

'So am I,' echoed Pia as she began hauling up a carton. 'But first, we have to carry all this stuff to the van.'

Just then, rather like a helpful genie, Ravi appeared before them.

'Let me help you with the stuff,' he offered. 'It has been a long day. The sooner you finish the better it will be.'

'We can manage,' Pia assured the young man.

'I won't hear of it,' he said. Clapping his hands, he summoned a couple of boys who had been employed for the evening and ordered them to carry the equipment. 'Just show them where the van is parked and they will do what is needed.'

'Thank you, Ravi.' Pia shook his hand and walked up to the road where she had parked the van.

It wasn't there. Puzzled, they looked all around. All the cars parked in front of the mansion had left and there was no trace of Gumma's van.

'Where did it go?' asked Meg. 'It seems to have disappeared into thin air.'

'It is simple. Gumma must have forgotten she had come with her friends and driven the van home. It happens when you are seventy plus. What a bother!'

'How will we go home now?'

'Let's speak to Ravi.'

Leaving Meg with the boys on the road, Pia ran back to the mansion and sought Ravi's help.

'I am so sorry, but my grandmother seems to have taken the van home, and we are stranded,' she explained to the amused man.

'That's no problem at all. I will arrange for the two of you to be dropped home,' Ravi said, adding, 'I would have dropped you myself but there are a few tasks to be finished before I end the day.'

'I wouldn't dream of dragging you away from your duties.' Pia threw him a grateful smile and added, 'Do drop in at the café sometime.'

'After all the rave reviews, there is no way I am going back to Delhi without a taste of your coffee.'

'You are welcome any time.' Pia dimpled. 'Thanks for coming to our rescue, Ravi.'

It was 1.30 a.m. by the time Pia walked into Elm Cottage. The first thing she noted upon arriving was that the van was not parked in its usual spot on the porch.

5

'How can the van disappear? It's not a sock or a stray pen, or a piece of jewellery, to go missing without anyone noticing.' Viclet's voice was shrill with annoyance. They were at the breakfast table the next morning. It was 9 a.m. and the lady had woken up with a headache. Late nights didn't suit her any more, although she refused to accept the fact. The few servings of her favourite gin-and-ginger punch had added to the headache. The news of the missing van had done nothing to improve her mood. 'It couldn't have driven off by itself, could it? And why didn't you call the police when you realized it was missing?'

'I assumed you had driven it home,' Pia explained patiently. 'It was only after I reached home and found it missing from the porch that I realized something was wrong. But it was too late to wake you or call the police. Besides, I was too exhausted to do anything.'

'It was foolish of you to assume that I had driven the van home. I am not senile enough to leave you high and dry at Bhandari Villa. Claire dropped me home. I would have informed you if I was driving back.'

Unwilling to add fodder to her grandmother's irritation, Pia didn't point out that the old lady had been a bit too tipsy to remember anything about last night. Much to her granddaughter's disquiet, Violet had imbibed a couple of goblets of punch.

'How could I drive away without taking the key from you?' demanded the lady, her eyes blazing. A sudden thought hit her and she narrowed her eyes. 'Don't tell me you forgot to lock the van.'

'Ramsar is such a safe place that I never lock the van,' Pia said, hanging her head sheepishly as she toyed with her breakfast. 'I am sorry, Gumma, it was careless of me.'

'Did you forget to apply the handbrake?'

'Of course I didn't,' retorted the young girl. 'I haven't forgotten the basics of hill-driving. Now, don't shout at me, please. Not so early in the morning. I said I am sorry.'

'I have been using that tin box for decades and never have I forgotten to lock the van. You use it for one day and look what happens.'

'Gumma, please stop shouting. It's not good for your blood pressure. How many times should I say I am sorry?'

'Well, don't sit there and apologize. Call the police station and report the theft.' Violet shook her finger at the girl. 'Better still, call the young chap. What's his name?' She snapped her fingers in an irritated manner. Her memory was playing games that morning. The hangover didn't help anyway.

'Which young man are you talking about?' Pia raised her left eyebrow enquiringly.

'I mean the young police officer who was following you around last night.'

'You mean Timothy Thapa? For your information, he was not following me around. He's too decent to do that,' grumbled the granddaughter as she scrolled through the contact list on her phone. Tim had obliged her with his number when he visited the café.

She dialled. His number was busy.

'Go to the police station and meet him,' ordered Violet. 'It will do you good to take a walk.'

'Gumma, I have a café to run. I can't be walking to the police station now,' objected Pia. 'I will try his number a few minutes later.'

Five minutes later, just as she was finishing her coffee, the phone rang. Glancing at the caller's name, she answered, 'Hi, Tim.'

Violet suppressed a smile as she perked up her ears to hear the conversation.

'What are you saying, Tim?' Pia's horrified exclamation reached her grandmother. The girl's face had paled. 'A dead body in my van? How's that even possible?'

'What's he saying?' Violet demanded to know.

'I will be there,' said Pia, raising her hand to quieten her grandmother, who was fidgeting in her seat. 'No, I don't have a vehicle.'

Violet strained her ears to hear Tim's reply. Minutes later, Pia ended the call, saying, 'Thank you! That will be nice.'

Turning an ashen face towards her grandmother, Pia said, 'They have found a dead body inside our van, which was pushed down the edge of the road. Tim is coming to pick me up. I have to go.'

'Oh, my God! A dead body in my van? How did it get there?' Violet shook her head. After the initial shock of Pia's words wore off, she let out her steam. 'It just goes to show that you can't leave your car unlocked these days. Not even in Ramsar. You are likely to pay a heavy price for the carelessness, my dear.' Leaning on her walking stick, she stood up and said, 'You are not going alone. I will accompany you to the place.'

Noting the grim lines on her grandmother's face, Pia knew a storm was waiting to break. Violet had no scruples about ticking off people. Sometimes without reason. 'No, Gumma, you are not coming with me,' she objected.

'Try and stop me,' Violet countered, her jaw set at a stubborn angle. 'I won't allow the police to haul you over burning coals just because you were careless enough to leave the van unlocked.'

'No one has accused me of anything. Not yet, anyway. I don't see why you should accompany me. For God's sake, I am a grown-up and I can deal with such situations.' Although she knew Violet was unbending once her mind was made up, Pia tried once more.

'That's what you think … I am going with you and that's final. So, don't you—'

Just then the doorbell rang, interrupting them.

'Good morning, Mrs Williams,' Tim greeted the lady cheerfully. 'Good morning, Pia.'

'I am ready,' said Pia, picking up her bag.

'So am I,' Violet declared.

'No, you are not coming with us,' the girl said, putting out a hand to stop her grandmother.

'I agree with Pia. You shouldn't take the trouble of visiting the accident site,' Tim told the adamant lady. 'It's just a minor procedure and Pia's presence should be enough. All she has to do is identify the van in which the body was found.'

'It is my van, young man. I am the owner. Technically, you should be taking me and not Pia.' Violet tapped her walking stick impatiently on the floor.

'Well…' Tim hesitated.

Without pausing for a reply, Violet walked towards the police vehicle and waited for the police officer to help her into it. A couple of minutes later, having clambered heavily to the co-driver's seat, she sat staring ahead. Resolute and stone-faced. Tim smiled and shook his head.

With an exasperated sigh, Pia shrugged her shoulders and got into the vehicle. As they approached the site, they saw that a small crowd had gathered on the road. Everyone was peering down into the ravine where a crane was at work. An ambulance stood waiting near it, and the accident site had been cordoned off.

Tim parked the police vehicle near the tow truck, which had been summoned to winch the van once the police had finished with their task. The crowd of curious onlookers switched their attention to Pia and whispered among themselves.

'Violet's granddaughter was driving the van last night,' mumbled a man. 'She must have parked the van carelessly, and it went down the slope.'

'Isn't she the girl who runs the coffee shop?' asked his companion.

'Get back, get back,' shouted Constable Sharad Pant, aka Shirt Pant, waving his stick to emphasize the words. 'Make way for the police.'

The crowd parted obediently to allow Tim and Pia to make their way to the spot where the van had come to a stop after plunging down the steep slope into the gorge, its descent arrested by a large boulder. Violet remained at the edge of the precipice, staring ruefully at the badly damaged vehicle. Its windscreen was in smithereens.

With a hand from Tim, Pia went down the slope.

'Careful,' he warned her. 'Don't touch those innocuous-looking shrubs. They are quite deadly.'

Pia clung closer to the officer as she picked her way carefully towards the spot where the van had nosedived.

The doctor and a few police personnel were already at the site and bustling around. The photographer shot pictures of the body, vehicle and the surrounding area, while a forensic expert busied himself with the other details.

The colonel, who was one of the first to arrive, was hovering around the area, examining the van and its surroundings, his keen eyes missing nothing. A wave of nausea swept over Pia as she looked at the corpse, which had been extricated from the driver's seat and laid on the ground. The face was a bloody mess, and the clothes were splattered with blood. The area around the van reeked of petrol, which had spilled from the damaged petrol tank.

Her mouth felt like paper and her knees buckled. Instinctively, she gripped Tim's arm and turned her head away.

'You don't have to look at the body,' he muttered under his breath. 'Just identify the van and I will take you back.'

'It is my grandmother's van,' she whispered. 'But I don't know the dead man.'

They stood side by side, Pia's face averted from the scene.

After checking the body temperature, and estimating lividity and rigor mortis, the doctor gave his opinion. 'According to the preliminary physical examination, I find the deceased suffered maxillofacial trauma that has resulted in nasal and maxillary fractures.'

'Can you put it in simpler words?' requested the colonel, who was looking at the areas pointed out by the doctor.

'To put it simply, the nose as well as the frontal teeth are broken due to the impact of the crash. There is laceration of the face and contusion in the chest region because of the body being slammed into the steering wheel.'

'Is it possible for you to establish the cause of death? I know that it takes an autopsy to provide the details.'

'I can only make a guess.' The doctor smiled. 'From the preliminary examination of the body, it appears the death was caused by shock and haemorrhage because of multiple head and chest injuries. It is difficult to give a precise reading at this stage. The details can be determined only after an autopsy has been conducted,' concluded the doctor.

'Could you give us the time of death?' Tim asked.

'The exact time of death cannot be given at this stage, but taking into account the stage of rigor mortis, I would say it occurred about ten to fourteen hours back.'

'It is around 9.30 a.m. now,' said the colonel, glancing at his wristwatch. 'Would that mean the death took place between 7.30 and 11.30 p.m.?'

'Yes. But that's just an approximation. The autopsy report will provide a closer estimate,' the doctor hurried to clarify.

'Since the deceased was a guest at the Bhandari party, do you think he was drunk enough to have driven the van off the road?'

'I detected a strong smell of alcohol, but only an autopsy can determine how much alcohol the deceased had taken.'

'Thank you, Doctor, I think the mystery of the death will be solved only after we receive the autopsy report.'

'My job is over for the moment. You can send the body for a post-mortem,' said the doctor, pulling the cover over the dead man's face. 'The sooner the better, I would say.'

'I will do that immediately,' said Tim. He gestured to the ambulance crew to take away the body.

'Has the deceased been identified?' the colonel wanted to know.

'The deceased is Deepak Dabral. A mariner by profession, he was a colleague of Rohan Bhandari. Dabral was here to attend the wedding reception. The Bhandaris had put him up at Hotel Misty Meadows along with his wife and a few other guests,' Tim informed Acharya. 'In fact, the wife, assisted by a few guests, lodged a police complaint about the missing man.'

'Who discovered the body?' asked the colonel.

'This morning, we received a tip from a young shepherd who was collecting bichhu buti...'

'Bichhu buti?' Pia looked perplexed.

'It's a common perennial plant that grows wild throughout the Himalayan region. The locals of this place use it for medicinal purposes,' Tim educated the girl. 'It was the shepherd who informed Sharad about the van and he rushed here.' Noticing the confusion on Pia's face, Tim elaborated, 'Sharad Pant aka Shirt Pant is an overzealous constable who loves wielding authority on the simple folks of the town.'

'Is that the constable?' She pointed at Shirt Pant, who was strutting around importantly. From time to time, he hollered at the crowd and used his stick to push them back from the precipice.

Yes, that's the one.' With an amused smile dancing on his face, Tim added, 'He's a chap with an unbeatable sense of importance.'

'What time did Sharad arrive at this spot?'

'He was here at 8 a.m.,' Tim replied.

'When did the police station receive the report about Dabral's disappearance?'

'It was reported at 6 a.m. this morning.'

'That was fast work, I must say. Has the wife been informed of her husband's death?' asked Acharya.

'Yes, we have informed the wife as well as the Bhandaris, and they have identified the body. Mrs Nisha Dabral was inconsolable after hearing of her husband's death. The doctor had to give her a sedative to calm her.'

'Is she still at the hotel?'

'No, they have shifted her to a guest room at Bhandari Villa. The Bhandaris refused to let her stay at the hotel in her present condition.'

'Did anyone notice Dabral slipping out of the party last night?'

'Colonel, when there are 200 guests enjoying unrestricted access to alcohol, it is unlikely that anyone will observe a guy slipping out of the party. This is especially true if he is the inconspicuous type. The deceased, with his dark suit and unremarkable personality, was not very noticeable.'

'What about his wife? Wasn't she with him?'

'According to Nisha Dabral, he was circulating among his friends while she sat at one spot with a couple of ladies.'

'What does his wife look like?'

'She is around 5 feet 4 inches, slender and very attractive,' Tim described with a twinkle in his eyes.

'Now, how did I miss her? I can miss an inconspicuous guy but to miss an attractive lady … it's unpardonable.'

'Truly unpardonable, Colonel,' said Tim, tongue firmly in cheek.

'I hardly notice strangers at a party,' Pia said, shaking her head. 'I mean, one is too busy enjoying the party to pay attention to people one doesn't know.'

'Mon chére! When you are a sleuth by hobby, you carry the microscope of your observation everywhere. Even at a party. It's a nasty habit, of course,' Acharya said, chuckling.

Tim bristled silently. He was fond of the colonel and had great regard for his observation powers, but he resented the colonel's habit of stealing the thunder from under his nose. Here he was, trying to impress Pia, and the man was hogging her attention.

'I would like to speak to Mrs Dabral once the effect of the sedative has worn off,' the colonel said as Tim and Pia accompanied him back to where Violet was waiting in the police vehicle.

'I have asked the Bhandaris to call me the moment she is awake.'

'There are so many questions on my mind. Why did Dabral wander off from the party? Did his wife not notice his absence through the night? What was he doing in Pia's van?' muttered the colonel. 'Was he inebriated enough to take off in the van by himself?'

'That's exactly the point,' Tim responded. 'I have also been trying to figure out why Dabral was in the driver's seat.'

'I wonder if he was trying to move the van to make it easier for a neighbouring car to move out of its parking space?' Tim pondered.

'But the guests hadn't arrived when I parked the van, so I couldn't be blocking anyone,' Pia objected.

'You have a point,' Acharya stroked his chin thoughtfully and said. 'What puzzles me is that the van went straight down the slope. It could have turned turtle or on its side.'

'It was dark, so he may have driven the van right off the road and lost control,' Tim suggested.

'That's impossible!' Pia said. 'The ignition key was with me. The van couldn't have been started without the key.'

'My dear, there are ways of starting a vehicle without a key, but we won't go into that now. I think the issue needs thorough study. Let's go to the police station and put our heads together over it,' suggested the colonel.

'That's a good idea,' agreed Tim. 'I have to give a detailed report to the deputy superintendent of police.'

'Haven't you informed him of the accident?'

'I did that as soon as we received a report of the van lying in the ravine, but Bulldog is expecting me to get back with details about the deceased's identity and other elements.'

Bulldog was what Tim called the DSP in private. In fact, all of the DSP's buddies at the police academy called him by that epithet. It was a fitting one. Thick of build and short-limbed with broad shoulders, a short neck and broad jaw, the DSP resembled a bulldog, the colonel agreed.

Telling Sharad Pant to remain on the spot till further instruction, Tim left for his office with Violet and Pia in the police vehicle, while the colonel followed in his car.

6

The busiest place in the tiny Himalayan town of Ramsar was around the milestone at the central bus stand. With the nearest railhead at Kathgodam, buses of all sizes, SUVs and taxis were the preferred modes of transportation. The few roads that went through the town radiated from that point.

The adjoining bazaar, a favourite hangout of the locals, was a modest clutch of shops that stocked things essential for a simple life. For the fancier stuff, one had to travel to Almora, which took a leisurely two hours by bus. For those in a hurry, there were packed SUVs driven by reckless drivers, who were great believers in karma. When death had to come, it would come anyway was their philosophy. They kept up their spirits with this belief, aided by a dose of the local brew.

Apart from its quaint atmosphere, Ramsar boasted a Victorian clubhouse that had seen better days. Although it was strictly for those who wished to spend time in the company of owls and bats, nevertheless it was a club. Then there was a nine-hole golf course, which attracted the likes of the retired colonel and a few people of eminence. There was also a ramshackle movie hall and an eatery that went by a misnomer, Tasty Bites. The thick clump of trees that surrounded Tasty Bites and the beautiful sight to the north—of the rolling slopes and snow-clad peaks of the Himalayas—were its major draw.

Hotel Misty Meadows and Hotel Paradise were the only hotels that catered to the occasional wanderer who strayed into Ramsar. Although Misty Meadows promised a panoramic view of idyllic pastures, all that the guests could see from the windows were brightly painted houses with wooden doors and windows that lay pell-mell on the sides of a steep hill crowned by an ancient temple. As for the other hotel, it was anything but a paradise.

In keeping with the size of the town and its low crime rate, the police station in Ramsar was a small one with less than half a dozen police personnel to sort out local matters. Theft, drunken louts and local squabbles between neighbours were the crimes Ramsar faced. There had been just a few murder cases in the last decade and they had all to do with outsiders. The locals were a peaceful lot who preferred compromise over controversy. The police station, housed in a single-storeyed structure with a tiny lock-up, two rooms and a peaceful ambience, looked more like a house. On most days, there was little work to occupy the officials.

That morning, however, was a different story.

A grim air hung over the police station as Violet, Pia and the colonel faced Tim in his office. Pia's eyes took in the damp, bilious green walls and depressing atmosphere of the room. On an old wooden desk sat an ancient desktop computer, with a pile of dusty files stacked on a tray by its side. The effervescent personality of the young man sitting across the table seemed totally out of place. The sole window in the room overlooked a dirt track lined with trees, which provided a distraction to the dull routine of the police station. A posy of wild flowers placed in a jug on the table offered the only touch of cheer.

Tim ordered for tea, and the four of them were settling down to business when the phone rang. It was the DSP, Jung

Bahadur Singh, demanding Tim's report on the accident case. For the first two minutes, it was a one-sided conversation with Bulldog barking at the other end. Tim rose to his feet and, casting an embarrassed look at Pia, walked out of the room to take the call.

'Tim's boss is a finicky man, very hard to please,' Acharya explained.

'I know all about it.' Violet's lips twisted in an amused smile. 'I had the misfortune of running into him.'

'He's not a wicked man. Honest, hard-working and incorruptible but a bit of a plodder. JBS has an unimaginative mind.'

'I don't think it's a disqualification for a police officer,' Pia rose to the DSP's defence. 'In fact, it could be an asset.'

'Mon chére, being unimaginative is a disqualification in all professions. Just imagine trying to solve a murder case without an imaginative brain. One won't have an insight into the murderer's mind and motive. Being able to pry into the criminal's psyche is of utmost importance, and I speak from experience.'

'I agree with the colonel,' said Violet. 'Being able to pry into anyone's psyche is the biggest ability, I think.'

'Well, I think it's vital to understand human psychology while solving a case.'

'Perhaps,' Pia admitted.

'My dear child, it comes handy in every situation,' added Violet.

'Phew!' Tim strode into the room and expelled a lungful of breath. 'What a morning!'

'He let you have an earful, I guess.' Acharya smirked.

'You can say that,' Tim grunted. 'There is no satisfying the man. He wants the forensic details even before the autopsy has been carried out.'

'I hope he is not planning to come to Ramsar.'

'Not immediately. He has a couple of meetings to attend today. Thank God! It gives me some time to get hold of the details.'

Stationed in Almora, the DSP was the overall area in-charge. The hour-and-a-half-long drive could not keep the man away. A whiff of a case and Bulldog was sure to land up at the police station to demand an explanation. Because of his unyielding nature, the DSP was not a popular person at any of the police stations under his jurisdiction.

'What's the latest on the boss?' asked the colonel.

'According to the grapevine, there is talk of his transfer to one of the godforsaken towns where no one will go.'

'Isn't that too soon? The guy has completed just a year in Almora.'

'He has completed a year and ten months, and this has been the longest tenure of his career.' Tim laughed.

'Since we have no interest in your boss's tenure or transfer, are we free to leave? Or are we being detained?' The steely voice of Violet Williams broke into the conversation.

'I am sorry. It was rude of us to talk shop while you are waiting. Of course you are free to leave, Mrs Williams. All we need is your statement and signature, after which you can go home.'

'Well, get on with it then. We can't be sitting here the whole day,' snapped the old lady.

Suitably chastened, Tim rang the old-fashioned bell on his table to summon the clerk. It took just a few minutes for the statements to be recorded and signed.

'Could you drop us, or are we supposed to find our way back?' Violet snapped irritably.

'Ma'am, just give me a few moments and I will have you dropped at your residence,' Tim replied.

Pia blushed with embarrassment at her grandmother's rudeness. 'Gumma!' She tugged at Violet's arm. 'We can find our way back.'

'I hope you have no objection to my dropping them back,' said the colonel. 'You have a busy morning ahead.'

'None whatsoever.' Tim grinned. 'Thank you, Colonel.'

Bidding goodbye to Tim, the colonel trooped out with Pia and Violet in tow. As they drove towards Elm Cottage, the colonel told Violet, 'You may want to make an insurance claim for the damages to the van.'

'Do you think it is worth the trouble? The van is now a heap of metal. It was time for a new one,' Violet said. She did not mention that she had an emotional connection with the vehicle. It was the first and last gift from her truant son.

'I know the insurance guys in Ramsar, so I could help you with the claim. That is, if you are interested in filing one,' Acharya offered.

'Let me think about it. For now, I would be happy to get home.'

'Right away, ma'am.'

'Why is the DSP interested in this case?' Pia asked from the back seat. 'Doesn't he trust his ASP to solve a simple accident case?'

'JBS trusts no one but himself. That is his biggest problem.' The colonel chortled.

'That's rather impractical, isn't it?' said Violet. 'Considering that the DSP is based in Almora.'

'It may be impractical, but he considers it his duty to have a finger in every pie. You are fortunate that he isn't here this morning. He would have torn you to bits before he let you off,' Acharya said, chuckling as he imagined how JBS would tear the formidable Violet apart.

'Colonel, a man who could tear me to bits has not been born yet,' Violet retorted, her face breaking into a mischievous grin. Her mood had undergone a change now that they had left the police station. 'I would have chewed him alive.'

'Gumma!' Pia said, her eyes twinkling. 'Be careful of what you say. The DSP may just prove you wrong.'

'That will be the day!' Violet growled. 'Why is the case being given so much weight? I thought it was a simple accident case. Do the police suspect it otherwise?'

'Well, as of now, it is an accident case. But, as an investigating officer, Tim has to make sure it is nothing but an accident.' Manoeuvring the car around a bend, Acharya smiled to himself. The old lady was sharp. It would be worthwhile pitting his brains against Violet's.

'And what is your role in the case?' Violet asked.

'My role is totally unofficial,' said the colonel. 'The DSP and Tim are kind enough to allow me to indulge in a bit of sleuthing whenever opportunity arrives. Though there aren't too many cases to keep us occupied, we are happy to work together on the few that occur.'

'You are being modest, Colonel. Stories of your exploits are not unknown to Ramsarians. Even though I inhabit Firangi Colony, I am a part of the local milieu. I keep up with the local news.' Violet chuckled as she spoke.

Meanwhile, at the police station, Tim was dealing with an impatient young man.

'I have to leave on my honeymoon, officer,' said Rohan Bhandari. 'I can't believe I am wasting my time at the police station while my guests are leaving town.'

'I understand, Rohan,' Tim tried to pacify the mariner. 'But a man is dead and we have to carry out the required procedures.'

'You asked me to identify Dabral, and I did. What now?'

'I want you to answer some basic questions to clarify why he drove the van down the ravine.'

'Should you not be speaking to his wife? I am sure she is the best person to answer your questions.'

'I will do that. At the moment, I want to speak to you. Since you are leaving Ramsar for ten days, it is unlikely we will have time to question you later.'

'For heaven's sake, how would I know the state of his mind or the reason he committed suicide in Ramsar? On the day of my wedding reception, if you please. What an inconsiderate chap, I say!'

'Terribly inconsiderate of him, I agree,' said Tim, suppressing a smile.

'Look, Dabral was a colleague. In fact, he had joined the company not too long back. Also, I was in the engine department and he was in the deck department. We didn't have much interaction. When he heard I was throwing a reception in Ramsar, he wanted to be included in the guest list. Please be clear, I had no intention of inviting him or his wife. It was his request and I couldn't refuse. I can't tell you anything more than that. He was neither a friend, nor do I know much about him.'

'Do you have any idea why he wanted to be invited to Ramsar?' Tim's mind was processing the information. The man had invited himself for Rohan Bhandari's wedding reception. Why?

'How the hell am I to know that? Initially, he wanted to attend the event alone, and then requested that his wife be added to the guest list. Why don't you ask the other colleagues about Dabral? Maybe someone could tell you something important.'

'I will do that, Rohan. You are the first one leaving Ramsar, so you have to be questioned first. Do you have an idea about the quantity of alcohol he had consumed?'

'No idea at all,' snapped Rohan. 'Seriously, officer, did you expect me to keep tabs on the alcohol consumption of the guests? Especially since it was my wedding reception.'

'What about his movements before the party?'

'No idea about that either. All I know is that the pair arrived yesterday morning on the same train from Delhi to Kathgodam as a couple of other guests from Delhi. They were all picked up from the railway station and taken to Hotel Misty Meadows. Thereafter, most guests wandered around town and arrived in the evening for the party. This being my wedding reception, I was not involved in the arrangements. Ravi was looking after the guests, so he may be able to provide you with a few more details.'

'What you are saying is that you know very little about your guest.' Picking up a pencil and twirling it around his fingers deliberately, Tim stared thoughtfully at the flustered man seated before him.

'That's right. May I leave now?' Rohan got up from the chair.

'Just a few more minutes and then you can leave. Was Dabral in a state of depression?'

'Look, officer, since I am no psychologist, it is not possible for me to tell you whether he was depressed or thrilled,' Rohan's voice rose in irritation. There was silence as he gained control of his emotions. Curiosity getting the better of him, he asked. 'Do you think he committed suicide?'

'We are not ruling it out. Either the man was too drunk to know what he was doing or he deliberately drove the van down the gorge. Thank you for the cooperation, Rohan. You may leave now.'

'Thank you, officer.'

'I am sorry for the unpleasant event that ruined your day, but here's wishing you a happy married life.' Tim got up and clasped Rohan's hand in a warm handshake as he spoke.

A minute later, the phone on his desk demanded attention. It was the DSP.

'Have you spoken to the wife?' he wanted to know.

'Not yet. The doctor has given her a sedative. I will question her as soon as she is awake.'

'That should have been the first thing to do. She is the most important link in this case. In fact, she could be the only person who knows why her husband left the party. Stop dragging your feet and start working,' chided Bulldog.

Much as he disliked doing so, Tim was immediately on the defensive.

'Sir, I was interviewing Rohan Bhandari.'

'What did Rohan Bhandari have to say?' The DSP was curious.

'He didn't have much to offer as he knows very little of Dabral's personal life. According to him, the deceased invited himself to Ramsar.'

'Well, that explains it. Dabral intended committing suicide in a remote place and so he got himself invited to Ramsar. I suspected so from the very beginning. No sane man would drive a vehicle down the ravine.'

'I agree.'

'I want you to get cracking on the matter. It's an open-and-shut case, so it shouldn't take you time to close. Let me tell you, the wife is the person to question. Inform her that the body can be collected after the autopsy. Ask her to call immediate family so they can assist her. The insurance guys will come nosing along once Violet Williams files a claim.'

'Yes, sir.'

There was no point in disagreeing with Bulldog. Parroting 'yes, sir' was the easiest way to handle the man. Tim had learnt to remain calm in the face of stress.

It was likely to be a very busy morning. Well, whatever was left of it. He had to speak to Dabral's colleagues at Hotel Misty Meadows before they left Ramsar. And then there was the wife who lay sedated at Bhandari Villa. Tim would have to speak to her soon.

7

Tim left for Hotel Misty Meadows to speak to Deepak Dabral's colleagues. Turn by turn, he summoned the guests to ask about the deceased's habits, nature, family and work. The colleagues were keen to help, but none of them could provide much information. What he had gleaned after an hour of gruelling questions amounted to almost nothing.

Tim looked ruefully at the notes he had made while questioning the colleagues.

1. The ship on which they worked had docked in Mumbai a fortnight back.
2. Four of them, including Deepak Dabral, lived in Delhi.
3. Although they were in the same city, Dabral did not socialize with them.
4. Dabral was a loner who mostly kept to himself.
5. The man was surly and often rude by nature.
6. He had joined the company recently and was a conscientious employee.
7. He was not the partying kind, but loved his drink.
8. Although none of the colleagues knew much about his family, they knew that Dabral's wife was working as a marketing executive for a private company.

9. Dabral was an avid reader. He always had a book, mostly thrillers, by his side.
10. Nisha Dabral was a vivacious, charming and friendly person, according to Dabral's colleagues.
11. She had come back from the party with them since Dabral had left the venue to meet someone.
12. The guests went back to the hotel at around 12.30 a.m., most of them inebriated.
13. Nisha knocked on the neighbouring guest's door at 5.45 a.m. and informed them that Dabral had not returned at night.
14. Worried, they went immediately to the police station and reported him missing.
15. The Dabrals and the other guests from Delhi had booked tickets to leave by the night train from Kathgodam.

It was past noon when the Bhandaris called to inform Tim that Nisha Dabral had woken up. He rushed immediately to Bhandari Villa and found her walking listlessly around the lawn in front of the bungalow.

Her anorexic figure draped in a silk kurta, a woollen shawl flung over one shoulder, eyes haunted, she presented a forlorn picture.

'Hello!' Tim greeted her before introducing himself. 'I am ASP Timothy Thapa.'

Nisha threw him an appraising look. Her eyes were red and puffy from weeping, he noticed. There were times Tim hated his job, and this was one such time. Subjecting a grieving relative to questioning was awkward.

'I am sorry about your loss.' He cleared his throat and began speaking, 'I know it is painful to speak about your husband, but I will have to ask you a few questions.'

'I understand,' she mumbled. Nisha Dabral looked at him. Her eyes were luminous with unshed tears.

'Shall we sit down somewhere?' he asked.

Nisha nodded mutely and followed him to the gazebo in a secluded corner of the garden.

'When did you last see your husband, Mrs Dabral?' Tim began.

'I last saw him at the party.'

'Why did he leave the party?'

'He had to meet someone.'

'Do you know whom he was meeting?'

'Deepak was to meet his cousin Umesh Gudyal at 9 p.m.'

'Umesh Gudyal?'

'Yes, Umesh is Deepak's cousin. He stays at Negi Mansion.'

'But you didn't stay with the cousin.'

'Deepak was not on good terms with his cousin,' Nisha Dabral spoke in a flat and emotionless voice. She sounded like an automaton.

'So, your husband went to meet his cousin Umesh Gudyal at 8.30 p.m.?'

Nisha laced her fingers together, making a steeple on which she rested her chin. There was a brief pause before she replied, her voice low, 'Yes.'

'And he didn't return to the party?'

'No. He didn't return to the party.' Nisha fixed her gaze on the rose bush near the gazebo.

'Did that not worry you?'

'I thought Deepak was held up because of the discussion. The matter had been weighing on his mind for a while and he wanted to sort it out.'

'But he did not return till midnight. That should have been a cause for worry.'

'I am used to my husband's ways. He does not always tell me his plans, and I am not a nosy person. I thought he had decided to spend the night at Negi Mansion. They were cousins, after all.'

'Would he do that without informing you?'

'Yes. It has happened in the past.'

'Would you say that the two of you were happily married?'

'Yes. We were happy,' she whispered. Then, noticing the quizzical look on Tim's face, Nisha continued in a confident voice. 'We were unique individuals with distinct personalities. He was an introvert and I am an extrovert. Also, I am a non-judgemental and easygoing person. I understood where Deepak was coming from and was happy to accommodate his sensitivities. Most marriages break up because the partners don't understand each other.'

'You are a wise woman, Mrs Dabral.'

A servant arrived with two cups of tea and placed the tray on the wicker table before them.

'I really needed the tea.' Tim took a sip of the steaming brew. It was strong, milky and sweet. 'Just the way I like my tea,' he remarked, smacking his lips with satisfaction.

Nisha let her tea go cold.

'What was Deepak's state of mind when the two of you came to Ramsar?' He continued the questioning.

'He was his usual sullen self.'

Tim wondered if there was a trace of bitterness in her voice.

'He wasn't feeling depressed?' Tim probed.

'I don't think so. Anyway, do you think he would tell me he was planning to commit suicide?'

'So you think it was suicide?'

'I am so confused,' she said, placing her palms on her eyes. 'I don't know what to think any more.'

He waited for her reactions, but she clammed up.

There was silence for a few moments. Nisha Dabral played with the fringe of her shawl, while Tim gazed at the row of flowers nearby, trying to prepare himself for the next step. He hated having to talk about the autopsy and the morgue with the lady.

'They have taken the body for an autopsy and you should be getting it tomorrow. Is there anyone you wish to inform? The body has to be collected from the morgue.'

She was silent.

'Mrs Dabral …' Tim mumbled.

She wept softly.

'I heard you, officer,' she replied after a brief pause. 'I was trying to gather my thoughts. It has been an enormous shock.' Nisha Dabral leaned back in the chair and dabbed at her eyes.

He waited.

'Deepak's parents live abroad with their elder son. They would not be able to travel back in a hurry. Frankly, Deepak's relationship with his brother has not been very smooth. I doubt he would rush here to claim the body.'

Nisha Dabral struggled with her emotions. Tim felt sorry for the woman.

'Is there someone from your side who could come? A brother, parents?'

She raised her tear-streaked face. 'I can't think of anyone,' she stated plaintively. 'My father has a heart condition and my mother is no more.'

'Brother … sister?'

Nisha Dabral studied her hands, which lay on her lap. The fingers were long and artistic, Tim noticed. She took a long time to reply.

'Yes, I can call my brother,' she finally said. 'Maybe I will call him.'

'I think you should do so immediately.'

'I have a splitting headache. I am exhausted, officer. Can your questions wait for a few hours?'

Without waiting for his reply, she got to her feet.

'I am sorry, Mrs Dabral. Of course, the questions can wait.' Tim stood up.

'Thank you for understanding.'

He watched her walk to the house, her back straight and unyielding.

After returning to the police station, Tim sat back and chewed on his pen. He wished the colonel had accompanied him to question the guests. Two brains were better than one, he believed. But Acharya had been busy with Violet's insurance claim.

It was late afternoon. Tim, who had had a busy morning, was drowning exhaustion in his fifth cup of coffee, specially brought from Pia's café. Lately, he had taken a fancy for caffé mochas, or mochaccinos as Pia called it, and nothing else could satisfy his coffee craving. The first order of the day invariably came from the police station as soon as Pia's Peaberry was open. Sometimes she found the constable outside, waiting for her to open the café. Shaken and stirred, nothing of the original flavour remained when the brew landed on his table, but Tim was happy.

Tim sat back to enjoy his coffee. He had sent the body for the autopsy, interviewed Pia and Violet, and the wife and colleagues of the deceased. The van had been winched up and towed to the police station. That was a lot of work for one morning.

He was scrolling through the messages on his phone when the colonel walked into the office.

'What brings you back to the police station, Colonel?' Tim asked Acharya, who laid his polished rosewood walking stick aside and sauntered towards the window that overlooked the dirt path. 'I am surprised you aren't playing golf this afternoon.'

'That lazy bum of a professor is reluctant to partner me today. He is giving backache as an excuse. I would commiserate, if I didn't know better.' The colonel chuckled. He paused for a moment to light up his cigar before commenting, 'Did you get an earful from the boss?'

'How did you know that?'

'The sullen expression on your face is a clear giveaway, my dear chap.'

'Am I sulking? Well, I am used to JBS's unreasonable ways. Here I was, busy getting a signed statement from Pia, questioning Rohan, tying up with various agencies and pushing for an early autopsy, but he thinks I spent the morning twiddling my thumbs.'

'What did he want?' asked Acharya, taking a seat across the officer.

'He needs no excuse to holler. This time he reprimanded me for not contacting the deceased's family.'

'I hope you have done that.'

'It wasn't a straightforward job. Questioning Dabral's wife took me a while. She is in shock and I didn't want to upset her some more by asking her about the mental state of her husband and the state of their marriage.'

'That's true. It's difficult to interrogate a grieving wife. One has to balance sensitivity and pragmatism,' agreed the colonel. 'How is the wife coping with the tragedy?'

'Mrs Nisha Dabral sounded upset but took the news in her stride. Despite her fragile appearance, she is a strong woman.' Tim spun the glass paperweight on his table. 'Would you like a cup of coffee, Colonel?' he asked as an afterthought. 'Pia's mochaccino is excellent. Coffee with chocolate is a match made in heaven.'

'I am sure there is another match in the making.' The colonel chuckled.

'I didn't get you,' Tim responded.

'Never mind, it was a joke. I wouldn't mind a cup of cappuccino, if you can get it.'

'That's not a problem at all. Shirt Pant can fetch it for you and, while he is at it, I wouldn't mind another cup of mochaccino.'

'Don't overdo the stuff, Tim,' advised the colonel. 'Both coffee and chocolate are addictive, as addictive and lethal as love.'

'I don't get you,' repeated Tim, a slow blush spreading over his face.

'I think you do, but let's leave that for the moment. When are you expecting the autopsy report?'

Tim called for the constable and instructed him to fetch the coffee before responding. 'The doctor conducting the autopsy was on the job when I last spoke to him. Unless there is a suspicion of death due to poisoning, he has promised to furnish the basic report by tomorrow morning. I will try to get a report unofficially this evening. Once the doctor confirms the cause of death, we can close the case.'

'What did the wife have to say about the deceased's state of mind?' Acharya steepled his fingers and closed his eyes. His mind was on overdrive.

'He wasn't depressed, she claimed. But she thinks it could be suicide. I couldn't probe too much as she begged to be excused from further questioning.'

'That is understandable.'

'I wish you had come along. You have a better approach with women.'

'Is that a compliment? Well, don't let Laila hear you or I will spend the rest of my life in the doghouse.' Acharya chortled.

'Your secret is safe with me, Colonel.'

'I wonder if it was suicide,' muttered the colonel, limping towards the window once again. 'If so, what could be the cause? What could have driven the man to take his life? Was it finances, health, or a relationship complication that led him to commit suicide?'

'It would be impossible for us to know that. Bulldog is convinced that the man committed suicide, and I would go with that. The state of his finances, mental or physical health and the troubles in his relationship do not concern us. Unless it is homicide, those factors lie beyond police purview.'

'You think so too?' Acharya turned towards Tim. 'It would be convenient, yes. There are so many questions that remain unanswered. Is it really a suicide case? Are we taking the easiest route to solving the death? Could it be anything other than suicide?'

'Well, whatever I gleaned from Rohan Bhandari fits that deduction,' Tim got to his feet and walked across the room towards the colonel.

'What did Rohan Bhandari tell you?'

'He told me that the deceased had invited himself to the wedding reception. Rohan had no intention of inviting Dabral. According to Bulldog, Dabral had come here with the sole intention of committing suicide. It explains the man's strange behaviour.'

'True! It is a plausible explanation,' agreed Acharya. 'What about the things found in Pia's van? I would like to look at them.'

'There was very little in the van, most of it unimportant. They are there on that table.' Tim pointed at the items heaped on a table in a corner of his room.

'May I take a look?' asked the colonel, walking towards the table.

'By all means.' Tim grinned. 'There is nothing precious or important.'

Acharya rummaged through the stuff. There was a can of orange juice, a packet of potato chips, a small container of baking powder and one of cocoa, some broken crockery and a lipstick. A marble rolling pin lying nearby arrested his eyes.

'We found the rolling pin on the floor of the van,' Tim replied to the questioning look thrown by the colonel.

He picked it up and weighed it in his hand. 'It's quite a heavy one. Fortunately, Pia is not married. Imagine her husband's plight were she to wield this on him.' Acharya laughed

'I guess the guy should ensure she got rid of it before they married.'

The constable, who had arrived with the coffee, halted at the threshold of Tim's office, wondering if the DSP had arrived. A moment later, he entered the room to find the two men laughing. He heaved a sigh of relief.

'How are you, Sharad?' Acharya addressed the grinning constable, who placed the brew on Tim's table.

'I am fine, sir.'

'Thank you for the coffee, Sharad.'

The constable threw him a salute and walked out, saying, 'Mention not, sir.'

'I think it is a clear-cut case,' said Tim, sipping his sixth cup of coffee that day.

'I have a suspicious mind. Any case that seems simple never fails to rouse my suspicion.'

'It is not fair to doubt everything in pursuit of excitement, Colonel,' Tim reproached.

'You are right. I will be happy to be proved wrong. On account of the unfortunate incident as a young officer, I realized how important it was to be cautious. My instincts have been on overdrive ever since.'

Tim knew all about the incident the colonel was speaking of.

It happened years ago, when, as a junior captain, Acharya was posted in a militant-infested area of Nagaland. One night, tipped off about a couple of militants who were hiding in a village at the fringes of a forest, Acharya was ordered to carry out a night raid to nab them.

On that cold and moonless night the team set out for the forest. Keyed up and alert, they walked through a tall grass field, their nerves on edge. Assisted by shaded torches, they traipsed, starting at each sound. Unnerved by a sudden movement in the grass, an edgy Acharya made a vital error of judgement. He shot in the dark, triggering a volley of retaliating fire from the militants. It was a blunder. His leading scout caught a bullet and died instantly. He was responsible for the death of the jawan.

The successful rounding up of the militants thereafter did nothing to erase the incident from his mind. He continued to be haunted by nightmares.

The incident proved to be a turning point in Acharya's life.

8

It was 7 in the evening when, at Rhodo Cottage, the four men sitting around a card table ended a game and discarded the idea of another game in favour of discussing the stranger's death.

The colonel was the first one to plonk himself on the comfortable couch at the other end of the room. Eager to know more about the case, the others followed his example.

'The man must be crazy,' opined the professor, cautiously biting into a steaming samosa. 'Mmmm, delicious!'

'What is delicious? The deceased's craziness?' teased the judge.

'Don't be daft, JJ. You know what I am talking about.'

'Well, I suppose he had a peg too many of the expensive whisky,' said the doctor. 'He definitely had no idea he would be taking a shortcut to heaven when he set out.'

'The guy could have been reversing the van to create space for his car,' said the professor.

'You are becoming senile, Prof. The guy was an outsider. He hadn't come in a car,' reminded the doc.

'In that case, he might have been helping someone park the car.'

'Would he get into a stranger's van in order to help another stranger? No. It doesn't explain his actions.'

'In that case, he might have just been drunk. I am satisfied with that explanation. It was a rambunctious party and most of the guests, including yours truly, had had too much to drink,' said the professor, picking up yet another samosa from the plate lying on the centre table. 'I am sure JJ had a few more drinks than his usual quota.'

'Speak for yourself, Professor,' the judge teased his friend. 'Not only were you drinking, you were also ogling the pretty young things at the party.'

'Well, what's wrong with that? It's rare to see so many comely lasses. A sight fit to warm the cockles of a man's heart.'

'Shame on you for hitting on women at your age,' scolded the doc. 'Now, if I were to do something like that ...'

'Just because you are a bachelor?'

'Not just a bachelor, but an eligible one,' the judge came to the doc's rescue.

'Let's drop this dangerous discussion. I will be heading to court if my wife hears us,' laughed the professor, taking a sip of tea. 'We might as well get on with our game.'

'I am in no mood to play tonight,' declared the doc.

'Nor am I,' said the judge.

'Each time there is an unexplained death, our game goes for a toss,' complained the professor.

For once, the colonel maintained a stony silence as his friends speculated on the death of the stranger. Brushing off an imaginary speck of dirt from his impeccably tailored albeit old blazer, he picked up the newspaper and began reading. The disinterest he feigned did not fool the judge.

'The pretence of indifference doesn't suit you, Colonel,' taunted JJ. 'The case must have churned your brain cells. So what is your take on the subject?'

'According to the police, it is a case of suicide,' replied Acharya.

'And you agree with them, of course.' His friend sniggered.

'I have found no reason to disagree. Not yet, anyway.'

'There are easier ways of committing suicide, one would think. Why create such a big mess?' the professor said.

'I agree.' The doc nodded.

'Painless too. Do you think he suffered?'

'It depends on how long it took for him to die.'

'I mean, he could have swallowed a bottle full of sleeping tablets and died peacefully,' the professor continued his stream of thought. 'Instead, what does the man do? He comes all the way from Delhi to Ramsar, seeks out an old van and drives it down the ravine. Strange are the ways of the mind.'

'What bothers me is why he chose to go down in Violet's van,' the doc wondered. 'There were at least twenty cars on that road that night, yet he chose the dilapidated van. What if it had stalled? It was a chilly night and we all know the moody behaviour of old engines. I would have driven the MLA's Mercedes down the ravine if I wanted to commit suicide. One should die in style. On second thoughts, I would have chosen sleeping pills.'

'I think it was very considerate of him. The man didn't want to destroy a new car.' The portly professor laughed.

'What nonsense!' JJ butted into the discussion. 'It is simple. All new cars come with an automatic lock system. The older models are easier to unlock.'

The colonel said, 'Dabral didn't have to bother about unlocking the van. Pia had forgotten to lock the door. All he had to do was try the door.'

'How can you be sure it was suicide?' JJ raised his bushy eyebrow questioningly.

'According to the statement given by Rohan Bhandari, Dabral invited himself to Ramsar for the wedding reception. The police think he came here with the sole intention of committing suicide,' replied Acharya, folding the newspaper and placing it back.

'And you are convinced?'

'Like I said, there is no evidence to suggest that it was anything other than suicide. In fact, I am waiting for Tim for an update on the matter.'

'The wife was at the party, I am told,' said the judge. 'What does she say? She should be in the know of her husband's mental state. Was he suffering from depression?'

'Tim asked her the same question,' said Acharya, placing his cup on a peg table. 'She claims he was his normal self. There was no trace of depression while they were at the party. However, she supports the suicide theory.'

'That's interesting!'

'It is! There being no evidence of foul play, all we can do is wait for the autopsy report to confirm this theory. Once that comes in and there is no evidence to prove it wasn't suicide, the police will close the case, I guess.'

'Tim should have been here by now. It is past 7,' muttered the judge, glancing at the vintage cuckoo clock hanging on the wall.

Geeta, who entered with yet another refill of steaming ginger tea, heard his remark and replied, 'He called up half an hour back to say he would be delayed.'

'You mean he is still working?'

'I don't know about that. Apparently, he is waiting for a report from the pathologist's office.'

'The pathologist's office doesn't work so late,' quipped the judge. 'He must be up to some mischief.'

'Your nephew is not the kind to spend time at his office when his favourite biryani is being cooked here.' Geeta chuckled. Everyone knew of Tim's partiality for her cooking.

'That's true,' agreed JJ. 'Something important must have kept him at his desk.'

'As far as I know, Tim is hoping to hear from a friend who works at the hospital.'

'Let's hope he is here soon,' said the judge.

'I am not leaving without hearing the forensic report, at least the reason of death,' declared the colonel.

'Isn't anyone interested in a game of bridge while we wait for that guy?' asked the professor, hoping his friends had changed their minds.

'Have a heart, Professor. We are discussing the mysterious death of a stranger in Ramsar and all you can think of is king, queen and knaves,' retorted Acharya.

'For your information, I have my heart in the right place. A death has occurred, I agree. But is there any point in speculating over it? The matter is being handled by the police. We have no business gossiping about the whys and wherefores of the death. The four of us gather at this cottage for an evening of fun, laughter and card games. So, let's continue with that.'

'I am in no mood to play,' said the colonel. 'You guys go ahead without me.'

'You know that is not possible. How can three of us play bridge?'

'Count me out too,' said the doc, getting wearily to his feet. 'It is time for me to leave. I had a long day.'

'Since everyone has decided to boycott the game, there is no point in my hanging around. I will leave too,' said the professor.

The two of them had stepped out on to the porch when, his face flushed and eyes shining with excitement, Tim burst through the gate of the cottage. Eager to hear the verdict, the doc and professor followed him into the hall. One look at Tim's face and Acharya knew that the forensic examination did not support the suicide theory.

'It isn't suicide, right?' He raised an eyebrow enquiringly. 'I bet it wasn't an accident either.'

'You have hit the nail on the head,' Tim exclaimed, striding up to the sofa. He plonked his weight down and rubbed his tired eyes. A minute later, he directed a searching glance at the colonel. 'I was wondering what made you doubtful about the suicide theory right from the beginning.'

'Should we assume it was homicide?' the doc piped up.

'That's right.'

'Well, that calls for some more discussion on the subject.' The professor, who loved mystery, looked at the group with enthusiasm.

Once again, their expressions serious, the men assembled at the card table.

'We will do that. First, let me fetch a cup of tea from the kitchen,' said Tim, stretching his long legs before springing up. A couple of minutes later, while the others were engaged in a lively debate on the causes of Dabral's death, he returned with tea, followed by his aunt.

Eager to have her say in the discussion, Geeta joined the men at the table.

'What exactly did your friend say about the cause of death?' asked the colonel once they had settled and everyone looked expectantly at Tim to spill the information.

'Well, the detailed report will follow. All he told me was the estimated time and the cause of death,' said the police officer. 'The death was caused by a heavy blow to the back of the head and the estimated time of death is between 8 and 11 p.m.'

'It was not suicide, then?' Geeta interjected. 'Who would kill a stranger in Ramsar? And why?'

'That's what the police have to find out,' JJ told his wife.

'I think someone with a grudge killed the man,' opined the professor. 'That guy could have followed Dabral here and clobbered him on the head.'

'Why would he follow him all the way to Ramsar? Your speculation falls flat on its face.' The doc rejected the professor's theory. 'I think the killer was at the party.'

Ignoring their inference, Tim continued, 'Dabral couldn't be dead at 8 p.m. since he was with his wife at the party till 8.30 p.m. Thereafter, he left the venue. So we can safely assume that the death took place after 8.30 p.m.'

'That's right,' agreed the colonel. Taking off his glasses, he polished them meticulously with a piece of microfibre cloth while he took in the information. Having worked with him on a few cases, Tim knew the colonel's mind was busy processing the facts.

'Colonel, what is your opinion on the matter? Who do you think killed the man from Delhi?' asked the professor.

'My dear friend, it is not possible to say anything now. The death has to be investigated, people have to be questioned and evidence collected, only then can we come to any conclusion,' replied Acharya, a trifle testily.

There was silence for a while.

'I would like to meet Mrs Dabral,' said the colonel. 'Before the storm breaks,' he added after a moment's pause.

'Storm?' Tim raised an eyebrow.

'I expect Bulldog to visit the police station tomorrow morning, so be prepared to face a hurricane.' Acharya's lips stretched in a smile. 'Does he know it is not a suicide?'

'Not yet. I will share the details after receiving the autopsy report. An unofficial report doesn't warrant sharing, I think.' Tim grinned.

'No, it doesn't.'

9

At 9 a.m. the next day, while on the way to Bhandari Villa, Tim and the colonel decided that Dabral's wife would not be informed that her husband's death was not suicide. Not until they received the official autopsy report at the police station. The colonel was eager to get her version of Dabral's death, before they told her it was homicide. He told Tim it was possible to catch a lie by matching two statements.

'I want to hear what she has to say before Nisha Dabral receives the forensic verdict. It could give us some important clues.'

'Do you expect her to add something to the statement she gave earlier?' Tim asked sceptically.

'You will be surprised. Often people get trapped in their statements. Ask them the same question a few times, and you may get a different reply after a while.'

Nisha Dabral had barely finished a breakfast of a couple of toasted slices of bread and orange juice in her room, when she was informed of their arrival. They were waiting for her in the study, she was told. Brushing away the crumbs of toast from her lap, she prepared herself to face the men.

White suits her, was the colonel's first thought as Nisha Dabral walked into the room, where the duo was waiting for her. The other members of the Bhandari family made a discreet disappearance as the trio settled down for the discussion.

Her face composed, the lady was dressed demurely in a white embroidered kurta and tights. Her thick hair was caught in an enamelled clip. Nisha Dabral displayed none of the nervousness of the previous day, Tim noted. The eyes were carefully made up to camouflage the remains of puffiness. The lips that had been dry and chapped were now smoothened with a natural lipstick. Her face was devoid of expression.

The woman looks like one of those anorexic models that come out of an assembly line. The vacant and expressionless face will make it difficult to read her thoughts, reckoned Acharya as he stood up to greet the woman. 'Good morning, Mrs Dabral,' he said. 'I am Colonel Arjun Acharya, a retired army officer. My sincere condolences for your loss.'

'Thank you,' she murmured, her dark eyes gauging him. If she felt surprised at his presence, she gave no indication of it.

'I wish we didn't have to bother you in your time of grief, but we have to complete the procedures,' Tim said. 'I hope you are feeling better this morning.'

'It's all right,' Nisha murmured. 'You have a duty to perform.'

'Were you successful in calling your brother?' Tim asked.

'Yes, he will arrive by the morning train tomorrow.'

'Good,' said Acharya. 'Do you mind if we ask you a few questions?'

'I don't really see why I am being subjected to interrogation,' she baulked, her eyes blazing. 'Yesterday by the officer and now by you. Should I assume that I am under suspicion?'

At last, a sign of emotion. The colonel chuckled.

'It's not an interrogation,' the colonel hastened to reassure her in his best avuncular manner. 'It is just an obligatory exercise. A death has taken place and we have to go into the reasons of its sudden and violent nature. Since your husband was a stranger here, there is no one else who can give us the information.'

'And where do you come into the picture, Colonel?' she demanded coldly. 'I can understand the police's right to question me, but I am baffled by your standing in the matter. I don't think I am obliged to respond to your questions.'

This is no wilting lily. She is sharp, the colonel thought. 'Let me explain,' he began. 'I assist the police in local investigations. Unofficially, of course. The ASP could ask you the questions, if you prefer.'

'It is better if you cooperate, Mrs Dabral. It will be quicker and save you a lot of headache.'

'Are you issuing a veiled threat, officer? What if I refuse?'

'It will be very inconvenient for all concerned. Either we will have to return to complete the questioning or you will be summoned to the police station to do so,' Tim informed grimly. 'It will simply delay matters and you may have to stay back in Ramsar for a while.'

There was a brief pause as Nisha Dabral weighed the consequences of not cooperating with the police. She studied the grey-haired colonel sitting across. There was a benign expression on his sharply etched features. Coming to a decision, she nodded her head.

'All right, I will answer all your questions, although I still don't understand the colonel's involvement in the matter.'

Ignoring her barb, Acharya cleared his throat and shot his first question at her.

'How long have you been married to Deepak Dabral?'

'We would have completed eighteen months next week.'

'How old was your husband?'

'He was thirty-nine.'

'I know it is rude to ask a woman's age, but how old are you?'

'I am thirty-one.'

'There was an eight-year difference between the two of you. Am I right?'

'Where are we going with that question, Colonel? Are you trying to insinuate something?"

'Absolutely not! I am trying to get a clear picture of the case and to do that, I have to ask several questions,' saying this, Acharya threw her a disarming smile. He paused for a while to dig out a cigar case from his pocket. Thereafter, he proceeded to lob the cigar cap, his actions slow and deliberate. Finally, he lit up the cigar. It was a diversionary tactic to keep the suspect squirming. He had given up smoking a long time back. It was a promise he'd made to Laila. The cigar was just a convenient tool, he assured her, and she compromised.

After a puff of the cigar, he resumed the questioning. 'Would you say that the two of you had a happy marriage?'

'I replied to that question yesterday. You can ask the officer.'

'Let me reframe the question. How was the relationship between the two of you?'

Tim was amused. By now he was familiar with most of the tactics of the colonel, and he enjoyed the cat-and-mouse game Acharya played with suspects.

'I have replied to that question also,' she stood up and said. 'It's a waste of time repeating the same thing. Besides, I don't think the age difference between Deepak and me or the level of happiness in our marriage has anything to do with my husband's death. Good day to you, Colonel,' she concluded.

'Just a minute, Nisha,' Acharya said, getting up on his feet. 'These questions are essential to the case. We are trying to establish the cause of your husband's death, and to do that we have to examine all his relationships. We expect you to cooperate with us.'

'I am willing to cooperate, but the officer asked the same questions. Having answered them, I don't see the point in repeating them. Also, isn't it insensitive to harass me while I am in bereavement?' Nisha resorted to emotional pressure.

'We understand your grief,' soothed the colonel. 'It gives us no pleasure to subject you to grilling at this moment. However, the police have to investigate your husband's death.' He spread his hands in a helpless gesture. 'Waiting to carry out investigations till the mourning period is over is not an option anyway.'

'Please calm down, Mrs Dabral,' Tim exhorted. 'We are trying to understand the mysterious death of your husband. If it was suicide, we have to determine the reasons for the same. Was the deceased in a healthy state of mind or was he emotionally upset is what we are trying to find out. Kindly answer the question.'

Nisha eyed Tim's determined face and realized that he meant business. The police officer had placed himself strategically near the door to block her exit. Drawing a deep sigh, she sat down heavily on the sofa.

She looked at Acharya uncertainly. His kindly eyes met hers across the distance. Not strictly handsome, with an impressive personality nevertheless, the colonel carried himself with a soldierly bearing. Sympathetic and avuncular, he appeared harmless. 'All right! I will answer all your questions,' Nisha Dabral yielded. Her shoulders sagged in a dispirited manner 'I will narrate the details of our marriage. That will provide you with all the answers, I hope,' she said.

'Thank you. That will be nice,' replied the colonel encouragingly. He looked wryly at the cigar, which was now extinguished.

'Deepak was introduced to me by a common friend during a formal party. Although he was years older than me, we got along reasonably well. He was looking for a wife, the friend had told me, since he knew that I was also looking for a life partner. Unlike most women, I have a fascination for older men. Call it a father fixation, but I feel older men are mature and experienced. We didn't fall in love overnight. It happened over a few months. In fact, it took a lot of time for him to broach the subject. He was not a man to take a sudden leap into matrimony, nor was he a communicative person. I guess he was old enough to realize the intricacies of the relationship. To be honest, I found his diffidence endearing. Finally, the two of us tied the knot,' Nisha said. There was a pause and she picked up the glass of water sitting on the side table.

After a few sips of water, she continued with the story. 'One thing I had understood was that there are no perfect relationships or marriages, so I had no unrealistic expectations from Deepak. To reply to your question, whether we were happy, I would say, yes, we were reasonably happy. You can say we were more comfortable than happy. It helped that we were not wearing rose-tinted glasses and had no lofty expectations from each other. Ours differed from most marriages. It was a live-and-let-live relationship. We allowed each other the freedom to do what we liked. Early on in the marriage, the two of us had decided not to stifle each other with demands. I am a working woman and have my own set of friends. Deepak was a loner. He didn't have friends. In fact, three months after our wedding, he sailed away on work. We have been together only for eleven months out of the eighteen months of marriage. Our marriage was too fresh to have unpleasantness. Who knows if disagreements would have entered the relationship after a while? Deepak didn't live long enough for me to experience that.'

There was another pause as her eyes misted and she grappled with her emotions. *Was there a fleeting expression of regret on her face?* Acharya wondered. *Regret at not having spent enough time with her husband because of his unexpected death, or was it an excellent piece of acting?*

A knock on the door was followed by a servant bringing them a tray of tea and biscuits.

'Madam wants to know if you want anything,' said the elderly retainer, placing the tray on the table before them.

'Bring me a glass of water,' Nisha ordered the man.

While they waited for the water, she resumed her narrative. 'We differed greatly from each other. I loved parties. He hated them. I am an extrovert. He was an introvert. I did not meet a single friend of his in the eighteen months of our marriage. In fact, I met a few of his colleagues for the first time at the party. I was surprised when he said we were invited to attend the wedding reception of a colleague. I was still more surprised when told by Rohan Bhandari that Deepak had invited himself to this place,' she confessed, a baffled expression on her face. 'Deepak was not the kind of person who would travel so far to attend a reception and the least likely person to invite himself for it.'

'You didn't ask why he wanted to attend the reception at Bhandari Villa?' Tim asked.

'Of course I asked him. I didn't want to travel all the way here to attend the reception party of a person I had never met,' she replied.

'What did your husband have to say to that?' Acharya was curious to know the reply.

'He said it would amount to killing two birds with a single stone,' her eyes lit up with amusement as she spoke. 'His sense of humour was weird.'

'What did he mean by that?'

'Deepak was a tight-lipped man. I asked for an explanation, but he was not forthcoming. I assumed he had other fish to fry while he was attending the party of a colleague.'

'When was the last time you saw your husband?'

'I saw him last at around 8.40 p.m. He left the party soon after.'

'Did he say where he was going?'

'He had mentioned something about getting late for an appointment, which was at 9 p.m.'

'You have no idea who he was meeting?'

A guarded look suddenly appeared on the woman's face. It didn't escape Acharya. It was as though the shutters had come down, wiping away all signs of emotion from the face.

'Didn't you mention that your husband had gone to meet a cousin?' Tim intervened. Taking out a notepad from the pocket, he continued. 'Let me jog your memory. You said Deepak Dabral had a meeting with Umesh Gudyal that night.'

'Yes, I remember now. He had gone out to meet Umesh,' Nisha said, throwing a scathing look at Tim.

'Any idea why he went to meet Umesh?' prodded Acharya.

'Deepak didn't share the details with me, but I remember him mentioning some property dispute with his cousin.'

'Was it the first time he was meeting his cousin?'

'I have no idea if the two of them had met earlier. All I know is that my husband had gone to meet his cousin for a discussion.'

'You mean to say that you don't know if your husband had come to Ramsar earlier?'

'I don't think he had come to Ramsar before the reception party thrown by the Bhandaris. As I have already said, Deepak wasn't a very communicative person and didn't keep me informed about every move of his. To be honest, I don't know if he had come here earlier without informing me.'

'That's understandable,' the colonel said, trying to soothe her ruffled feathers. He did not want her to stop cooperating with the police. But the woman decided she had spoken enough.

'I would like to leave, Colonel, if you are done with the questioning. I have told you everything I could. If there is anything else, please come back after my brother arrives.'

For the second time during the interview, Nisha Dabral stood up and threw a dismissive look at Acharya.

'Thank you, Mrs Dabral,' said the colonel, getting up from his seat. 'You have been a big help.'

'I hope you have enough evidence to prove that my husband committed suicide.'

'I hope so too,' murmured Acharya.

Without a backward glance, she left the room.

'What a woman!' Tim remarked as they drove towards the police station.

'Make no mistake, Tim. We are not dealing with a grief-stricken widow here. Nisha Dabral is a very intelligent woman. She is composed, careful and in full control.'

The autopsy report was waiting on Tim's table when the two men reached his office. He pursed his lips and let out a brief whistle as he read through the report before handing it over to Acharya, who was tapping a pencil on the table.

'As per the report, Dabral's death was caused by blunt-force trauma. It mentions a medium-sized scalp laceration in the left parietal area.' Acharya pursed his lips as he read the report aloud. 'The skull reveals a fracture in the parietal bone. The brain is oedematous with subdural and subarachnoid haemorrhage. Injuries are ante-mortem in nature and recent in origin.' The colonel flipped the page. 'There is a lot of medical jargon, but we need not go into those details.'

'Medium-sized scalp laceration in the left parietal area … Would that mean that the person inflicting the injury was standing slightly to the left of the victim?' Tim asked.

'You are absolutely right. Dabral was hit on the left side of the head, from the back. It means that the person had crept up behind the victim to deal him the death blow.'

'And now that we have received the report, it is time to call Bulldog. I dread the thought of aggravating the acid attack on his innards.' Tim winked at the colonel as he picked up the phone to call the DSP.

The DSP's chronic dyspepsia and his constant need for a glass of cold buttermilk with a pinch of roasted cumin powder to cure it was a joke among the police officers under him.

As expected, Bulldog burst an artery at the news. Till the forensic report arrived, he had comforted himself with the suicide theory. The matter would have to be treated as a homicide now, making it impossible to avoid extensive investigations. It would mean constant shuttling between Almora and Ramsar, added pressure from the top and an aggravation of dyspepsia.

'It is almost 11 a.m. now. I will be there by 12.30,' barked the DSP. 'I expect you have made some headway in the case. Make sure that the report along with all your findings are on the table. We have to get cracking. There is no time to lose.'

That was another problem. Bulldog wanted all crime cases to be solved within twenty-four hours. His methods were often crude and unimaginative.

'Sir, we have been informed that Nisha Dabral's brother will arrive today. Thereafter they will collect the body from the morgue and take it to Delhi for cremation.'

'If he is taking the morning train from Delhi to Kathgodam, he cannot reach Ramsar before 4 p.m. I will be there much before he reaches, so don't worry about the brother.'

Tim knew that the morning trains from Delhi reached the railhead around noon, and the drive from Kathgodam to Ramsar would take around four hours, so Bulldog was right.

'The body will remain in the morgue till I reach a decision,' bellowed the DSP, his voice rising with every word. 'No one is to leave town till I give permission. You are to ensure that Dabral's wife or his colleagues do not leave Ramsar. Is that clear?'

'But sir ...'

'No buts,' Bulldog interrupted Tim. 'I want to question each of the deceased's colleagues who were present at the party.'

'The colleagues have already left for Kathgodam in the morning.'

'You should have detained them,' JBS bellowed. 'How could you let them go?'

'I found no valid reason to detain them. I had already questioned them. Also, Dabral's death was assumed to be a case of suicide, so I gave them the clearance to leave town. However, the autopsy report throws doubts on that theory,' Tim explained.

'We will decide that after I have seen the report. I am starting right away.'

'Yes, sir.'

Tim put down the phone and inhaled deeply.

'Good luck to you.' The colonel chuckled, who had been listening to the conversation. 'I must leave before the cyclone hits the police station.'

'This is not expected of you, Colonel. You are abandoning me,' Tim said in jest. 'In any case, you will soon have to face the cyclone. You are sure to be dragged into the case.' He laughed.

'I would love that, of course.' Acharya cackled. 'In the meantime, I wish you a happy encounter with Bulldog.' He brandished the walking stick in the air and walked out jauntily.

As predicted by the colonel, the cyclone hit the Ramsar police station a little after noon. Having driven at breakneck speed, Bulldog made it in record time. His heartburn intensified with the stress caused by the case, the agitated DSP began lambasting Tim. Letting off steam didn't bring relief from the dyspepsia, but provided him with an outlet for pressure.

'How could a van be stolen from right under the noses of 200 guests? Bhandari Villa was teeming with people that night. Someone would have seen the van being driven. Another point to consider is that there were quite a few cars parked on the road fringing the villa. Why then would a man take the trouble of stealing a dilapidated van? Wouldn't he steal the swankiest of cars?' the DSP thundered.

Tim listened patiently as the boss vented his ire. He knew it was important that Bulldog got his frustration out of his system. Sane discussion could follow only after the man was done with the fulminating.

'You were at the venue and so was the colonel. Did you not notice anything?' Bulldog asked.

'Sir, the villa is ringed by high walls. It is impossible for people to see the road from the lawn where the party was being held,' Tim explained. Tactfully, he avoided mentioning that the DSP had also attended the party. Although JBS had left the venue at 10 p.m., he had had ample opportunity to observe whatever he expected others to have observed. Besides, it was a party and everyone was there to have a good time. No one expected trouble.

'Have you questioned the girl who was driving Violet William's van?'

'I have recorded her statement. According to Pia, she did not know the deceased.'

'Have you questioned Umesh Gudyal? You informed me that Nisha Dabral had admitted that her husband left the party for an appointment with Gudyal at 9 p.m. That was the last time she had seen Dabral.'

'I haven't questioned Gudyal yet. I spent the morning questioning the colleagues before they left Ramsar. Thereafter, I went to Bhandari Villa and questioned the wife.'

'That is not enough. You should have recorded Gudyal's statement. It is simple. Dabral left the party to meet his cousin. Thereafter he didn't return. His body was found in the morning, which means Gudyal was the last person to see the deceased alive,' JBS surmised.

'We had assumed it to be a case of suicide,' Tim reminded his boss.

'Even if it was suicide, the fact doesn't change that Gudyal was the last person to see him alive.' JBS was fast losing patience. 'Reports of his violent temper have reached me earlier. That guy bashed up a person for a minor argument. Killing Dabral after a heated argument is not beyond Umesh Gudyal. Call the scoundrel to the police station right now. I want to question him.'

'Gudyal?'

'Who else would I mean? Don't you get it?' Bulldog had worked himself up. He closed his eyes, and like the doctor had advised, counted to ten and continued, 'It's Gudyal I want to question.'

'Yes, sir,' Tim said and picked up the phone to call Umesh Gudyal.

'Wait! I think it will be better to go to Negi Mansion to question the chap. I want to catch him unawares,' the DSP said. He drained the water from the glass placed on the table and stood up.

The two of them were about to step out of the office when Laxmi Badola rushed into the police station. Sharad Pant, his ears cocked to catch the conversation inside, was standing near the door to Tim's office. He stretched out his arm to block the woman from entering the room.

'Where do you think you are going?' he demanded importantly.

'I want to meet the police inspector.' Laxmi raised her chin defiantly. 'Who are you to stop me? Move out of my way.'

'The DSP is here and an important discussion is taking place,' Sharad said, barring the woman's path. 'You can't go in now.'

'Just you try to stop me,' challenged the woman. Pushing the constable to a side, Laxmi stormed into the room.

'I saw the stranger arguing in front of my house,' she announced.

Her words drew the desired attention. Tim and the DSP stared at the woman. 'Which stranger are you talking about?' hollered Bulldog, pushing his weight down on a chair once more.

'I am talking about the man who was found dead in the van.' Laxmi Badola waved the local newspaper under the DSP's nose. 'The man in this picture, he is the one I am talking about.'

There, on the front page, right below a photograph of the deceased, was the news about his death. The news item dwelled elaborately on the van and the death, along with the reporter's inference on how it could have happened.

10

'Sit down and tell me everything,' the DSP ordered the diminutive woman. Casting a victorious look at Sharad, Laxmi took a seat.

Bulldog faced the smug woman with sharp eyes. She was raring to speak. He pointed at the photograph in the newspaper and said, 'You have seen this man in Ramsar, you say.'

Her eyes bright with excitement, Laxmi Badola blurted, 'I have seen him two days back. Here in Ramsar. He was standing right in front of my house.'

'Start from the beginning and tell us everything in an orderly manner,' Tim commanded the woman.

Laxmi needed no further encouragement. She was just too happy to take part in a dramatic situation. Words tumbled out of the woman's mouth, almost incoherently.

'Take a deep breath and start again,' suggested Bulldog impatiently. He cast an eye on the wall clock and waved his hand to hurry her.

The woman took a deep breath and began talking. Gesturing with both hands to emphasize the importance of her narration she recounted the incident of the fateful morning when she had eavesdropped into the heated conversation between Umesh and Dabral.

'It was about 2 in the afternoon. I had finished lunch and was sitting in the living room when I heard two men arguing loudly on the road.' She didn't want to reduce the importance of her mission by admitting that she had been half-asleep after a heavy meal. 'Curious, I peeped out. And what do you think I saw? There, right in front of Negi Mansion, stood Umesh Gudyal and this man.' She pointed at the photograph in the newspaper. 'They were quarrelling about something.'

'Did you hear what they were arguing about?'

'Yes, it was something about letters, property and going to court. I couldn't hear everything since a strong wind was blowing away the words, but I distinctly caught the stranger shouting, "I have a share in the property. I will drag you to court if we cannot come to a mutually acceptable agreement."'

'What happened after that?'

'Suddenly Umesh took out a knife and said, "I will kill you if I see you in Ramsar again,"' she ended self-importantly. This was her moment of glory and she would not let anyone reduce it to nothing. Adding spice to a story came naturally to her. The woman did not hesitate for a fraction of a second before introducing a knife into the scene to make it dramatic. Embellishment was her forte.

Perking up his ears, Bulldog sat up at the mention of a knife. 'He threatened the man with a knife?' he asked.

'Yes, he did.'

'Sir …' Tim tried to intervene. He had heard all about Laxmi Badola and her tales. Everyone in town had had a taste of her gossiping. It was better to take her yarn with a large pinch of salt. He wanted to warn the boss.

'Later, Tim.' The DSP stopped him with a raised hand. He was convinced that the woman would lead them to the culprit. 'Let the woman complete her story. How big was the knife?' he asked Laxmi.

'It was this big.' She showed the length of her palm. Changing her mind, she pointed to a twelve-inch measuring scale lying on Tim's table and said, 'It was that length.'

'A footlong knife. Are you sure?' Bulldog looked doubtfully at her.

Realizing her folly, Laxmi Badola wondered about the length of a knife required to kill a man. She couldn't make up her mind. Would it be better if she stuck to the size of her palm? She wondered, *perhaps I should have mentioned a sickle instead of knife. A sickle comes in a standard size and it is easily available at the local shops. It is also a fixture in every house since the women use it for cutting grass to feed the goats and cows. It comes handy while threatening a person.*

'Maybe a couple of inches shorter,' she looked at the scale indecisively. 'Anyway, it was a long knife. To my mind, it was sharp and long enough to kill a man.'

'Are you sure Umesh Gudyal had a knife in his hand?' asked the DSP, suddenly doubtful of the woman's statement. 'Did you see properly? Could it be something else?'

'Of course I saw the knife.' The woman bridled at his tone. Now that she had stuck her foot in her mouth, she would have to keep it there. 'It was shining as though Umesh had sharpened it recently.'

'Sir …' Tim tried to warn Bulldog again.

'Let her finish.' Once again, the DSP stopped him from speaking. 'What happened after Umesh threatened to kill the man?' he asked the woman, who was preening importantly.

'Nothing! The stranger went away after warning Umesh that he would go to court.' The DSP seemed disappointed at the tame ending to the story. Noticing the expression on Bulldog's face, Laxmi quickly added some more fodder for thought. 'I think the stranger was so scared of Umesh that he drove the van down the ravine. After all, it is better to kill oneself than to be killed mercilessly by a person like Umesh,' she ended. Satisfied with her ability to craft a suitable ending, she sat back and waited. Laxmi wished she had something more to add to the story, something dramatic like having witnessed the actual event.

'Well! Thank you for coming forward with the information.' The DSP got up and steered the woman towards the door. 'We will seek your help when required. Now go home and don't discuss this with anyone.'

Clearly disappointed at the DSP's approach, Laxmi Badola shook her head. She had expected a little more appreciation from him, along with an offer for a cup of tea. And maybe some pakoras. This was no way to treat someone who had come forward with important information.

Anyway, it was an achievement. Not everyone gets to meet the senior police officer who had come all the way from Almora. She had his full attention too. It was an achievement, all right. She would invite a few women for tea that evening. It would be nice to share the experience of meeting the DSP.

Wrapped up in her plans, the woman was walking out of the police station when she almost collided into a man. It was happening once too often. Laxmi rebuked herself for being unmindful.

'Sorry!' he apologized, walking past the woman.

Her head still in the clouds, she smiled at the man. Then she halted and turned to stare at his back. The face seemed familiar. *My mind is playing tricks*, she decided. *He couldn't be familiar. How could I have met this stranger?* She was being silly. Energized by the mental picture of goggle-eyed women as she shared the story of her visit to the police station, Laxmi Badola walked towards her house.

His mind cogitating over the woman's story, the DSP paced the room. An amused Tim watched his superior pondering over Laxmi Badola's embellished story.

'Things are falling in place,' muttered Bulldog. 'Umesh Gudyal must have killed Dabral. It is logical. The two men argue over Negi's property and Umesh ends up threatening Dabral. In the evening, he carries out the threat. All we have to do now is arrest the scoundrel and give him the third degree. Once that is done, he will soon be singing.'

'I am sceptical about the woman's story. She is a big gossip, and everyone in Ramsar is aware of her tendency to spice up stories. The knife bit is definitely an embellishment, I feel,' Tim said.

The DSP stopped pacing the floor and looked at his junior. 'We can't discard the story. It has to be true. Why would the woman walk into the police station and spin a yarn? Most people do not want to get involved in a death case. The woman must have seen them arguing. I agree that the knife part struck me as a figment of her imagination. She was looking for sensation, I felt.'

'That's exactly the problem. Laxmi Badola likes to sensationalize everything. She is a lonely woman. Such stories make up for the lack of excitement in her life,' said Tim.

'Well, we will discard the knife and take the rest of her story with a pinch of salt.'

'Yes, sir,' Tim nodded his head. Going with the DSP's theory made life simpler. He decided to investigate the matter with the colonel's help and present the findings to the senior officer. Only after they had found the murderer.

'Let us go to Negi Mansion,' said the DSP, picking up his cap from the table. 'First, I want to question Umesh Gudyal, after which I would like to interview Nisha Dabral at Bhandari Villa.'

'Would you like to have a sandwich before we go to Negi Mansion? It is past 1 already.' Tim looked hopefully at his senior. He could feel his stomach rumbling. A ham sandwich and a cup of coffee at Pia's Peaberry seemed a good idea.

'That will not be possible, Tim. There is a lot of work to be done and I have to be back in Almora by 5 p.m.,' replied the DSP, demolishing Tim's hopes of a quick tête-à-tête with Pia while sipping his coffee.

Tim wondered if Bulldog would want to interview Pia too. He could suggest it once they had finished with Umesh Gudyal and Nisha Dabral. A coffee then would be equally enjoyable.

Realizing that the DSP was raring to go for Gudyal's jugular, Tim followed Bulldog out of the room. The two were walking down the short corridor when they heard a pleasant, well-modulated voice asking for the ASP. Turning the bend in the corridor, they spotted a smartly dressed man arguing with Sharad.

'I want to meet the ASP,' the man was saying.

Never one to miss an opportunity to show his importance, the constable shook his head. 'You can't meet him now. He is busy.'

'Look, it is important that I meet him immediately,' the man insisted.

'Didn't I say he is busy?' Sharad Pant glared at the visitor. Pointing to a bench, he said, 'Wait there. I will inform you when he is free to see you.'

'I am warning you, constable…'

'Warning, eh? You are warning me?' Tim heard Shirt Pant's belligerent tone and knew that the constable would spare no effort to detain the stranger. Challenge brought out the worse in him.

'What is it, Sharad?' asked the DSP. 'Who is this man?'

The constable stood at attention and saluted the DSP. 'He is…' Turning to the visitor, he said, 'Tell your name to sa'ab.'

'I am Sudhir Sabharwal, Nisha Dabral's brother,' said the man.

Tim darted an envious look at the well-built visitor who towered over him. Not an extra inch of fat or flesh. *That body must have come from endless hours of working out at a gym*, he mused. Tim was a fitness fanatic and spent no less than an hour sweating it out at the local gym, but he had a long way to go before he could attain Sudhir Sabharwal's kind of body.

Ruggedly handsome in a pair of worn blue jeans and a leather jacket over a blue-and-white checked shirt, Sudhir extended his hand towards the DSP.

'I am DSP Jung Bahadur Singh,' responded Bulldog. 'You arrived early? The morning train doesn't reach Kathgodam before 11.30 and then it is a four-hour drive to Ramsar.'

'We were not expecting you so soon. Were you not scheduled to arrive later?' Tim asked. 'Your sister told me…'

'That's right. According to the plan, I was to take the morning train. However, I was eager to reach Ramsar and be by Nisha's side. So I took the night train instead. Although the Bhandaris are taking good care of her, it is not the same as having a family member by one's side. The tragedy has shaken my sister. She needs emotional support to tide her over the death of her husband.'

Tim did not think Nisha Dabral was suffering from shock. He got the feeling that she was in full control of her emotions. 'What time did you reach Kathgodam?' he asked.

'The train reached at about 6.30 in the morning. Thereafter, I checked into the hotel and freshened up.'

'You are staying at a hotel?' Tim asked with surprise, adding. 'I thought you would stay with your sister at Bhandari Villa.'

'I thought it improper to impose myself on the Bhandaris. They have been kind enough to accommodate my sister.' Sabharwal scratched his left hand, which was covered with angry red rashes.

'Are you planning to stay in Ramsar for some time?' the DSP wanted to know.

'There are a few formalities before we can collect the body from the morgue, I am told. Also, the arrangements for cremation have to be tied up. I am not familiar with the town, so it will take me longer to arrange everything.'

'You are not taking the body back to Delhi?' The DSP was surprised to hear of it. 'You want to cremate it here in Ramsar?'

'Nisha and I reached the decision after a long discussion over the phone.' Sudhir Sabharwal spread his palms in a gesture of resignation. 'Deepak's parents are with his elder brother in the USA. It would take some time for his brother to travel from Seattle. Considering that the two brothers were not on good terms, it is highly doubtful he would take the trouble of travelling to Delhi to attend the cremation. Our father lives in Patiala. He is ailing and too feeble to attend the cremation. Since Nisha and I are the only ones available at the moment, we decided it was better to have the cremation here. Carting the body all the way to Delhi makes little sense, under the present circumstances,' he said while scratching his hand again.

The DSP shrugged his shoulders. It was none of his business where the body was cremated once the autopsy had been done. 'It is your sister's prerogative to decide where she wants the last rituals to be conducted. The police have no objection to the cremation being performed here,' he said.

'In that case, I will go to the morgue and finish the formalities.'

'Before you do that, I have a few questions to ask.'

'Shoot! I am here to answer all your questions.' Sudhir smiled pleasantly.

'I am in a bit of a hurry at the moment. We have to step out for a while to deal with some urgent matters. You will have to wait here till we return.'

'In that case, I will have lunch and return in an hour's time,' said Sudhir. 'I didn't have breakfast this morning,' he confessed sheepishly.

The mention of lunch reactivated Tim's hunger pangs, and he wished he could take off for a quick bite.

'Come back in an hour,' the DSP looked at his watch before replying. 'Don't be late.'

'I will be here at 2,' said the young man, throwing a mock salute at Bulldog as he walked out briskly.

Tim was staring admiringly at the man's back when the DSP commented, 'Smart alec.'

'Yes, he is rather smart,' agreed Tim. 'If only he didn't keep scratching his hand. It reduces the man's charm.'

'Don't dawdle, Tim,' the DSP snapped. 'It's time for us to meet Umesh Gudyal.'

11

The drive to Negi Mansion was a silent one. Bulldog was in a crabby mood. There had been too many interruptions since his arrival. Convinced that Umesh Gudyal was behind the crime, he was keen on getting his hands on the guy.

Umesh Gudyal was enjoying his lunch when the two of them reached Negi Mansion. A look of annoyance crossed his face at the interruption.

'Tell them I am eating,' he growled at his mother. 'They can wait.'

'It is not just the local inspector. He has brought a high-ranking officer from Almora to speak to you,' she whispered. 'It must be an important matter. Besides, he looks annoyed. You should not make him wait.'

'It doesn't worry me. I have done nothing wrong to warrant a visit from a high-ranking official. I will see them after finishing the meal. Ask them to wait. Why don't you offer them a cup of tea?'

'Beta …'

'Don't bother me … go out and speak to them.' Umesh continued eating in an unhurried manner.

Sita lingered apprehensively. An inherent fear of the police stopped her from going before them.

'What is happening? Why is Umesh Gudyal hiding?' the DSP bellowed from the hall, the smell of stale cigarettes bothering him. 'Do you want me to drag you to the police station?'

The warning drew Sita Gudyal from the kitchen. 'He is having his lunch,' she said, her eyes darting towards the door. 'He will be here in a minute. Please take your seat.' She led the two men towards a couple of chairs. 'While you are waiting, I will make tea for you.'

'Do you think we have time to waste?' bellowed the DSP, refusing to take a seat. 'What cheek, having lunch while we wait for His Majesty! Tell him to come out right now, or I will grab him by the collar and haul him to the police station.' Turning to Tim, he ordered, 'Drag that chap here right now.'

Tim hesitated. He saw no point in creating a furore.

'You heard me?' barked Bulldog.

'There is no need for anyone to grab me by the neck,' said Umesh Gudyal, walking into the hall. He was cool and unruffled. 'You can't barge into a house and drag a guy by the collar. There is something known as law and order in the country.'

'You will teach me about law and order?' the DSP fumed.

Umesh Gudyal stood before them, his muscular body tense and waiting. Eyes narrowed, he appraised the DSP, while his foxy face remained impassive. 'What brings you to Negi Mansion?' he asked. Far from being cowed by the DSP's hollering, he stared arrogantly at the police officers.

Provoked by Gudyal's words, the DSP lost the last trace of control. 'You don't know what brings us here?' he shouted.

'I don't.'

'Sit down, Umesh,' Tim intervened. He had no desire to witness a verbal brawl. His fingers fisted, Bulldog was pacing around restlessly, waiting to pounce on the man.

'Are you aware of the death of a stranger that took place two days back?'

'It is impossible to miss news printed on the front page of the local newspaper.' The unapologetic man smirked. 'May I?' he asked. Without waiting for permission, he lit up a cigarette.

'It will be better if you stick to facts and give the correct reply to our questions,' suggested Tim.

'Stop smoking before it suffocates us,' shouted Bulldog.

'Have it your way, officer.' Umesh stubbed out the cigarette and faced his interrogators. 'Yes, I know about the death. And before you ask, let me tell you I also knew the man.'

'How was he connected to you?'

'Deepak Dabral claimed to be my cousin, but I have never met him before coming to Ramsar. I could not verify his claim.'

'Why did he meet you?'

'Dabral wanted a part of Negi's property. He claimed to be a nephew of late Major Ratan Negi. We, my mother and I, are the legal inheritors of his property, as far as I know.'

'So, you are not sure that he is your cousin?'

'My uncle, Ratan Negi, had three sisters. Deepak claims to be the son of the eldest sister. I have not had the time to substantiate that claim yet. The second sister died childless. My mother is the youngest sister.'

'Your mother should be able to identify him.'

'My mother ran away with a man at an early age. After the scandal, the Negi family struck Mother off the roster of relatives. My parents married in Kathmandu, which was his ancestral place. We lived there for most of our life. We had a hard life. My father was a lowly clerk, who struggled to make ends meet. Mother toiled night and day to keep us clothed and fed. It wasn't a happy life. The Negi family refused to accept my father till his death. They kept no contact with us either.

'We were the poor relatives, fit to be shunned and ignored. They assumed we would come begging for financial help. We never did. My parents were proud people. They brought me up the best they could. I don't have the best education, but they took care to educate me. It was only after I completed my studies that we came to India and I took up a job. We tried to get in touch with my uncle, who served in the army. In fact, I met him a few times at his house in Kathgodam. By then, he was suffering from severe liver damage. For some strange reason, he took a liking for me. Perhaps he was repentant for having severed all connections with us or maybe it was because the others never cared to meet or take care of him. Since I was staying with my mother in Haldwani, I visited him as often as I could. Ratan Negi reciprocated with a few visits to our place. At one time, Ratan Negi had been very fond of his youngest sister. Meeting her after decades brought back many memories. It revived the relationship.'

Tim nodded understandingly. 'Did he speak of his other sisters?' he wanted to know.

'He mentioned them with regret. "No one wants to look after a sick man," he said. It is a selfish world.'

'He didn't mention leaving the property to you?'

'There was not much talk of the property, though he once mentioned that the ancestral property in Ramsar should not be allowed to go to seed. He regretted not having kept it in good shape. Just a couple of months before death, he instructed me to take care of Negi Mansion after his death.'

'Was there any witness to that conversation?' asked the DSP. He had cooled down after the initial outburst.

'No.' Umesh Gudyal shook his head. 'That day, just the two of us were present at Uncle's Kathgodam house. Towards the end of his life, he began thinking about Negi Mansion. My uncle had happy memories connected with the house. "We must not allow it to fall apart," he told me.'

There was a tinge of sorrow on his weather-beaten face. Umesh Gudyal was the same age as Deepak Dabral, but a tough life had left its imprint on the man. It had turned him into a surly, taciturn and pessimistic person. The effects on his mother were irreversible. An early marriage to a man who struggled to keep up the pretences of a decent life and left her a widow, deprived of family support and the love of her siblings, had left Sita Gudyal with nothing to offer to society.

'This is the first time I am speaking about all this.' Umesh nodded his head sadly. 'I pretend to be nonchalant, but it is tough being poor and ostracized.'

'You were the last person to see Dabral alive,' bellowed the DSP. 'He was murdered soon after your meeting on Sunday night.'

'I assure you that I met him at 2 in the afternoon. He must have met a hundred people after we met. What makes you believe I killed him?' Umesh laughed. 'Pray, why would I take the trouble of killing someone I barely knew?'

'But you can't deny that you met Dabral again later that night,' bellowed the DSP, trying to browbeat the fellow. 'He was murdered soon after the meeting.'

'Look, officer, we were to meet at 9 p.m. that night at Negi Mansion, but Deepak Dabral never made it to my house.'

'Why did you want to meet him? From what I heard, the two of you had an altercation over this property and parted on a hostile note, with you threatening to kill him.'

'That's true,' agreed Umesh Gudyal, 'we parted on a bitter note. However, my mother and I discussed the matter once he left. She felt that we could talk it over and come to an agreement. It was on her plea that I agreed to a meeting at our place.'

'At 9 p.m.?' Tim asked.

'Yes, at 9. The meeting was to take place here, at Negi Mansion.'

'And he didn't turn up?'

'No. He didn't.'

'That's unbelievable,' said the DSP. 'The deceased's wife, Nisha Dabral, clearly stated that her husband left the party at around 8.40 p.m. to keep an appointment with you.'

'I repeat, we had arranged to meet at 9 p.m. but Dabral did not turn up. I waited for him till 10 p.m. but he did not come. In fact, I told my mother that he was not interested in a patch-up and that we should not waste our time.'

'Do you expect me to believe that?'

'I don't expect you to disbelieve it either. I am telling you the truth. What you deduce is up to you.'

'Don't be cheeky,' scolded JBS. 'The deceased stepped out of the party at Bhandari Villa to meet you. We also know that you had an altercation over your uncle's property the same afternoon and had a compelling motive to kill the man. That is enough for the police to arrest you.' Bulldog shook his index finger angrily at Umesh.

'I can't stop you from arresting me, but I have not killed Dabral, and that's the truth.' Umesh Gudyal shrugged indifferently. There was no trace of fear or apprehension on his craggy face. 'In any case, I have an alibi. My mother will confirm that I did not leave the house at any time during the night.'

'Your mother will swear to anything in order to save her only son,' retorted JBS.

'In that case, there is nothing further to discuss.'

Frustrated with his indifferent attitude, JBS thrust out his chin challengingly. 'Do you know we have a witness who swears you had a brawl with Dabral on the same day as his death?'

'It was not a brawl. Dabral and I had a heated argument. That's all.'

'Did you not flash a knife and threaten to kill him?'

'Knife?' Umesh threw back his head and laughed. 'That's absurd! It is the figment of someone's overactive imagination, and I can guess the identity of your witness.'

'So, you confess there was a heated argument?'

'Of course I confess. As for your star witness, Laxmi Badola, I can only advise you to take her statement with a large dollop of salt.'

'That is for the law to decide. For the moment, you are not to leave Ramsar without the permission of the police,' warned the DSP. 'I forbid you to leave town.'

'You can't expect me to do that,' protested Umesh. 'I have a job, DSP.'

'This is a murder case and you are a suspect. We have a witness who swears that you threatened to kill Dabral. You should have thought of your job while killing your cousin.'

'That's ridiculous,' fumed Umesh. 'Just because you have an unreliable witness swearing of a brawl and a knife, you put me on the list of suspects. You don't care if I lose my job. It's not fair.'

'A murder is not fair either,' the DSP shot the words at Gudyal. 'You should be grateful that we have not arrested you. But remember that you have been warned against leaving town.'

Turning to Tim, he ordered, 'Let's go.'

The two of them took off for Bhandari Villa to interview the widow.

The wedding guests having departed, the villa wore a quiet air. The family was at lunch when the police officers reached the place.

'Bhandari Sa'ab wants to know if you would like to join him for lunch,' asked Ramprasad, the elderly retainer. 'The family has just begun their meal and will be happy if you could join them.'

'There's no need for that,' said the DSP. 'We don't have the time to have lunch. Just inform Mrs Dabral that we are here.'

'But sa'ab, she is not here.'

'What? Where is she?' Bulldog was outraged at the woman's absence.

'Do you know where she has gone?' Tim asked the bewildered man.

'No, sa'ab, I have no idea.'

'Did she not say anything?'

The man shook his head.

'What time did she leave?'

'Madam's brother arrived here, and then the two of them left about forty-five minutes back.'

'That scoundrel promised to be present within the hour at the police station. I had planned to speak to his sister and get back to the police station to question the chap,' raged the DSP, his mood getting blacker by the minute. He had been fuming ever since the interview with Umesh Gudyal. The man's cool arrogance had disturbed Bulldog.

'We could go back to the police station and wait for Sudhir Sabharwal,' Tim suggested cautiously.

'We will wait here for the two of them,' the DSP decided. 'I want to speak to Nisha Dabral.' Turning to the servant, he asked, 'While we are waiting, can you fetch me a glass of cold buttermilk with a pinch of rock salt and cumin powder?'

'Yes, sa'ab.' The retainer bowed deferentially. He shuffled away to do the bidding of the DSP.

A few minutes later, having downed two glasses of cold buttermilk, his heartburn mellowed, the DSP was in a better mood.

'We might as well have our lunch, sir,' Tim suggested.

'Maybe we should do that.' For once, Bulldog approved of Tim's idea. 'I had a small breakfast this morning and an empty stomach aggravates dyspepsia. We could grab a quick sandwich at the place you were suggesting.'

Tim smiled, elated at the thought of meeting Pia. 'It will take just a few minutes. Thereafter, we could either return to this place or call the brother and sister to the police station.'

'Do you have the phone numbers of Nisha and her brother?' asked the DSP.

'The colonel had taken her number during our first meeting with her. Shall I ask him for it?'

'Do that. Speak to the widow and her brother once you get the number. Tell them to report at the police station immediately.'

'Yes, sir,' said Tim, punching the colonel's number on the phone. A couple of minutes later, having taken the number from the colonel and spoken to Nisha, Tim climbed into the driver's seat of the police vehicle and the two officers took off for Pia's Peaberry.

'Hey there,' Pia greeted the duo warmly. She threw an enquiring look at the DSP and smiled. 'I guess you are Tim's boss.'

Her endearing smile seemed to take the edge off Bulldog's mood, and he returned the smile. 'Hello!' he said. 'I have heard a lot about your coffee shop from the ASP. So, what can you offer? We are in a hurry.'

'How would you like some coffee with a piece of freshly baked walnut cake?'

'That sounds good,' Tim said. 'Is it possible to get some sandwiches before we have the cake and coffee?'

'Sure! How about a chicken-and-mayonnaise sandwich? I could make a mushroom-and-herb omelette to go with it.'

'That will take long. Won't it?' asked Bulldog doubtfully.

'Can you give me ten minutes?' Pia asked, throwing an engaging smile at him. 'Or would that be asking for too much? Preparing food in a hurry or eating it in haste is not good for anyone's health, I have read.'

'Take fifteen,' replied the DSP generously. The girl's bright smile and gentle manner had worked like magic. Suddenly, he felt himself thaw.

Tim was surprised to find his boss in an amiable mood after the disagreeable episodes at Negi Mansion and Bhandari Villa.

Pia instructed Meg to prepare the sandwiches while she got busy with the omelettes.

'This is a nice place.' The DSP surveyed the lively decor in the sunny café and nodded his head appreciatively.

Forty minutes later, sated and relaxed after a satisfying meal of sandwiches, omelettes, coffee and cake, the two officers stepped out of the café.

'Why don't you request the colonel to join us at the police station?' the DSP ordered Tim. 'It would be good to learn his thoughts about the case.'

Although he hated to admit it, Bulldog had a lot of respect for the colonel's opinion and methods. Despite all reservations, he admired Acharya's cool-headed approach to a case.

Tim relayed the message to the colonel, who confirmed he would reach the police station in fifteen minutes.

12

Nisha Dabral and Sudhir Sabharwal were yet to arrive when the DSP and Tim returned to the police station. The news of their delay was enough to take away the DSP's geniality in a jiffy.

'I will put the scoundrel in the lock-up, just you wait and see,' he fumed and began pacing the floor in an agitated manner. Nothing bothered him more than indiscipline and insubordination.

Tim stood in a corner, making space for the DSP to continue his pacing. Knowing the wisdom of keeping silent when the boss ranted, Tim held his tongue.

'It is already 2.30 p.m., and I have lined up a meeting in Almora at 5. Call Nisha and tell her to be here with her brother within five minutes,' Bulldog commanded. 'Warn her of the consequences if they do not reach the police station on time.'

Tim was about to punch her number in when Acharya entered the room.

'Good afternoon,' the colonel greeted the duo cheerfully.

'Good afternoon, Colonel,' responded the DSP. His mood suddenly turned benign. Now that the colonel had arrived, he was sure the sleuth would come up with crucial ideas. Although he hated to admit it, Bulldog laid a heavy burden of expectations at Acharya's door. 'What have you been doing to this town, Colonel?' he remarked flippantly. 'The crime graph is heading northwards.'

'Well, we have to gird up to investigate the reasons for the zooming crime rate.' Acharya chuckled. He knew the DSP was not generous enough to share the credit of solving a crime, although the top brass were aware of his contribution. The colonel also knew that Bulldog loved hogging the limelight. The balm of flattery always worked on the pompous man. 'I am sure you have the latest murder case under control. So how is it going?'

'Not too bad,' grunted the DSP in reply. He had no intention of admitting that the police were clueless about the murderer. 'We are working on some clues and are heading in the right direction. But I have my hands full in Almora and have little time to spare. Rushing to Ramsar every day is putting a lot of pressure on me. It could ease a bit if you took an interest in the investigation.'

'That goes without saying, JBS. Tim and I are aware of your workload,' said Acharya, his tongue firmly lodged in his cheek. A little sweet talk could soften the toughest man. 'You need not worry about this case. Tim and I can do the preliminary investigation and call upon your expertise when we are stuck.'

As expected, the statement pepped up the DSP's mood. 'Thank you, Colonel. I know we can depend upon your help,' he said grudgingly. Throwing a glance at the wall clock, he began drumming his fingers on the table impatiently. Wanting to benefit from Acharya's views on Nisha and Sabharwal, he continued, 'We are waiting for Nisha Dabral and her brother to arrive. Would you like to be present while we question them? We can exchange notes after we finish the questioning.'

'I am at your disposal.' The colonel smiled. He knew Bulldog well enough to realize how difficult it was for the egoistic man to seek help. 'Her brother is here in Ramsar?' The colonel raised an eyebrow questioningly.

'He arrived a few hours back,' Tim informed.

'I was given the impression that he was to come by the morning train.'

'He says he took the night train.'

'So where is he now?'

'The two of them are enjoying a meal at Tasty Bites,' JBS growled.

'And Nisha is with him?'

'That's right,' Tim replied. Turning to his boss, he asked, 'Should I call her or give them five more minutes?'

'Call her right now. I don't have time to waste.'

Tim was about to punch in Nisha's number on his phone when they heard voices. Minutes later the widow and her brother entered the office.

'Have you been waiting long?' the brother asked. Without waiting for a response, he added, 'Nisha was brooding, so I took her out for lunch at Tasty Bites. It is a lovely place with a spectacular view, which more than makes up for the insipid fare.'

'You don't have to narrate the details of the restaurant. We know all about the place,' grunted Bulldog. 'Did you not promise to be at the police station in an hour? It is almost two hours now.'

'I am sorry. The service at Tasty Bites is very poor. The waiters should be dismissed if they want to attract more people.'

The colonel suppressed a smile at the reply. The young man's cockiness was sure to rile up Bulldog, he knew.

'Do you realize that while you were enjoying the scenery and a laid-back meal, we have missed ours?' bellowed the DSP.

'Sorry about that.' Sudhir threw an engaging smile at him. 'Why don't we go to Tasty Bites right away? We can have a chat in an informal setting while you enjoy lunch. I wouldn't mind a round of the frothy lassi. That's the only decent item on the menu. I am sure you have tasted it.'

Tim struggled to maintain a straight face.

'Listen, Sabharwal, I have no time for frivolities,' the DSP thundered. 'We are waiting to question the two of you, and you are talking of lassi.'

'Question us? Why? We are not criminals, and we don't owe you explanations for going out to lunch. Don't you cross the line, officer. I can act tough too,' the man said as the winning smile on his face was replaced by a scowl. He scratched his left hand, which displayed remnants of angry rashes. 'You can save the belligerence for local chaps. I am not here to listen to nonsense.'

'Are you threatening me?' the DSP's voice boomed. Red in the face, he pointed a finger at the man. 'Let me warn you, Sabharwal. One more word from you and we will put you in the lock-up and no one will be able to do anything about it.'

'What the hell?' shouted Sabharwal. 'All we did was go for lunch. As per my knowledge of law, that's no crime.'

Nisha pulled at his arm and conveyed a silent missive. 'There is no point getting into trouble with the DSP,' she whispered.

Realizing the gravity of the situation, he sat down and tried a fresh approach. 'Look, officer, let's not get into a disagreeable situation. We have gone through a tragedy recently and want no more unpleasantness in our life.'

'It is better that the two of you answer the questions without creating any fuss,' Tim suggested gravely. 'It could get rather unpleasant otherwise. I am sure you wouldn't want that.'

'I don't understand…' spluttered Sabharwal.

Nisha put a restraining hand on her brother's arm and took over. 'We are ready to answer all your questions. The two of us want the culprit to be punished and we will help the police in doing that. We are happy to provide any information needed to solve the case.' She threw a gentle smile at the DSP. 'We also know how busy you are, so shoot your questions and we will answer.'

Placated with the reassurance, JBS took a deep breath and gulped down a full glass of water. Relaxed, he sat back and began speaking.

'Do you know anything about your husband's claim to Negi Mansion?'

'No.' She shook her head. 'Deepak did not share any information about his dispute with his cousin regarding the property. All I know is that he had a stake in it.'

'But you know that he went to meet Umesh Gudyal on the afternoon of the party.'

'No. I know nothing about it.'

'You mean to say that he didn't inform you while going out of the hotel?' asked the DSP. 'And you didn't bother to ask him where he was going?' There was an expression of disbelief on his face.

'Deepak informed me that he was going out to meet someone. I don't know whom he met.'

'Do you know that your husband did not commit suicide? He was murdered!' Bulldog threw the bait at the smug woman.

'Murdered?' The information shook the woman. 'Deepak was murdered?' she asked in a trembling voice, her face ashen. 'Oh, my God! This is unbelievable.'

Acharya shot a quick look at the brother. Sudhir Sabharwal looked equally shocked at the news. The young man's jaws tightened, and he clenched his fists to control the emotions. 'Who would murder Deepak? He had done no harm to anyone. Besides, few people know him in Ramsar,' he finally said.

'That is what the police are trying to find out.' Tim responded. He felt sorry for the widow and her brother. They were a pair of young people caught in a web of undesirable events and were struggling to come to terms with a grievous loss.

'I think his cousin killed Deepak,' Sabharwal gave his verdict. 'Nisha told me that he left the party at 8.40 p.m. to meet his cousin. Thereafter, he neither went back to the party nor returned to the hotel.'

'We know that,' said Acharya. 'What we want to know is if he really went to meet Umesh Gudyal, or if he went somewhere else. We all know there's many a slip between the cup and the lip. At present, we have just your sister's version—that her husband had a rendezvous with his cousin.'

'Why should you disbelieve her? She has no reason to tell a lie. Deepak was her husband, dammit!' Sabharwal banged his fist on the table in an agitated manner. Almost immediately, he was contrite. 'I am sorry. Look, if Deepak said he was meeting his cousin, we have no reason to believe otherwise. The night was too cold to go gallivanting around town. Not to forget, Deepak had no friends in Ramsar. Besides, we have found a note that proves he had gone out to meet his cousin.' Turning to his sister, he said, 'Show them the note you found in the book.'

'What note? What book?' The DSP wanted to know. Having formed an unfavourable image of Sabharwal, he was convinced that the young man was up to some trick. 'Don't pull any stunts,' he warned.

'It's not a stunt.' Sabharwal threw a derisive look at the officer. 'You have a suspicious mind, I must say.'

'Police officers are always suspicious of anyone who produces evidence like a conjuror producing rabbits from a hat,' said Tim, defending his boss. Turning to Nisha, he remarked, 'You didn't mention the note in your earlier statement. So where did this come from?'

'I want you to read this message before you cast aspersions on us.' Nisha handed a piece of paper to the DSP.

Bulldog glanced quickly at the note before passing it to Tim, who read the same and handed it to the colonel. It was a note from Umesh Gudyal asking Dabral to meet him at Negi Mansion at 9 p.m. so they could discuss the property issues.

'Where did you find the note?' Acharya folded the note carefully before giving it to Tim for safekeeping.

'It was in a book Deepak had been reading,' Nisha informed the men.

'Why didn't you show it to me the day Tim and I met you at Bhandari Villa?' asked the colonel.

'I didn't show it because I had not found the note then.'

'How did you find the note?'

'And when did you find it?' Tim lobbed the question at the widow. It was a tactic the colonel and he often used. They would rain questions on the suspect. It was a stratagem to confuse the person, giving them no time to come up with a lie. Bulldog intervened from time to time, enjoying the game.

'Our bags were brought from the hotel to Bhandari Villa the day after the party. After Deepak's body was found, I was too distraught to go through his stuff. It was only after Sudhir arrived that the two of us went through the contents in the bags. In fact, it was my brother who found the note. He was riffling through the book Deepak had been reading when we arrived in Ramsar, when he found the note.'

'I see,' grunted the DSP. 'So, it was through sheer accident that you stumbled upon the note?'

'Yes!' after a quick glance at each other, both Sabharwal and Nisha replied together.

'Well, you—' The colonel's sentence was interrupted by the noise of a loud argument. The altercation was taking place in the corridor.

'You can't go in now.' They could hear Sharad ticking off someone. 'There are many people in sa'ab's office. They are having an important meeting.'

'You can't stop me.' Tim heard Laxmi Badola's belligerent voice. 'I have something important to tell them, and it can't wait till they finish. You think I have nothing better to do than loiter in the police station?'

'You always have something important to tell everyone.' The constable laughed. 'By the way, you can share the important news with me. If it is really important, I will convey it to sa'ab.'

'Why should I share the information with you?' asked Laxmi.

'In that case, you can keep waiting for the sa'ab to be free.'

There was a pause. Tim could visualize the woman trying to decide if she should share the information with the constable. The DSP, Colonel, Sabharwal and Nisha had stopped talking and were listening to the argument. Curiosity piqued, they waited to hear the woman's statement.

'I saw a stranger at the bus stop at 10 in the night.' Laxmi's shrill voice reached everyone sitting in Tim's office. The woman was unstoppable.

'And that information is important enough to interrupt the meeting, you feel?' Sharad scorned the woman, dismissing her information.

'It is important. That's the reason I have come all the way to share the information with sa'ab. It happened the night before Deepak Dabral was found dead in the van. What if the man I saw had something to do with the accident?' Laxmi's voice had risen by another notch.

Acharya nodded at Tim, who stepped out to intervene. 'What is it this time?' he asked the constable.

'Sa'ab, it is another one of Laxmi's cock-and-bull stories. She claims to have spotted a suspicious man at the bus stop and wants to disturb everyone with her tall tales. I told her you were in a meeting with the big boss.'

'Inspector sa'ab ...' began Laxmi. 'Shirt Pant is not allowing me to meet you. It is a significant piece of information, but he refuses to listen. The man I bumped into that night was wearing a false moustache.'

'How do you know it was a false moustache?' The constable sniggered. 'You have never used one.'

'I can recognize one. The moustache was coming off at the edge on one side of the nose...' Laxmi insisted.

'Ridiculous!' commented the constable. 'She can't see very well at night, and she noticed the false moustache coming loose on one side.'

Tim put up his hand to silence Shirt Pant and turned to the woman. 'It is all right, Laxmi. We will listen to your story, but you will have to wait till the meeting is over.'

'I told her the same thing,' said Sharad. 'But the adamant woman refuses to listen to me.'

'But...' she began.

As Tim turned his back on her, he heard the constable saying, 'Are you happy now? I told you to wait. Sit on that bench and twiddle your thumbs till the meeting is over.' He pointed at a bench in the corridor.

'I can't wait,' grumbled the woman. 'I have a lot of work waiting at home.'

'Then come back tomorrow.' Sharad chuckled. 'You can add a couple of stories to this one.'

Sighing, Tim went back to the office.

'It is Laxmi Badola, isn't it?' asked the colonel. 'What did she want now?'

'What is all this about seeing some stranger with a false moustache?' Bulldog wanted to know.

'She is a big nuisance,' replied Tim, settling down in his chair. 'Now that she has had a taste of importance, she will fabricate several stories to gain attention. This time it is about running into a suspicious character at the bus stop. She claims he was wearing a false moustache and a monkey cap to cover his features,' he said dismissively.

The colonel's eyes strayed to the door. 'I hope it's not something important. Do you think she would have taken the trouble of coming all the way for some trivial bit?'

'Laxmi can walk a long distance for gossip.' Tim's eyes twinkled with mirth as he spoke.

'Coming back to the note, now that we know that Dabral's death was not an accident or suicide, it assumes greater significance. As I said earlier, it doesn't prove that Dabral met Umesh Gudyal. It only confirms that his cousin sent out an invitation to the deceased. We can consider it as circumstantial evidence, of course,' the colonel gave his opinion.

'That's true.' JBS nodded his head in agreement.

'I don't understand why the police are refusing to take the note seriously. It is a clear pointer of the cousin's intention to kill Deepak. Why else would he invite Deepak to the mansion at night?' Sabharwal asked exasperatedly. He scratched his hand furiously, his nails leaving red welts on the skin.

'Are you collecting the body from the morgue now?' Tim asked.

'Yes, I went to the crematorium and made arrangements for the cremation after meeting you at the police station. All we have to do is take the body from the morgue to the crematorium. I hope you have no objection to our going ahead with it.'

'We have no objection,' replied the DSP gruffly.

Nisha's face crumpled at the mention of the morgue. Loud, torturous sobs racked her body. The brave front she had put up for the past two days left her suddenly. The keening widow hugged herself to control her body from shaking. She tried to stand, but her legs buckled under her and she collapsed into the chair once again.

Sabharwal quickly rushed to her side, murmuring soothing words in her ear as he held her. 'Shush! I am here.' He rubbed her back comfortingly.

Tim held out a glass of water to the grieving woman, who shook her head. She continued to cling to her brother for support.

'Take a few sips,' said Sabharwal, pressing the glass of water to her lips. 'It will help.'

She raised her tear-stained face appealingly at him and wailed, 'Why? Oh, why did this have to happen?'

'Everything will be all right,' he said, continuing to hold the glass at her lips. 'The police will arrest the culprit soon, I am sure.'

Nisha Dabral took a couple of sips and nodded her head.

'Officer, have you finished? My sister needs rest,' said Sabharwal, helping his sister to her feet. Ashen-faced, she leaned against him weakly. 'May I take her back to Bhandari Villa? With your permission, of course,' he added sarcastically. He stood back and scratched his hand once more.

'Yes, of course,' said the DSP unhappily. He would have liked to grill the duo for some more time, but the widow seemed to be in no shape to withstand further questioning.

Watched by the three men, the young man walked out of the door, still murmuring soothing words in his sister's ear. His brawny arms supported her trembling body, forcing her to keep step with him.

'Colonel, what is your impression of those two?' the DSP asked, pointing to the door through which the brother and sister had just walked out. He didn't trust Sabharwal. There was something fishy about the guy. Bulldog wondered if the colonel felt the same way.

'I can't say offhand,' Acharya mused. 'It is difficult to read the two of them. Either they are consummate actors or they are genuinely grieving. Nisha Dabral has come across differently on the two occasions I met her, making it difficult for me to gauge the truth.'

'She appears to be shocked by Dabral's death, if you ask me,' said Tim, who was feeling sympathetic towards the widow. 'Her grief appears genuine. It can't be acting.'

'Maybe!' the colonel commented. 'The note has to be examined by a handwriting expert before we know if Gudyal really wrote it.'

'Do you have any doubt about that?' Tim asked. 'I don't think Sabharwal or Nisha would dare to forge his handwriting.'

'My dear chap, there is always an element of doubt when a note suddenly comes into the picture. Why didn't it appear earlier? Why now?'

'Although I distrust the brother, I don't think he had anything to do with the brother-in-law's death. The guy had neither the motive nor the opportunity,' opined the DSP, spinning a paperweight lying on the table.

'The widow has a rock-solid alibi. She remained at the party through the evening and went back to the hotel with Dabral's colleagues,' Tim recounted the facts. 'Early in the morning, when Dabral had still not returned, she sought the help of the colleagues, and they reported the matter to the police. According to the doc, the death had occurred sometime between 7.30 and 11.30 p.m., so that puts her out of the list of suspects.'

'It is Gudyal who killed Dabral,' the DSP said. 'He had the motive, opportunity and time. He sent a note to Dabral to meet at 9 p.m. Knowing that the man would step out of the party to meet him, Gudyal waited near the van. He must have killed Dabral soon after he left Bhandari Villa. Thereafter, it was easy to place the body in the van and push it down the slope.' He darted a quick look at his wristwatch and stood up hurriedly.

'Well, I will leave the two of you to decide if they are genuinely grieving or acting. I have to rush back to Almora now. Tim, I expect you to update me tonight.'

'Yes, sir,' said Tim, standing up to walk his boss to the vehicle.

He found the colonel in a thoughtful mood when he got back after seeing the DSP off.

'What is your gut feeling?' Tim asked. 'I know you didn't want to disclose your thoughts in front of Bulldog.'

'According to Bulldog's assumption, Gudyal killed Dabral near the van. I am not convinced by that theory. There are a few gaping holes. Why would Dabral go near the van? Wouldn't he have walked towards Negi Mansion? And if Gudyal was hiding near the gate and killed him when he came out of the house, would he take the chance of dragging the body across the road? It is an arduous task for a man to drag a body alone. It would take a reasonably long time to do so, and then place it inside the van before pushing it down the ravine,' remarked the colonel. 'It's too pat a solution.'

'There must be some explanation for your questions. Gudyal is a healthy man. Dragging Dabral after the murder, placing the body in the van and pushing it down the slope would not be too difficult for him.'

'Yet those questions trouble my mind. We have to find logical explanations for them before we zero in on Gudyal as the murderer.'

'The boss is convinced that he is our man. In fact, he has tasked me with another questioning session with Gudyal. Most likely, JBS will want the man arrested tomorrow.'

'I would like to be present at the questioning session,' said Acharya. 'Are you planning to go there now?'

'I am wondering if we should attend Dabral's cremation. The morgue called to inform me that the brother will collect the body in a short while. He must have called them right after leaving the police station. According to the morgue in-charge, the body was being taken to the crematorium directly. The distance is not much, anyway.'

'I think we should be there. What time is the cremation?' the colonel asked, picking up his walking stick.

'Sabharwal must have taken the body to the crematorium. Since it gets dark by 5.30, I don't think they intend delaying the cremation. We should leave now if we want to attend it,' Tim said, picking up the keys to his vehicle.

'Let's not delay. I want to be there.' With Tim at his heels, the colonel walked out of the office. 'Don't forget that we have to speak to Laxmi Badola. She may have seen something.'

'Although I doubt she has something important to tell us, I will summon her to the police station tomorrow morning,' promised Tim.

'Never ignore a person's claim or a clue,' advised Acharya as the ASP gunned the engine of the vehicle. 'Even if it comes from a braggart like Laxmi Badola. I have a feeling the woman's information could be of significance.'

13

The usual cheer and laughter that accompanied high tea at Elm Cottage was missing as the four women sat down to discuss the unexpected happenings in Ramsar. For once, the usually effervescent Violet Williams was in a grim mood. She lit up yet another cigarette, which was an indication of her stress. Some of her tension conveyed itself to the others in the room.

'Murdered! Not for a minute could I have imagined that the man was murdered. I still think it is a case of suicide. The man got into the unlocked van and drove it down the ravine for some silly reason. And that was it. I only wish he had chosen some other vehicle for his purpose. It would have saved me a lot of bother.'

'Initially, the police also believed it to be suicide,' agreed Mary.

'So what changed that belief?' demanded Violet.

'They must have discovered something new that points to murder,' commented Nancy. 'It is not likely that the DSP will jump to conclusions without some firm evidence.'

'You don't know that man. He is the most obstinate fellow I have ever met.' As an old resident of Ramsar, Violet had seen enough of the DSP's crude methods and had no respect for them.

'Even if the DSP were mistaken, I am sure Tim wouldn't play along with his theory. He's an intelligent and fair man.' Nancy picked up a piece of almond cake from the platter lying on the coffee table and closed her eyes as she savoured the taste. 'This is delicious, Violet,' she complimented the hostess.

'I agree with you. Tim is one of the most sincere and modest young men in town,' Claire said. Picking up the teacup, she took a dainty sip of the flavourful tea.

'Everything has gone for a six. With this murder business, I wonder if Tim will agree to attend the surprise party we are planning.' Violet sighed.

'Don't fret, Vee. I am sure he will find the culprit much before the birthday party,' said Nancy, unwavering in her faith in Tim's efficiency. The three friends occasionally called Violet by that name, especially in times of distress.

'I have full faith in Colonel Acharya's capability,' declared Claire. 'He has solved the few murders we have had in town. Remember that complex case of the film star's murder? There were so many suspects, but he singled out the killer.'

'And then there was that murder of the businessman and the two mysterious break-ins that had shocked the entire town.'

'Look, girls, there is no point in debating about the case. It will ruin the mood, that's all. I suggest that we continue with our plans for the party,' suggested Mary, the practical one. 'There may be enough reasons to celebrate by that time. We still have ten days before the event. I am sure the colonel and Tim will nab the killer much before that.'

'Now that we have decided to continue with the party plans, let's get on with our game of canasta,' agreed Nancy.

'I am really in no mood to play.' Violet sighed. Stress never failed to give her an attack of migraine, and she could feel it knocking on the right side of her head. 'The insurance guys have been pestering me the whole morning. Despite the colonel's assurances, the fellows seem hell-bent on trying to find excuses for not paying for the damages. To add to the troubles, the police have confiscated my marble rolling pin, and Pia has failed to find a suitable substitute. I had bought the marble one from Jabalpur a few decades back. They made good stuff those days. I wish the police would return it to us.'

'Why did they confiscate the rolling pin?' Mary asked, the vertical lines on her forehead gathering together to create parallel tracks.

'According to them, the rolling pin could have been used as the murder weapon.' Violet rolled her eyes and took one last puff of the cigarette before stubbing it out in the ashtray lying near her. 'They want to conduct some DNA tests, whatever it is, on the tissues found on the pin.'

'They can't pin the blame on Pia just because her rolling pin has some unknown tissues.' Claire snorted. 'For all you know, the tissues could have come from your cat, Tabby.'

Everyone in Firangi Colony knew Tabby. The fat, furry cat had been Violet's companion for a long time. It had a free run of the house and exhibited a special attachment to the winged chair in the library. Tabby's reign continued till Pia arrived on the scene and banished the feline from the library, much to her grandmother's annoyance.

'Since we have decided against playing canasta, why don't we decide the menu for the party?' Mary suggested. She wanted to distract her friend from thinking about the murder.

'Not today. My mind is too unsettled to concentrate on anything. God knows where all this is heading.' Violet furrowed her eyebrows. Her headache was threatening to intensify.

The women nodded in understanding. They knew how much their friend loved her granddaughter. Her rigid attitude had vanished after Pia arrived in Ramsar. The girl had suffused the house with vitality and laughter, giving a second lease of life to the old lady. In some ways, she had touched the lives of the three friends too. It was always nice to have a young person around.

'How does Pia feel about the whole affair?' asked Nancy.

'The girl is trying to go about her business, pretending that the case doesn't bother her. But I know her better. She would not share her concerns for fear of upsetting me. Besides, the guilt of leaving the van unlocked hasn't left her.'

'It's not her fault that a stranger climbed into the van and drove it down the abyss, or got killed in it.'

'I know it is not her fault. It could have happened with anyone. Pia was under too much pressure that night. It was her first catering order, and she wanted to do a good job.' Although her granddaughter had not confessed the worries, Violet had sensed Pia's anxiety.

'Well, you can't undo whatever happened. I will drop into the café and have a chat with the girl,' said Nancy. She patted Violet's knee consolingly. 'If nothing, it will give her a chance to vent her feelings.'

'I have never seen you so disturbed,' commented Mary, glancing at Violet, who had lit another cigarette and inhaled deeply. 'I always took you to be a strong woman. I wish you wouldn't smoke so much, Violet. It's not good for your lungs.'

The others nodded their heads in agreement.

'Strong! My foot!' Violet exclaimed. 'My dear, the strength you see is a facade. It's a pretence. I have had a tough life. But I never let the unfortunate events shatter my confidence. It's not been easy to endure the constant pain of a broken body. I went through life without complaining, but this is too much. A murdered man in my van is the last thing I expected to handle.'

'Don't worry, things will get resolved,' consoled Nancy, taking Violet's hands in her own. 'Give it a few days. Let the police do their job.'

'I wish they would.'

Less than a week ago, they were planning a surprise party to bring two young people together, but a stranger's murder had thrown everything out of gear.

The afternoon light had faded outside. Warmth fled, and the shadows lengthened, turning the room cold. The chill stretched and reached out for the disenchanted hearts huddled around the coffee table, each woman reflecting on the capriciousness of life. The party broke up soon after.

It was to a dark house that Pia returned.

'Gumma! Where are you?' she called out. Stepping into the lounge, she groped for the light switch. Violet grimaced and shaded her eyes as Pia switched on the lights. 'Are you all right? Why are you sitting in the dark?' the girl asked anxiously.

The effects of the unpleasant event on her grandmother had not escaped her attention. For the umpteenth time, Pia wished she had locked the van before entering Bhandari Villa. One act of carelessness had caused so much grief. No one knew when or where it would end.

14

The cremation was a quiet affair with a handful of people in attendance. Nisha Dabral, calm and composed, stood leaning against her brother, her face inscrutable. Apart from Sabharwal and Nisha, there was Ravi, whom the Bhandaris had chosen as their representative. Umesh Gudyal stood all by himself at one end of the ground, arms crossed across his chest, his face impassive. For once, he was not smoking.

A couple of curious Ramsarians stood on the fringes of the motley gathering, their eyes missing nothing. Tim noted a reporter and a photographer from the local newspaper. The small town had little to offer in terms of sensational news, and the newshounds were not likely to let go of a mysterious murder.

Acharya's eyes scanned the people present at the crematorium. Like Tim, he was also surprised to see Gudyal at the cremation.

Once the cremation was over, people walked up to the widow and her brother to express their condolences. Some said a few words, others conveyed their sympathy with a silent nod of the head. Her head lowered, eyes dry, Nisha stood with folded hands near Sabharwal. Exhaustion and lack of sleep had left their mark around the young man's eyes. Together, the two acknowledged the commiserations.

After everyone left the ground, the colonel walked towards the duo and squeezed Sabharwal's hands to express his sympathy. 'May the Almighty give you the strength to cope with the tremendous loss,' he murmured. His manner avuncular and kindly, he approached Nisha and folded his hands and said, 'Take care.'

Tim joined the colonel and nodded his head at the grieving woman. He loathed cremations, since they reminded him of his parents' death. The two of them had died in an accident, leaving him orphaned at an early age. Theirs was the first cremation he had attended, and he wished it had been the last, but his profession required him to attend them frequently.

He walked over to Sabharwal and patted his shoulder. 'When are you leaving for Delhi?' he asked in a low voice. It was not the right place or occasion for the question, he knew, but it was imperative to know the answer.

'We are planning to leave tomorrow, after collecting the ashes,' Sabharwal replied. 'There's no point in remaining in Ramsar, now that the cremation is over. I expect the police will keep us informed of the progress in the case. Let us know when you arrest the murderer.'

'Definitely!' said Tim. Raising his hand in goodbye, he joined the colonel, who was waiting for him.

As they began walking towards the exit, Acharya noticed Gudyal walking towards Nisha and her brother. He had been waiting for the others to leave.

The colonel halted in his tracks. 'Slow down,' he said to Tim in a low voice. 'I want to catch the duo's reactions to Gudyal.'

The two of them stopped a few feet from the widow. Extracting his phone from the pocket, Tim pretended to be speaking to the caller in a hushed voice while watching the trio. From their vantage point, the colonel and the officer could hear the conversation that was taking place.

Clearing his throat, Gudyal began speaking. 'I am sorry. It is rather unfortunate that we have to meet under tragic circumstances. I am Umesh Gudyal.'

'You are sorry?' Sabharwal mocked. 'You have the cheek to attend the cremation after killing your cousin? Why should you be sorry?'

'You killed my husband.' Her eyes blazing, Nisha jumped into the fray. 'You are a murderer.'

'I didn't kill …' Gudyal flinched at the sudden attack by the brother-and-sister duo.

'Fire drives the wasp out of its nest,' muttered Acharya.

'You have no right to make such accusations,' retorted Gudyal, who had recovered from the initial recoil. 'There is no point attacking me. You should look for the murderer instead of trying to pin it on me. Just because I had the decency to come here …'

'Decency! That word does not figure in your dictionary,' growled Sabharwal, cutting Gudyal off mid-sentence.

'Deepak claimed to be my cousin, and he died in this town. I had no intention of attending the cremation, or speaking with you. It was my mother who insisted that I do so.'

'Does your mother know you killed him, or is she a conspirator in the murder?'

'Watch your tongue,' shouted Gudyal. 'I won't tolerate anyone badmouthing my mother.'

'You killed Deepak because he had demanded a share in Ratan Negi's property,' Nisha accused in a shrill voice. 'Even the police are convinced about your guilt.'

'How many times do I have to repeat myself?' Gudyal snapped, clenching his fists. 'As for Ratan Negi's property, where was your husband when the man was dying? Did any of you ever check on him? Not a single relative was by his bedside when he died. I was there throughout his sickness, holding his hand, running errands and summoning the doctors for him.' Gudyal's voice went up by a few decibels.

For a few seconds, there was a hushed silence. The siblings were not prepared for Gudyal's counter-attack. Acharya could imagine the duo's brain ticking for a fitting reply. He chuckled silently as Nisha came up with a rejoinder. That woman had nerves of steel.

'You were with Ratan Negi in his last moments because you wanted to take control of his property. Do you think we can't spot the plans of a scheming mind?' she demanded.

'Can you see nothing good in a person? I had no ulterior motive in being by my uncle's side. He was suffering from a painful collapse of his liver. His plight could have moved even a stranger. Only an unscrupulous person would see deviousness in my actions.' Gudyal shook his head sadly. He had no wish to quarrel with the duo. His mother had warned him repeatedly against an angry response, but Nisha and her brother seemed bent on provoking him.

'Did Ratan Negi leave a will?' Sabharwal demanded. 'How do we know he left the property to you?'

'Yes, he left a will,' replied Gudyal. 'He left his entire property to me.'

'I don't believe you.' Nisha directed a disdainful look at the man and asked, 'I want to see the will. As the widow of Deepak Dabral, I have a right to see Ratan Negi's will.'

'Ask your lawyer to get in touch with me,' came Gudyal's curt reply.

'We will do that.' Sabharwal thrust out his chin challengingly. 'I hope you know that Nisha will have a right to the entire property when you go behind bars.'

'Why should I go behind bars?' Gudyal tried to restrain the anger building up inside him.

'Why should you be arrested, you ask?' The brother laughed derisively. 'Aren't all murderers supposed to be behind bars?'

'I am warning you.' Gudyal shook his finger threateningly. 'You call me a killer one more time and I won't be responsible for the consequences.'

The two men were evenly matched. Like gladiators in an amphitheatre, they sized each other up, looking for weaknesses.

'It's time to intervene. We don't want them to be locked in verbal or physical combat. A casualty in the crematorium would be rather tragic,' the colonel whispered to Tim, and they began walking towards the brawling men. 'Gentlemen, I think it is neither the place nor the occasion to brawl. Have a thought for the deceased,' he said.

The colonel's words seemed to dampen some of their anger. Neither Nisha nor her brother wanted to be seen in an aggressive posture by Acharya and the police officer.

'I came here to convey my condolences,' Gudyal addressed the colonel. 'I had no wish to get into any unpleasantness, but these two began accusing me of Dabral's murder. They went so far as to suggest that my mother is involved in the murder.'

Placing a consoling hand on Gudyal's shoulder, the colonel turned towards Sabharwal, saying, 'He came here in good faith. I don't think it was nice of you to accuse him of murder.'

'Can't you see through the man's pretence?' retorted Nisha. 'He killed my husband, and that's the truth.'

'We don't know the truth,' Tim remarked. 'Not yet, anyway.'

'That's right!' agreed the colonel. 'It's not fair to accuse anyone till the investigation is over.'

'Everyone is on our suspect list till we find the murderer,' added Tim. All the sympathy he had for Nisha had vanished after her unseemly conduct. 'That includes the two of you.'

Nisha looked surprised at Tim's statement. 'You mean I am also on the list of suspects?'

'Yes, madam. You are also on the list. In fact, I want the two of you to come to the police station before you leave for Delhi,' Tim ordered sternly. 'We have a few more questions for you.'

'Is there anything else you want, officer?' she asked sarcastically. 'I thought you had finished grilling us.'

'The grilling will continue till we nab the culprit.' Tim smiled amicably, aware that his statement had rattled the duo. They wanted no more questioning by the police. 'Not just for grilling, we want you at the police station for fingerprinting.'

His words had an unsettling effect on the two.

'Fingerprinting? Why, that's ridiculous,' Sabharwal exploded. 'We are not criminals.'

'It's a murder, and we have to take fingerprints of every suspect. That's the routine.'

'I should leave now,' said Umesh Gudyal, a triumphant smile playing on his face.

'Officer, you can't be serious.' All belligerence gone, Nisha's voice took on a grovelling note.

'There's no need for further discussion on the matter. I will expect the two of you at the police station,' Tim issued his ultimatum. Turning to Gudyal, he asked, 'How did you come here?'

'I came walking.'

'We will drop you home,' Tim offered. He knew that the colonel was eager to quiz the man.

'Thank you, but I don't need a drop. I am used to walking,' Gudyal replied.

'I insist,' Tim said, steering the protesting man towards the vehicle. 'We have something to discuss with you.'

'What do you want to discuss?' Gudyal turned to face him. He decided not to allow the police officer's words to rattle him.

'All in good time, Umesh,' replied Tim, rubbing the back of his neck. He turned it first to one side and then the other, to loosen the muscles. It had been a stressful time.

The colonel took the co-driver's seat while a surly Gudyal climbed into the rear seat.

A couple of minutes later, the three of them took off for Negi Mansion.

'Would you like to come inside the house to discuss whatever you have in mind?' Gudyal invited them after they reached the mansion.

Tim and Acharya exchanged a look and nodded their heads in agreement.

'It shouldn't take much time. We will ask a couple of questions and leave.' The colonel's tone was reassuring as he and Tim walked through the gate.

Negi Mansion was a two-storeyed structure with no semblance of uniformity, as though the architect had been undecided between the traditional and the modern. The second floor was restricted to a couple of rooms with dormer windows, housed under a slanting roof. The windows were sashed and a wide, covered verandah ran along the front. It was a house built by a whimsical man, but the structure fascinated the colonel.

The front yard was a riot of weeds and wild flowers, Acharya noticed. The grass needed mowing. A few apricot, pear and mulberry trees, probably planted in the initial years of occupancy, stood sentinel near the periphery wall.

'I intend to spruce it up, one of these days,' commented Gudyal, noticing the expression in the colonel's eyes. 'It's a difficult task to maintain an old house.' Tim had put himself in Gudyal's good books by ticking off Nisha and her brother. Gudyal now bent over backwards to put up a pleasant attitude.

They trooped into a sparsely furnished, scrupulously clean hall. A strong smell of cigarettes hung around the house. It had permeated every fibre of the upholstery.

A lumpy couch, a few chairs and a centre table took up most of the room. A large television occupied the wall space between two windows, with a rickety rocking chair placed before it. This was probably the space occupied by Gudyal's mother.

'Would you like a cup of tea?' offered the host. Tim and the colonel politely declined his offer.

'I have said all I had to say,' Gudyal began as soon as they had taken their seats. 'There is really nothing more to add. All I want to say is you are barking up the wrong tree. I did not kill Dabral.'

'Was this note written by you?' asked Tim, holding out the letter given by Nisha.

'Yes,' admitted the man after scrutinizing the note. 'I scribbled this note inviting Dabral for a discussion at Negi Mansion.'

'Why did you call him here?'

'Didn't I mention that?' Gudyal asked testily. The hostility was back in his voice.

He lit up a cigarette, inhaled deeply and coughed unapologetically.

'We want an answer to the question,' Tim stated. 'I don't want a counter-question from you.'

'You said that you wanted him to be at the mansion for a discussion,' Acharya butted into the conversation before it turned ugly. He could sense Tim's impatience. 'What did you want to discuss?'

'Isn't it obvious? Dabral was demanding a share in my uncle's property. He had no right to it, but refused to listen to reason. My mother suggested that I show him Ratan Negi's will, wherein he had left the property to me.'

'What brought on the change of heart?' Tim asked scathingly. 'We have learnt of your hostile reaction to Dabral's claim.'

'After the argument in the afternoon, Mother felt that I should have handled the matter amicably. She chided me for being belligerent. It was on her advice that I invited Dabral to discuss the matter in a mature and peaceful manner.'

'You called him at 9.'

'I did. He didn't turn up.'

'After the argument, when your mother chided you for the hostility, didn't you attempt to meet him at the hotel?' probed the colonel.

'Why should I? I saw no reason to pursue the man. If he had been a friendly person, I would have gone all out to be nice. Unfortunately, he was bent upon being nasty. It was only after my mother suggested that I invite him to the mansion that I agreed to send a note.'

'Did Dabral know anyone else in town?' Tim asked.

'How am I to know that? He was here to attend the Bhandari wedding reception, that's all I know,' Gudyal replied as calmly as possible, but it was obvious that he was getting all worked up. His body shook with a sudden spasm of coughing.

From the corner of his eye, Acharya spotted his mother hovering near the door. The son's coughing bout seemed to have brought her there.

'Look, Colonel, I have said all this a dozen times to each of you. Do you expect me to change my statement or do you intend to bulldoze me into saying something incriminating?' Gudyal bared his nicotine-stained teeth in a snarl. 'I am aware of the high-handed tactics practised by the police.'

'Let me assure you, we have no such intention. All we want is the truth from you,' assured the colonel, his manner gentle and placating. 'Let us know if you remember any other fragment from the conversation. Sometimes the mind throws up a vital piece of information that may have seemed insignificant earlier.'

'I will do that. Good day to you, Colonel.' Gudyal got to his feet. He wanted them out of the house.

'What is your intuition telling you, Colonel?' asked Tim as they climbed into the vehicle and he directed its nose towards the police station.

'The nicotine-stained teeth and fingers point to the fact that the man is a chain-smoker. His clothes, body and breath— everything smells of cigarettes. I could almost hear the guy's lungs crying for mercy. I wonder how his mother breathes in that house.'

It was not an answer Tim was expecting. He laughed at the colonel's attempt at distracting his attention. The astute sleuth would not divulge his thoughts till he had made up his mind. 'That's quite a sermon, considering you love your cigar. Speaking of cigars, I haven't seen you smoke a single one today.'

'I am under the high command's lens. Warnings have been issued and I am trying hard to toe the line. The nicotine craving is a real challenge, especially while dealing with a mystifying case.' The colonel pursed his mouth in a smirk.

No one knew better than Tim about the colonel's habit of leaning on the cigar crutch to get his brain activated. 'It will be interesting to see how long your resolution lasts.'

'That is something I can't promise.' Acharya chuckled. 'I am trying. No one can blame me for not trying. Coming to your question about my thoughts on the man, I agree that Gudyal is a brash and unsocial man. However, I can't see him as a killer.' He shook his head. 'I doubt he killed Dabral.'

'Bulldog is convinced that he is the culprit. First, we have Laxmi Badola's statement about the heated argument between the two men and then his note inviting Dabral to Negi Mansion.'

'JBS excels at putting the cart before the horse. It is easy to find a scapegoat and slaughter it. Yes, Gudyal and Dabral had an argument and then there is the note, but these two things don't prove Umesh Gudyal's guilt. Instead of skimming the surface, we will have to dig deeper, my friend. Have you sent the tissues collected from Pia's rolling pin for investigation?'

'Yes, that has been sent. I am also despatching Sabharwal's and Nisha's hair samples for a DNA match.'

'Where did you find those?' Surprised with the information, Acharya turned to scrutinize Tim's profile.

'I had instructed the barber who performed a token shave on Sabharwal's head to save a few strands for the police.' Tim chuckled.

As per Hindu rites, the male member carrying out the funeral had to shave his head, but few young men liked to do so. Instead, a tiny patch of hair was shaved off to symbolize sacrifice, Acharya knew.

'As for Nisha's hair, all I had to do was instruct the Bhandari family retainer to hand over the dustbin in the guest room occupied by her. Sharad Pant found some strands the widow had discarded after brushing her hair. I have sent the two hair samples for a DNA match with the ones found on the rolling pin.'

'That's ingenious, Tim. I am impressed,' the colonel complimented. 'I expect the rolling pin to have tissues of Dabral and the killer. When are you expecting the results of the DNA match?'

'The results will take a couple of days, at least. But a friend working in the forensic department has promised to update me with the report before it reaches here officially.'

'That's fantastic!' They had reached the turning of Oak Street. 'You can drop me near my house,' said the colonel. 'Would you like to step in for a cup of coffee? The standards may not be the same as Pia's coffee, but I can boast of an excellent brew at my place.'

'You are teasing me.' Tim smiled, turning the vehicle towards Acharya's bungalow. 'It's been a long day and I wouldn't mind a cuppa.'

'You still have the task of updating the DSP,' reminded Acharya as they halted before The Nook. Bullet's excited barking greeted them as soon as they got out of the vehicle and opened the flower-festooned gate to the bungalow driveway.

15

It was an unusually cold and windy night. The angry grey sky with its water-laden clouds continued to grumble throughout the day. By evening it had made up its mind and a heavy downpour with squally winds attacked the town. The gale made the trees bow with reverence and littered the street with debris. Water gurgled down the asphalt into already overloaded storm drains. Loud and unreserved thunderclaps punctured the thick evening silence.

At 8.30 p.m., after a frugal dinner, Laxmi settled down in front of the TV to watch her favourite soap. She raised the volume to offset the roar of the natural elements. It was her favourite time of the evening, when movies and soap operas gave wings to her imagination and she lost herself in the make-believe world presented by the idiot box.

Snug in an age-softened quilt, her feet tucked under her, Laxmi Badola lolled on the lumpy couch, watching the drama unfolding on the small screen. An emotional woman, she was moved by the heroine's misfortunes, and let the tears flow down her weather-beaten cheeks.

Someone knocked on the door. Her attention momentarily diverted from the soap, she tried to listen. *I am imagining things.* She shook her head. Sometimes the wind played tricks. The knocking reached her ears once again. Lowering the volume of the television, she tilted her head and cocked her ears to confirm if someone was really rapping on the door. This time, she heard it clearly. The knocking continued. Insistent. Louder. Surprised, she looked up at the clock on the wall.

It was a few minutes past 9 and she wasn't expecting any visitors. Few people ventured out on a wild night full of wind and rain. It was unlikely for someone to knock on her door at this time of the night, unless it was an emergency.

Who could it be? Has someone lost his way? Or is it a neighbour in trouble?

Reluctantly, she roused herself from the couch. Pushing aside the comfortable quilt, she padded towards the window and parted the curtains to peer outside. The woman could see no one. The street light, yellow and vaporous, cast a weak light on the deserted road. A wind-tossed branch of a pine tree tapped on the bedroom window. Laxmi willed the person to go away.

She debated against the thought of remaining silent. *What if I do not open the door? The visitor would go away after a few attempts.*

Just as she had made up her mind to remain unresponsive, she heard the determined rapping. *It must be someone in need. I will have to open the door.*

'Who is it?' she raised her voice. There was no response. She had definitely heard a loud knock on the door. So why was the person not responding to her question?

'Who's it?' she demanded in a shaky voice. A feeling of uneasiness gripped the woman as she waited for a reply. All she heard in reply was yet another clap of thunder. 'I will not open the door till I hear a reply,' she announced in a loud voice. 'Whoever you are, answer my question.'

A muffled voice came in response to her demand. The knock was repeated. Louder and insistent. She pussyfooted to the door and cocked her head against it, trying to catch a reply. Outside, the wind continued to howl. All she could hear was its keening.

'Why don't you reply? What do you want?' Laxmi asked in a voice tinged with anxiety.

'I have something for you,' the reply came in a barely audible voice, loud thunder drowning the words. The drumming sound grew louder as rain pummelled the tiled roof of her cottage.

Laxmi caught a few words. Could it be a gift from Badri, her son-in-law? Her anxiety evaporating, she relaxed a little.

'A gift?' she asked, her eyes lighting up in eager anticipation.

Although Badri rarely visited her, the scoundrel sent her an occasional gift through friends who passed through Ramsar. Sometimes a sari, sometimes a warm woollen shawl, or a fancy purse he had bought during one of his trips to the city. Once, during Diwali, he had sent her some money to buy herself a gift. The gifts, however, were few. In the twelve years he had been married to Laxmi's daughter, he had sent her a sari on a few instances. In the first two years after the wedding there had been a gift each year, which petered down to one in two years, and then to one every five years. Not that she blamed him. With a modest job and so many mouths to feed in the family, there was little money to spare. Her daughter, of course, had no say in the matter.

It must be an unexpected gift from my son-in-law. The festive season was just a few weeks away. Perhaps he wanted to make up for the past lapses. Maybe he had been waiting for a friend to pass through town. It had to be a very close friend. No sane person would deliver a gift on a night like this, but she was not one to look a gift horse in the mouth.

She would provide Badri's friend with a modest meal if he had not eaten, Laxmi decided.

'Have you come from Bageshwar?' she asked, trying to confirm the joyful news.

Laxmi heard a faint murmur in response to her query. Sighing, she opened the door and screwed her eyes to stare at the tall man standing outside. She could not figure out who it was, it was dark outside. The hood of his jacket pulled low over the head, to protect from the rain, made it difficult for her to see the face.

He was soaked to the skin. The visitor paused for a moment to stub out his cigarette in the bougainvillea pot next to the door. *What a thoughtful person.* Laxmi watched appreciatively as he wiped his shoes carefully on the doormat.

A gust of wind blew a sheet of rain into the room, making him hurry inside and shut the door quickly. His back turned to her, the man stood near the door and shook off the raindrops that clung to his clothes.

Poor man, he is totally soaked, and all for my sake. 'Wait here while I fetch a towel,' she instructed, rushing towards the bathroom.

His back was turned to her as Laxmi returned with the towel. 'Here, wipe yourself dry before you catch a cold. In the meantime, I will get some hot ginger tea for you.'

'That won't be necessary,' he said. Pushing back the hood from the head, he turned to face her. 'I won't be here for long.'

A slow smile curled his lips upward, giving a boyish look to his face. The smile didn't reach his cold eyes. Something was terribly wrong. Laxmi's breath quickened and her heart hammered with unease.

'Who ... who are you?' Laxmi stepped back, stammering. Her eyes widened with fear. A warning bell clanged in her brain. The man could not be one of Badri's friends. Her fingers curled into fists, nails digging into the palms. Her legs twitched, fighting the impulse to whirl around and sprint out of the house.

He didn't reply. Instead, he moved towards her ominously.

Stepping back, she collided with the television. It fell from its perch on the rickety table with a loud crash, the glass screen splintering into fragments.

'Sit down,' the man ordered in a stern voice, his eyes running over the room. That voice. Laxmi had heard it before, and recently too. She recognized the low, menacing tone.

She let her body drop heavily on to the couch, her eyes following the man as he paced the room in a leisurely manner. Laxmi felt fear torturing her guts, churning the stomach in tense cramps. She wanted to use the toilet. Time dragged its feet in slow motion, each second passing like an hour.

'Sad.' He shook his head regretfully and mumbled, 'It's really very unfortunate. Visiting you was not on my agenda.'

There was no hurry in his manner. Each movement was measured and deliberate.

What does he mean? His words made no sense to her. Her tongue was paralysed, the muscles frozen in place, but her senses remained heightened. Pure terror coursed through her veins, its icy arrow aiming for the heart. She trembled with the chill of fear.

With all her energies concentrated in her mind, it began functioning at its optimum. Among her friends, she was known for two attributes—acute observation and a razor-sharp mind. Both the faculties were on full alert now. His presence in her house was not without reason. *But what could it be? He mentioned the visit to be an unplanned one. Did it have anything to do with the alarming events that had taken place in town?*

Her mind did a quick recap of the events of the last few days.

On the very day she heard Umesh Gudyal arguing with the stranger, Laxmi had gone to attend the wedding of a friend's daughter at the other end of town. Images of that evening, strong and vivid, rushed through her mind.

It was around 10 that night, she remembered. Dressed in a bright orange sari with zari, her jewellery in place, she was returning home with a couple of women from the neighbourhood. It was a long walk, but that didn't worry the women, who were in high spirits. The evening had been rather satisfying, what with the lavish meal and a box of expensive sweets given as a return gift. It had been one of her happiest evenings lately. It was likely to be her last evening of happiness. She sighed.

Chattering and laughing, the women had walked past the bus stand, where a few people huddled together to ward off the cold.

'You are a nosy woman.' The stranger's flat and emotionless voice jerked her back to the present. 'You gossip too much for your own good.'

She was sure now. It had all to do with her going to the police.

He turned slowly and faced her. She saw him take out a thin nylon rope from the pocket of his jacket. He was going to kill her, she realized. Her breath ragged, Laxmi felt her innards freezing with fear. Adrenaline coursed through her system and a fight or flight instinct took charge.

Her eyes darted furiously, looking for an escape, but her legs felt leaden.

He stood towering before her. 'Why are you so tense?' He put his mouth near her ear and whispered, 'Just relax.'

Taking out a piece of duct tape, he slapped it on her trembling mouth. 'It won't hurt,' she heard him say. For a moment he contemplated if he should tie the woman's hands and then shook away the thought. It was not required. How much of a fight could she put up, anyway?

Paralysed with fear, she again spotted the nylon rope pulled taut between his fists. Whatever doubt had remained in her mind was now pushed aside. The woman knew that her end was near.

The scream that rose in Laxmi's throat died quietly as he looped the nylon rope around her neck like a noose. Slowly and steadily, he began pulling the ends apart.

The woman struggled against his grip. She would not allow him to kill her. Her desperate fingers clutched at everything within reach.

'There is no point.' The voice was cold and menacing. 'Fighting the inevitable will make it more painful. Let go. It will soon be over.' He twisted hands and pulled the nylon cord harder. Her lungs burned, desperate for a breath of air.

Gathering the last bit of strength and resolve, Laxmi fought. It was a silent battle. She clawed, thrashed and kicked with her hands and feet, but to no avail. The noose around her neck grew tighter with every move. Her eyes bulged, legs flapped impotently as he pulled the rope tighter, cutting off the air supply. Still he tightened the noose. She twisted, choking and fighting for breath as life slipped away. A final gasp for breath and her body went limp. The head lolled to a side, and the tongue slipped out of the mouth.

Like an artist giving last touches to a painting, he laid the woman carefully on the couch, and covered her with the quilt. Tucking a cushion under the woman's head, he gently closed her bloodshot, bulging eyes and stood looking at her for a moment. He had not enjoyed killing the poor woman, but it was necessary. Why couldn't she have kept her nose out of his business?

Satisfied with the setting, the visitor slipped out of the house, pulling the door behind him. He darted a quick glance down the road, before walking out into the rain. The grandfather clock on the wall struck ten times, announcing the hour. It had taken him very little time to commit the crime.

Unaware of the tragic death of the gossipy woman, the Ramsarians remained tucked in the comfort of their quilts.

16

It was a calm morning. The storm that raged through the town died a little after midnight, and the rain stopped pelting the ground. Mist rose from the valley and swathed the mountains. The best time to catch the mountains at their best was early in the morning. Wrapped in a thick woollen coat, the hood covering his head, the colonel set out for his morning walk. This was his favourite time of the day when, undisturbed, he could ruminate on the issues that bothered him.

The eagle-headed walking stick in hand, he soldiered along the long and snaking Ridge Road that led towards the top of the hill. On a good day, he covered three bends that tallied to 3 kilometres each way. With Beethoven's *Moonlight Sonata* tantalizing his ears, Acharya strode bravely up the incline, pausing briefly at the second bend. He gazed at the dense pine forests that flanked the road and took a deep breath of the pine-scented breeze. For the umpteenth time, he patted himself on the back for having chosen Ramsar as his post-retirement haven.

Untouched by tourists, grime and greed, it was a utopian place. Dotted with red-roofed bungalows, snaking roads, pine forests interspersed with blazing rhododendron blooms, and with a sweeping view of the magnificent mountains in the north, the town was a dreamer's delight. Not that he was a dreamer.

The colonel walked leisurely down the steep road, invigorated and eager to face the day. With each stride, he could feel the cobwebs that had clouded his brain disappearing bit by bit. By the end of the walk, as he rounded the last bend, he had decided to share a cup of tea with Laxmi Badola.

The woman had barged into the police station to share some information, but the police had been too busy to give her a patient hearing. Acharya was aware of Laxmi's reputation. He knew that the lonely woman was in the habit of blowing minor incidents into major events, so no one took her seriously.

Led by his intuition, he decided to hear what the woman wanted to share with the police. He had heard snatches of her argument with the constable, and gathered that she had spotted an unsavoury character at the bus stand. The man's portrayal could be exaggerated, but she couldn't have conjured the person from thin air. The woman must have seen such a person, he was sure.

Attention to minor snippets often paved the way to a bigger picture, the colonel believed.

Although he had wandered through Pinewood Street a couple of times, he was not fully familiar with the houses on either side of the street. Now, as he ambled past the houses, looking for Laxmi Badola's residence, Acharya noted the houses on both sides of the quiet street. He knew the woman lived across Negi Mansion. Armed with that knowledge, he began looking for the specific building.

Ten minutes later, he was standing before a single-storeyed brick house opposite Negi Mansion. It was a modest house constructed by Laxmi's husband on a patch of land inherited from his parents. Ever since her husband's death about ten years ago, the woman had lived alone in the house. Her son had followed the footsteps of his father to join the army and the two daughters were happily married. It was only during the infrequent visits from her children that the woman's house echoed with laughter.

A picket fence with flaking white paint surrounded the house, which was fronted by a small garden displaying a medley of flowers planted in a haphazard manner. A variety of flowers stood guarding a patch of kitchen garden, which was exhibiting a healthy growth of tomatoes, brinjals and green chillies. A bougainvillea creeper drooped over the main door, its magenta flowers lending colour to the fading paint on it.

Failing to find the doorbell button, Acharya rapped on the door with his walking stick. No one responded to the knocking, so he rapped again. He could sense no movement or activity inside the house as he waited. Unable to evoke a response to repeated rapping, the colonel pushed the door after a few minutes. It swung open without offering any resistance.

He called out the woman's name and hit his stick repeatedly on the door before entering. Something was amiss. Warning bells clanging in his brain, the colonel rushed into the room.

The first thing he noted was the furniture in disarray and scrape marks on the floor. The floor was littered with pieces of broken glass from the television, which lay toppled. The entire room looked as though a fracas had taken place in it.

His eyes swivelled towards the couch. Laxmi Badola lay covered with a blanket. He knew the woman was dead even before he touched her. There was a look of pure terror on her waxy face. The bottom lip, blue and tortured, jutted out like a pout. Her hands were clenched into fists and the nails had a bluish tinge. From experience, the colonel knew that she had been dead for some hours. The body was in a state of full rigor mortis, so the death would have taken place at least six to eight hours ago.

He pushed the blanket aside, and studied the woman's neck. There were ligature marks on the lower third of the neck, a clear sign of strangulation. He had read enough forensic books to know that Laxmi Badola had been strangled to death. A ball pen lying on the floor attracted his attention. Picking it up with his handkerchief, he pocketed it.

Wasting no time, Acharya took out his phone and called Tim.

'I am at Laxmi Badola's house,' he said. 'She has been murdered.'

Tim would hurry to the place as soon as possible, the colonel knew.

While he waited, his sharp eyes scanned the room carefully. Groaning, he put his walking stick aside and bent down to look under the couch. He found a thick layer of dust. Laxmi's arthritic bones wouldn't have allowed her to clean under there, he realized.

An object lying under the sagging couch attracted his attention. Cursing his uncooperative knee, he used his stick to help him bring out the tiny tube of medicine. Using his handkerchief, he held up the tube and hauled himself up with a Herculean effort. Thereafter, he went near the window and read the composition on the tube, before putting it into his pocket.

Tim had not arrived, so the colonel began wandering through the house. Apart from the drawing room, there were two bedrooms, a kitchen and a tiny store with a door that opened into an alley.

The rooms were neat and sparsely furnished. Laxmi lived a simple and uncomplicated life. *If only her death had been as uncomplicated as her life.*

Tim arrived just as the colonel emerged from a bedroom after searching for clues.

'Good morning,' the officer greeted him cheerfully. The exuberance of youth never failed to amaze the colonel.

'Not a very good morning for Laxmi Badola,' Acharya replied sardonically, and pointed at the corpse. 'The poor woman will never see another morning.'

'What brought you here in the first place?' Tim wondered why the colonel had thought it necessary to visit the woman so early in the morning.

'It was a strong hunch that brought me here. Not many young people would agree with me, but morning walks are best suited for rumination. This morning I recalled that Laxmi had walked into the police station demanding to speak with you. She insisted that she had important information to convey, but Shirt Pant didn't allow her to meet us.'

'She always had some important information.'

'No, Tim. It is sad that she was not taken seriously. Observant people should not be taken lightly. They notice what others fail to observe. Laxmi had sharp eyes and a sharper mind. The woman must have seen something that brought her running to the police station. One of us should have heard her story. It could have saved her life.'

'How could we have saved her life?'

'Isn't it obvious? In all likelihood, the woman was killed to stop the information from being relayed to the police. Had we allowed her to speak, murdering her would have become pointless.'

'You think she really had some vital information?' Tim sounded sceptical.

'Yes, I am convinced that it was important. It was the desire to hear her statement that brought me here this morning. Unfortunately, I was too late.' Acharya's eyes mirrored unhappiness at his failure to prevent the woman's death.

'Don't blame yourself, Colonel. Going by your logic, the DSP and I are equally guilty,' Tim reminded him.

'The DSP isn't a very astute man, so it doesn't matter if he paid no attention to the woman. Your carelessness can be excused on grounds of inexperience. But how could I make that mistake?'

Realizing the truth in Acharya's words, Tim stared ruefully at the woman.

'Let's not waste time in regrets,' said the colonel briskly. 'The only way to atone for the blunder is to bring the culprit to justice.'

'The doctor, photographer and the forensic guy will be here in a few minutes. You were the first to arrive at the scene, so you must have noticed something. Did you find any clues that can lead us to the murderer?' Tim had immense faith in the colonel's observation powers and sixth sense.

'There are a few things I noticed. First, the door was unlocked but there was no sign that it had been forced open. Whoever killed the woman did not break into the house. He was let in by her, so I assume he was known to Laxmi. Second, there are signs of struggle, so she must have put up a valiant effort to stop her murderer. Third, rigor mortis shows she has been dead for at least six to eight hours. Since the temperature last night was quite low, the time of murder could even be nine hours ago or a little more.'

'What time did you arrive?'

'It was exactly 7.30 a.m. when I entered the house.'

Tim did a quick calculation. 'That would place the likely time of death between 10 p.m. and 1 a.m.'

'Yes, give or take an hour here or there,' agreed Acharya. 'That's my estimation. Let's see what the doc has to say. We will know better after the post-mortem, of course.'

'Is there anything else you noticed?'

'My initial observations lead me to deduce that the woman has been strangled. I have limited knowledge of forensic science, so we will have to wait for the doctor's verdict.'

Tim let out a whistle. 'How did you conclude she had been strangled?'

The colonel led Tim to the body and pointed at the ligature marks on the neck. 'Do you see the mark on the neck? It is the mark left by a rope. A ligature mark on the lower third of the neck suggests strangulation. Now, observe the congestion and cyanosis of the face. These are additional pointers that the woman had been strangled to death.'

Tim nodded appreciatively. 'Did you find any other clue?' he asked eagerly.

'I found two objects while exploring the room. One of them is a pen.' Acharya took out the ballpoint pen and showed it to the police officer. 'And the other is a tiny tube of ointment.' With a flourish, he produced the other item.

'Hydrocortisone cream,' Tim read the label. 'We will have to ask the doc about it.' He proceeded to examine the pen. 'The ballpoint pen is a golden Cruiser Makellos. By the look of it, I think it's an expensive pen. Not many in Ramsar can afford such a pen, so it shouldn't be difficult to find the owner.'

'You don't have to bother. The pen belongs to Umesh Gudyal. I have seen it in his pocket,' Acharya said. 'And it costs close to twenty thousand bucks. The cap is crafted from 24-carat gold. I checked on the internet just now.'

'What is Gudyal doing with an expensive pen like that? I don't think he can afford to splurge such a big amount on a ballpoint pen. Do you think he has stolen it from someone?'

'We will have to ask him that.' The colonel chuckled, amused at Tim's puzzled expression.

'I will send both these items for fingerprinting.' Tim dropped the two objects in a ziplock bag. 'And before you ask me, I have informed the DSP. I called him right after hearing from you. So he should arrive shortly.'

The arrival of the doctor, ambulance, forensic guy and photographer caught the attention of the neighbourhood. The last few days had brought a few unexpected events to Ramsar. To their mind, the sudden arrival of the police and doctor could only mean one thing. Something untoward had taken place in Laxmi Badola's house. Word spread. Drawn by curiosity, a crowd of onlookers began gathering in front of her house. They stood gossiping and speculating about the dead woman.

Inside the house, the colonel and Tim watched as the body was photographed and examined, and fingerprints were lifted from the door latch and other objects.

'What is your opinion, doc?' Tim asked the doctor after he had finished examining the body.

'The woman's death was caused by strangulation. As for the time of death, I can only give a rough estimate. I think she died between 8 and 11 last night. We will know more after the autopsy.' The doc unclenched Laxmi Badola's fists and examined the fingernails carefully. 'There's no doubt that she didn't go down without a fight. There are enough signs of struggle, contusions and lacerations to prove her resistance.'

'Is there anything that could point to the identity of the killer?' Tim asked, leaning closer to look at the woman's fists.

'I would say there is,' the doc affirmed. 'The victims often leave indications that serve as evidence. Sometimes we get lucky and find pieces of cloth, buttons or hair of the assailant in the deceased's hands. This is caused by cadaveric spasm.'

'Did you get lucky this morning?' The colonel wanted to know.

'Yes, I think so. Look at this.' He took out a pair of forceps and picked up a strand of hair lying in Laxmi's fist. 'In fact, we have been doubly lucky this morning. Apart from the hair, there is tissue debris under the deceased's fingernails.'

The doctor handed a magnifying glass to Tim and pointed with the forceps. 'If you look carefully under the nails that bear signs of cyanosis, you will see the tissues. There are enough remnants of tissue for the forensic team to work on.

'Here's something interesting for you,' the doctor called out to the forensic man, who studied the fingernails for underlying debris.

'A gold mine,' he remarked as he collected them in a sterile container.

The entire team continued to work swiftly and efficiently, while Tim and the colonel scanned the premises for some more evidence. The body was being taken away for the autopsy when their ears picked up sounds of commotion. Looking outside, Tim saw Sharad Pant shooing away the bystanders, saying, 'Make way, make way for sa'ab.'

Minutes later, JBS burst into the house, not unlike an elephant in a porcelain store.

'What's the matter?' he demanded. 'Haven't you finished searching the premises yet?'

'Good morning, sir,' Tim greeted the boss, his spine straightening of its own accord. 'We have gone through the room and found a couple of things.'

'Did you look outside the main door?'

Tim exchanged a look with the colonel. They had not had the time to search the area around the house.

'Snap up, Tim! It's one of the first things you should have done. No wonder you failed to find an important piece of evidence,' declared the DSP triumphantly. Like a clever conjuror, he waved a cigarette butt under their noses.

'Where did you find this?' asked Acharya, cursing himself for not having noticed the butt.

'It was in the flowerpot near the entrance,' informed the DSP. He loved nothing better than a chance to haul up others, especially the officers serving under him. He never missed an opportunity to snub the colonel too. 'Negligence in a murder case can result in disaster.' He shook his head.

Tim knew he had been caught on the wrong foot. 'We were planning to search the outer area ...' he began sheepishly.

'Are you telling me that you intended to examine the external area after the scene of the crime had been contaminated by the curious crowd of onlookers?' The sarcasm in JBS's voice was impossible to miss. 'You have forgotten the very first rule of investigating. A criminal case can be made, or lost, at the crime scene. It is the place where the greatest margin of error occurs,' quoted the DSP. Never one to lose an opportunity to sermonize, he continued, 'Proper collection and retrieval of evidence is of utmost importance. Police records are full of culprits who were nabbed because they left their calling card at the crime scene. Chewing gum, saliva, hair and cigarette butts are just some of the items that may be left behind by a criminal. These items often help detectives determine who was present at the crime scene.'

Aware of the truth in the DSP's statement, Tim and Acharya nodded their heads dutifully. The colonel knew many cases had been screwed up because onlookers had picked up something without realizing it could be an important clue. Sometimes, unscrupulous elements would remove weapons, wallets or some personal items from the victim or the surroundings. There was also the danger that the onlookers would leave a multitude of foot- and fingerprints traces of clothing and bodily fluids that contaminate important pieces of evidence at the crime scene.

Carefully, the DSP held out the cigarette butt for Acharya to examine. 'Can you identify the brand, Colonel?'

Acharya screwed up his eyes to study the butt. 'Careful, Colonel,' cautioned the DSP, removing the butt out of Acharya's reach. 'There might be latent fingerprints, which can help us identify the murderer. A DNA profiling test on the saliva traces could reveal the culprit.'

'Yes, of course,' Acharya agreed. He stopped himself from retorting. He, more than anyone else, knew the danger of obliterating fingerprints by careless handling. 'Let's bag the evidence and study it later.'

'That would be wise.' The DSP nodded triumphantly. The ever-pompous man was delighted at finding an opportunity to put the colonel in his place. He resented the fact that Acharya had made a remarkable impression on the police commissioner with his sleuthing skills. 'Let's wrap up matters here and seal the house. Thereafter, we can discuss the details at the police station.'

17

An hour later, having sealed the scene of the crime and bagged the evidence, Tim drove the DSP and colonel to the police station.

'I missed breakfast,' declared Bulldog as soon as they entered Tim's office. 'Do you think the coffee shop will be open?'

Acharya and Tim exchanged amused glances. Clearly, Pia's coffee shop had made the right impression on the DSP.

'It is past 10 now,' Tim replied, glancing at the wristwatch. 'I will call Pia and find out if the café is open. I am sure she will oblige us with some sandwiches. Should I ask Sharad to fetch some coffee and sandwiches for you?'

'Yes, you should do that.'

As he had expected, Pia informed Tim that the café was open and she could take the order for sandwiches.

'What should I order for you?' putting the call on hold, Tim asked the DSP.

'Any kind of sandwich will do,' responded Bulldog, who didn't know much about the variations available at the café. As an afterthought, he asked, 'What did we have the other day? Order the same stuff. That was quite good.'

'If I remember correctly, you had a chicken-mayonnaise sandwich and a mushroom omelette.'

The DSP grunted his approval. 'Order some coffee to go with that,' he added.

'What about you, Colonel? Would you like some sandwiches and coffee?' Tim asked.

'I don't want sandwiches, but a cup of cappuccino would be nice,' Acharya replied.

He got up and walked towards the window.

'So, who do you think killed the woman?' asked JBS after Tim had sent the constable on the errand. 'Is it the same person who killed Dabral?'

The colonel turned and faced Bulldog, but remained standing with his back to the window. 'It may or may not be the same person. The mode of killing is different in the two cases. However, the two may have been connected. My gut feeling is that Laxmi Badola was killed because she knew the killer. The poor woman had come here to share the information, but we ignored her.'

'That may be true. But I am convinced that Umesh Gudyal is the murderer,' JBS said. 'After he killed Dabral over the property dispute, he learnt that Laxmi Badola was likely to identify him as the killer. So he walked across to her house and strangled her to death. The cigarette butt is just one of the pieces of evidence he left behind. That man is a chain-smoker and must have been smoking when he reached the woman's house.'

'The matter needs to be investigated carefully. We have to be sure of his involvement before we accuse Umesh Gudyal,' said Acharya, who didn't agree with the quick solution provided by the DSP, but didn't want to antagonize Bulldog by disagreeing. 'I doubt he would have been smoking while at Laxmi's house. The cigarette butt might have been dropped on an earlier occasion. It might be better to wait till we receive the DNA report of the tissues found under the victim's nails.'

'I am sure the DNA profile of the tissues will match with those of Umesh Gudyal.' The DSP lifted his chin and stared challengingly at Acharya. 'Not just that, a third-degree treatment will have him singing in no time.'

Looking at his stubborn canine face, Acharya wondered, as he had wondered many times before, how had Bulldog reached his present rank? An obstinate and judgemental man, the DSP was quick to jump to conclusions. He never failed to find a scapegoat.

'Tim, I want you to send all the items for DNA profiling with instructions that they should be accorded priority. I will speak to the forensic lab in-charge to hasten the reports,' Bulldog ordered.

Further ruminations were set aside for a while as Sharad Pant entered the office with the sandwiches and coffee. Overjoyed to have the opportunity of commandeering the police vehicle, the constable was grinning with pleasure, Tim noted.

The DSP busied himself with the food. 'The Williams girl makes superb stuff,' he grunted with satisfaction. 'I am not a coffee person, but I could easily get addicted to the caffé lattes made by her.'

Acharya threw a meaningful look at Tim, who was trying to suppress a smile.

It was while they were enjoying the coffee that a young lad burst into the room, followed by an irate constable.

'Where do you think you are going?' shouted Sharad Pant, grabbing the lad by the sleeve. 'Sa'ab, this fellow—'

'Who are you?' asked the DSP, staring at the emaciated teenager. Clad in a dark hooded jacket, he looked no more than fifteen.

Acharya had often seen the cheerful boy, who supported his widowed mother by delivering newspapers and running errands for the older ladies of Firangi Colony. A hard-working and honest chap, he sometimes substituted as a gardener for the colonel.

'He is Lalu, the newspaper delivery boy,' replied Sharad, tugging at the boy's arm. 'I told him—'

'What do you want?' Tim cut in.

'Sa'ab, I saw the murderer,' bleated the boy.

'Where and when did you see the murderer?' Tim asked, gesturing to Shirt Pant to let go of the boy. Thereafter, he beckoned to the boy to come closer. 'Now, tell us what you saw,' he ordered.

Casting a nervous glance at the DSP, Lalu slunk closer to the table.

'Sa'ab, this morning, at about 6, I was delivering newspapers on Pinewood Street. I was on my bicycle, as usual. As I pedalled past Laxmi Badola's house, I spotted Umesh emerging from her house.' The lad paused. He looked around hesitantly, waiting for reactions to the information.

'You saw Umesh Gudyal coming out of Laxmi's house?' asked the colonel. He knew Lalu to be an alert and honest boy.

'Yes, sa'ab. Umesh was coming out of her house,' repeated the boy. 'He looked cautiously around before crossing the street and rushing into his house. I wondered why he had gone to Laxmi's house.'

'What did you do?' Tim wanted to know.

'I halted for a while, watching Negi Mansion. The newspapers had to be delivered so I couldn't loiter around for long. When Umesh did not come out of his house, I went away.'

'Did you see anyone else on the street?'

The boy thought for a while and shook his head. 'No, there was no one around.'

'You are sure Umesh went to Laxmi's house at 6 in the morning?' asked the DSP, his voice rising with excitement. He needed no further proof to indict Umesh Gudyal.

'Yes, sa'ab.'

'Thank you, Lalu.' Tim patted the boy on the back. 'Come and meet me if you remember anything else.'

'I will do that,' promised the boy, who had no love lost for Umesh Gudyal. A few months back, Lalu had been reprimanded by Umesh for whistling as he passed the mansion every morning.

'Do you still have doubts about the identity of the murderer, Colonel?' the DSP asked as soon as the boy left the office. 'As far as I am concerned, Umesh Gudyal is the man,' he said and thumped the table jubilantly. 'Tim, I want you to collate all evidence against the chap and arrest him for the murder of Laxmi Badola.'

'I still feel that we must dig a little deeper into the muck before we arrive at a conclusion.' Acharya gave up his resolution to do without the cigar. Extracting one from his pocket, he trimmed and lit it. The colonel had chosen the slim and mild variety for a change, Tim noted.

Drawing in the smoke with a satisfied grunt, Acharya savoured the tobacco flavour for a minute before giving vent to his thoughts. 'For a few minutes, let us presume Umesh Gudyal is the murderer. What do you think is his motive for killing Dabral?'

'It's for Ratan Negi's property, of course,' pat came the reply from the DSP, who thought that the question was facile.

'According to Gudyal, Ratan Negi willed his property to him. What would he gain by killing the cousin?' the colonel countered.

'Maybe he is lying. Maybe there is no such will.'

'That can easily be proved. If he has the will, I can find no motive for him to kill Dabral.'

'All right, I will go with your theory that Gudyal is innocent. The question remains: if he had the will, why did he want to meet Dabral?'

'According to Gudyal's statement, he wanted to mend fences with his cousin. I believe his statement.'

'In that case, what was he doing in the murdered woman's house that morning? We have an eyewitness who saw him emerging from Laxmi Badola's house. How would you explain that? What about the cigarette butt found in the potted plant at the entrance?'

'We should give him a chance to explain.' The colonel retrohaled, enjoying the fine blend of the tobacco flavours. He had perfected the art of drawing the smoke into the mouth and rolling it around, before forcing it out through the nose.

'For once, I will pander to your whim,' the DSP declared magnanimously. 'We will question him one last time. I hope he has a convincing explanation for the two pieces of evidence against him.' Turning to Tim, who had maintained discreet silence, he said, 'It is time to drag Gudyal to the police station.'

The colonel and DSP were waiting for Gudyal to be brought in, when Sabharwal made an appearance.

'Good morning,' he greeted cheerfully. Without waiting for permission, he drew out a chair and plonked himself on it. His manner smacked of impudence. 'I thought it proper to meet you before we left for Delhi. Also, I heard there was another murder last night. Ramsar is getting a bit too dangerous to loiter around,' saying which Sabharwal guffawed, his cockiness rankling the men in the room.

'Speaking of proper behaviour, don't you think it improper to enter an office without asking for permission?' the colonel remarked, taking the man down a peg or two.

'You should have asked for permission,' Tim joined the colonel in reproaching the man. 'Firstly, it is the right thing to do. Secondly, we were having an important discussion.'

'Sorry! It was wrong of me to have taken the liberty to interrupt your meeting.' Sabharwal smiled while scratching his left hand. 'I thought—'

'You thought it was proper to barge into an ASP's office without seeking permission,' the DSP bellowed. 'We don't like insolent people, especially those who have no business being so.'

Chastened by the cumulative attack, Sabharwal apologized, 'I am sorry—'

'Anyway, what brings you here this morning? I am sure you didn't come here to exchange pleasantries,' Bulldog cut in.

Disconcerted by the DSP's brusque manner, Sabharwal huffed, 'You are absolutely right. I have not come to exchange pleasantries or waste your precious time. Tim had asked me to see him before leaving Ramsar, so I came.'

'You will have to wait for a while for me to speak to you,' said Tim sternly. 'I had asked both Nisha and you to be here, so we could ask you a few questions. Why isn't she here?'

'Haven't you asked enough questions? My sister is not in a condition to face an interrogation yet again.'

Tim exchanged a look with the colonel, who nodded subtly.

'All right, we will do without her. Kindly wait outside till I summon you.' Tim got up and saw the man to the door.

'Will it take long? We are in a hurry since we have to reach Kathgodam in time to catch the train to Delhi,' Sabharwal said, subdued after the rebuke. He knew the police officer could detain him for as long as he wanted.

'Please wait!' was all Tim deigned to say.

'That man is a nuisance.' Bulldog shook his head. 'Do you want him to linger here?' he asked Tim.

'I wanted both Nisha and Sabharwal to come to the police station before they left Ramsar so they could be fingerprinted. I will ask him to wait for the forensic technician to take his fingerprints. Thereafter, the technician can visit Bhandari Villa to fingerprint the sister,' Tim informed.

'That may be a good idea,' growled the DSP. He had no intention of delaying his departure from Ramsar. 'Call the man inside and warn him against leaving without finishing the procedure.'

Sabharwal appeared visibly subdued when he presented himself before the three men.

'I think it was wrong of me to have barged into the office.' The winning smile remained pasted on his face as Tim told him to get himself fingerprinted.

A constable was instructed to arrange for the fingerprinting, and Sabharwal was dismissed.

'I won't be meeting you again.' Sabharwal cleared his throat awkwardly and said, 'Thank you for all your effort in trying to find my brother-in-law's murderer. Please let me know if I can be of help in the matter.' He shook hands with all the men before walking up to the door. He paused suddenly and, turning to the DSP, asked, 'Have you any idea who murdered my brother-in-law?'

'We are closing in,' replied the DSP smugly. 'I think he will be in the lock-up before you reach your destination.'

'Nisha will be happy to know that. Although I can guess the person's name, may I know who it is?'

'No, you may not,' Acharya retorted before the DSP could let the cat out of the bag. He would not allow Umesh Gudyal's name to be revealed to the conceited idiot. 'You will get to know eventually.'

'Yes, of course,' said Sabharwal. 'I thought I could share the information with my sister. It would have given her a lot of satisfaction to know that the scoundrel Umesh Gudyal is behind bars.'

'What makes you so sure that he is the murderer?'

Sabharwal remained rooted near the door, deliberating over his reply. 'Well, it's obvious that Gudyal invited Deepak for a chat and killed him. I heard that the woman who was murdered last night lived across his house. Maybe she saw something, so he silenced her.'

'Bravo!' Acharya stood up and clapped dramatically. 'Who needs the police or a sleuth when there are smart men like you?'

'I just stated the obvious,' snapped Sabharwal, smarting at the colonel's sarcasm.

'You will do well to leave the matter for the police to investigate.'

'I should leave,' saying this, the young man turned to the door once more.

'Yes, you should,' the DSP remarked impassively. 'Remember to leave all your contact numbers and addresses, including those of your sister, with the constable before you leave.'

'Are we under a cloud, then?' Sabharwal raised his eyebrow enquiringly, inadvertently scratching his hand.

At that moment, Sharad Pant, who had been despatched to bring Gudyal, strode into the room with his quarry.

Throwing a surprised look at the visitor, Gudyal asked, 'So you have been busy stoking the fire?'

'I don't have to stoke the fire. Everyone knows you killed Deepak.' Sabharwal smirked, relishing his target's embarrassment. 'Good luck, Gudyal!' He patted Gudyal's shoulder in a patronizing manner.

'You are a disgusting man,' Gudyal said, levelling a disdainful look at the loathsome fellow and shrinking away from him.

'Crime doesn't pay, my dear chap,' Sabharwal sermonized cheekily. It was obvious that he was enjoying the spectacle. 'Remember, the law always catches up with the criminal.'

'That will be enough,' shouted the DSP, getting to his feet. 'Get going, Sabharwal, before I lose my temper.'

'I am going.' He chuckled, hurrying towards the door, pausing for a moment to fire a parting shot at the seething Gudyal. 'No offence meant. I will remember you in my prayers.'

'What an obnoxious chap!' commented Acharya.

'The guy is being particularly offensive this morning,' agreed Tim.

'I guess he is feeling relaxed after the tension of the last few days,' opined the DSP.

'It could be the relief of getting away from the police and the town,' opined Acharya.

'May I know why I have been brought here?' enquired Umesh Gudyal, irritation writ large on his face. Sabharwal's caustic comments had added to his annoyance. 'I thought I had done all the explaining on the previous occasions.'

'We don't have to offer any explanation for bringing you here,' the DSP responded nastily.

'Investigations for a murder are not over till the murderer is apprehended,' interjected the colonel. 'And now we have a second murder to investigate.'

'I had nothing to do with either of the cases.'

'Every criminal professes innocence.' The DSP sneered. 'The police will decide whether you had anything to do with the two murders.'

JBS nodded at Tim in a tacit signal to continue the questioning while he busied himself with signing some papers. His ears, however, were tuned to catch Tim's questions and Gudyal's replies.

'You live across from Laxmi Badola's house, don't you?' Tim asked.

'Is that a crime?' A confrontational attitude was evident in Gudyal's response.

'When did you last see her?'

'I am not in the habit of socializing with neighbours, especially busybodies like Laxmi Badola.'

'Don't circumvent the question. When did you last see the deceased?'

'I haven't seen her in the past forty-eight hours.'

'That's a false statement. You saw her just before she was killed.'

'No, I didn't.' Gudyal stuck resolutely to his statement.

'We have evidence to prove you wrong.' Tim's tone was harsh. 'You got rid of Laxmi Badola because she was a threat. She had seen you murdering Dabral.'

'That's not true,' Gudyal said. He appeared exhausted. The past few days had been disturbing. Knowing that he was on the police's suspect list made him restless, and neither his mother nor he had been sleeping well. Despite all the posturing, Tim's accusation intensified his exasperation. 'I had nothing to do with her murder,' he rasped. He felt his throat drying and asked for water. 'May I smoke?' he requested after gulping down a full glass of water.

Without waiting for permission, he took out a fresh pack of cigarettes and tore the cellophane wrapper with trembling fingers. Extracting a cigarette with difficulty, he lit it in a slow and deliberate manner, trying to gather some self-control. Filling his lungs with smoke, he let it out in one long exhale before speaking.

'Prove me wrong, officer,' he challenged in a controlled voice, and directed a steady gaze at Tim. The moments of panic had passed.

'Your preferred brand of cigarettes is Gold Flake Filter, isn't it?' Tim asked, eyeing the pack of cigarettes placed on the table by Gudyal.

'So it is,' the man responded in an unflustered manner. 'It's not an offence, I think.'

'What do you have to say about this?' Tim took out the plastic bag containing the cigarette stub found in the potted plant flanking Laxmi Badola's door.

'What do you expect me to say?'

'This was found at the crime scene.'

'It proves nothing, officer. There are scores of people smoking Gold Flake Filter in this town. Anyone could have dropped it there.'

'Scores of people may be smoking that brand but this stub has your fingerprints on it.'

On the very day he had been fingerprinted, Gudyal knew that the police had listed him as one of the suspects. He knew they would match his prints with each and every piece of evidence discovered at the scene of the crime.

'It means nothing. I am a chain-smoker and tend to leave stubs all over the place. Anyone could have taken a stub and planted it at the crime scene to implicate me in the murder.' Gudyal kept his cool despite the provocation.

'Why would anyone do that?' asked Tim.

'I am not a popular person in this town. In fact, not many people like to exchange greetings with me.'

'Is that reason enough for someone to implicate you in a murder? I think not,' Tim retorted. 'It's not just the cigarette stub. We also have an eyewitness who saw you emerging from Laxmi Badola's house early this morning.'

'Nonsense!'

'The police do not feel it is nonsense,' said the colonel, who had been listening to the interaction silently. 'You have to come forth with a better explanation.'

'I refuse to comment on the figment of some nosy chap's imagination.'

'What do you have to say about this?' Acharya placed the golden Cruiser Makellos ballpoint pen on the table between them.

Gudyal made a quick move to grab the ballpoint pen but Tim quickly removed it out of his reach. 'Is that your pen, Gudyal?' he asked.

'Where did you find it?' asked Gudyal, lunging towards the pen once more.

'So you admit that the pen belongs to you? It's an expensive ball pen. How did you manage to buy it?'

'Did you steal the pen from Dabral?' interpolated the DSP, surprised by its sudden appearance. He made a mental note to tick off Tim and Acharya for not mentioning it to him.

'Why should I steal the pen?'

'As far as I know, you don't earn enough to indulge in fancy purchases.'

'The ball pen was given to me by my uncle. It was his last gift and I have an emotional connection with it.'

'How did it land up at Laxmi Badola's house?' Acharya levelled the question at the man.

'I lost it a couple of days back and have been looking for it. I don't know how it landed up at her house.'

'Your cigarette stub and ball pen must have an interest in murders. So they landed up at the scene of the crime.' The DSP's voice was loaded with sarcasm. 'Try a more convincing excuse, Gudyal.'

'It is not an excuse. I am telling you the truth. Someone must have stolen the ball pen and dropped it at Laxmi Badola's house.' Gudyal's desperation was evident as he lit another cigarette to calm his nerves.

'Apart from these, your fingerprints were found all over the place. What is your explanation for that?' Tim asked the man.

'I will offer no explanation,' Gudyal replied in a rude manner.

'Do you realize that we have enough evidence to arrest you for Laxmi Badola's murder?'

'Believe me, officer I didn't murder her.'

'We will leave that decision to the court. As far as I am concerned, you are the murderer,' the DSP stated with finality.

Turning to Tim, he ordered, 'I want the man arrested for the murder of Laxmi Badola.'

Realizing the futility of protesting, Gudyal remained silent. His shoulders sagged with the weight of helplessness. He needed time and help to prove his innocence.

The DSP departed a few minutes later, leaving Tim to deal with the paperwork. Dissatisfied with the way things were going, Acharya left the police station in a huff. He would have preferred to wait for the forensic reports before arresting Gudyal, but nothing he said would change the DSP's decision. Having worked with the man, he knew the futility of arguing with Bulldog.

18

It was a pleasant and sunny morning, ideal for exercise. In fact, it was a perfect one for a round of golf as well. Acharya, who had realized the morning's perfection while on his daily walk, decided to indulge in the game. It had been a couple of weeks since he had found time to swing his irons. At 9 a.m. sharp, having fixed a rendezvous with the professor, the colonel presented himself at the nine-hole golf course, which was the pride of Ramsar.

The professor, though he worked hard on improving his game, was a poor golfer and fell short of the average handicap. The swings he practised diligently on the lawn of his house added nothing to his expertise. He played golf as he would play cricket, the cricket bat being substituted with a golfing iron.

That morning when the duo met up for a game, the professor was at his worst. That didn't stop him from bragging.

'My practice swings have helped me improve my game. Just watch my swing,' swaggered the professor.

Suppressing an amused smile, Acharya watched his partner try a couple of swings before raising the club high above his head. The next minute, the professor swung it downward with full force. The club connected with the ball, making it take off in a high arc before disappearing in the air. The professor, whose eyes were trained expectantly towards the target green, was shocked by the thud created by the ball as it landed just a couple of feet away from him.

The colonel, who had expected the ball to land in the nearby waterbody, was surprised by the sudden change in the ball's destination. Every time he played, the professor unerringly managed to shoot off a couple of golf balls into the water, causing much amusement among the caddies.

'That was a lethal shot, Prof.' The colonel chuckled. 'I think it would be prudent for me to wear a helmet during our next game.'

'Damn! I used the wrong iron. I should have used number seven,' the professor muttered. Pushing the sunglasses up on his forehead, he narrowed his eyes to check the number of the club. His vanity hindered his game. Too vain to wear his glasses to the golf course, he never failed to choose the wrong club, shoot in the wrong direction or miss the ball.

'Don't bother to check the number,' Acharya remarked as he chose a club for a shot. 'You can either impress the players at the golf course or play a good game. Not that they would give you the time of the day, with or without your glasses.'

'You speak as though you are an ace at playing the game.'

'The proof of the pudding is in the eating,' quoted Acharya. 'Just watch this shot and you will know that,' said the colonel, his club poised over the ball. With his cap perched rakishly over the brow, dark glasses on the nose, he struck an impressive figure, no doubt.

This time, the colonel's ball sailed majestically before plopping into the pond. Not one to miss a chance, the professor jeered and clapped.

Despite much cajoling, none of the caddies were willing to dive into the cold water to fish out the ball. The game was now equally poised.

The morning was going badly for both the players, with their shots going awry and the caddies running all over the golf course to collect the balls. It didn't take too long for the game to end.

'My mind is not on the game this morning,' Acharya offered his usual excuse.

'Isn't that a lame excuse? All the while you were making fun of my game and when your ball landed in the pond, you declared that your mind is not on the game. Admit it, Colonel, you are no better a player than me.' It was the professor's turn to laugh. He thumped the colonel's back, saying, 'No offence meant, but with a handicap of eighteen, you are going nowhere and that is the truth.'

Back in the golf hut, they shared some sandwiches and jokes. It was 10.30 a.m. and the two friends were ordering a second round of tea when the colonel received a call from the police station.

'Can you come to the police station?' Tim asked.

'Give me twenty minutes and I will be there.' Acharya knew better than to question the importance of the police officer's request.

The order was cancelled and the two men stepped out. The colonel dropped his golf partner before making his way to the police station, his mind grappling with the statements given by Nisha and her brother. Then there was the matter of the two things he had picked up from Laxmi's house. He was missing a vital link. The tube of ointment he had picked up from the scene of the crime addled his mind. Acharya made a mental note to discuss the matter with the doc.

'How was the game this morning?' Tim smiled mischievously as Acharya eased his body in a chair across the table. He knew all about the professor's missed shots and the lost golf balls. He also knew that the colonel was no better.

'Same as ever,' grunted the colonel and said wryly. 'The professor doesn't know the first thing about the game. This morning, for instance, he swung his club like a cricket bat, and the ball lifted high into the air and landed at his feet instead of the green. It was a terrible shot. The next one went into the pond. The son of a gun has lost half a dozen balls in the last one week.'

'You have to admit that the professor is an optimistic person. Nothing can deter him from trying his hand at the game.'

'I agree. Considering the time he spends practising his shots, he should have been a pro by now. But you didn't summon me here to discuss golf, did you?'

'No, I didn't. In fact, an agitated Urmila Thapliyal awaits our attention. She insists that she has some important information to share with the police.'

'They all have important information.' The colonel sighed, his mind doing a recap of a similar visit from Laxmi not too long ago. 'Yet we are no closer to finding the culprit.' Taking out his cigar from his pocket, he busied himself with it. 'Well, what are we waiting for? Let's hear what she has to say.'

'She was Laxmi Badola's bosom pal,' Tim informed as he rang the old-fashioned desk bell to summon the constable and instructed him to fetch the woman to his office. 'The two women were close for a very long time.'

'I have wasted so much time waiting to speak to the police. Do you think I have no work?' The colonel heard her berating the constable as he led her into the room.

'Yes, only you have work. I guess you think that sa'ab is twiddling his thumbs in the office,' was Sharad Pant's mocking rejoinder to the woman's grumbling.

Undeterred, Urmila Thapliyal pushed him aside and hurried into the room. 'Sa'ab, I have something important to share with you but Shirt Pant refused to let me enter your office. I have been waiting for an hour.'

'An hour? Your watch runs at supersonic speed.' The constable smirked as he followed the woman into the room. 'It's barely ten minutes.'

'Now that you are here, stop complaining,' Tim told the woman. It was at his order that Sharad had kept the woman waiting. Tim had wanted the colonel to be present during his conversation with Urmila Thapliyal. Turning to the grinning constable, he ordered, 'You can leave now.'

The woman directed a blistering look at the retreating Sharad and resumed her complaint. 'Sa'ab, that fellow does not allow us to speak to you. You don't know—'

'All right, what did you want to tell us?' Tim interrupted the sulking woman.

'I hope you will keep the information secret,' she whispered and looked around fearfully. 'I don't want to be killed like my friend.'

'You can speak without fear,' Acharya added in a kindly manner and handed her a glass of water. 'Whatever you say will remain within these four walls. We will also ensure your safety.'

'Sa'ab, Laxmi had seen the person who murdered the man from Delhi.' Her eyes sparkling, she began speaking animatedly. The woman had tried to hold back the information, but guilt had got the better of her. It was clear that the desire to get her friend's killer punished had forced her to approach the police station.

'Did she share the identity of the person?' the colonel asked worriedly. He didn't want Urmila to suffer the same fate as Laxmi. The killer was ruthless. He wouldn't spare anyone he perceived as a threat.

'No,' the woman said, shaking her head regretfully.

'Is it Umesh Gudyal?' Tim wanted to know.

'I don't think so. She said it was a stranger.'

'When and how did she meet him?'

Urmila shifted her weight on the chair till she was comfortably settled. Taking a deep breath, she launched into a lengthy story. 'It happened the evening before the first murder. We had gone to attend a wedding at the other end of town.'

'You mean Laxmi and you?'

'There were four of us, including Laxmi. All of us live in the same neighbourhood, so we went together. We were there the whole day and enjoyed ourselves. It was only when we were returning home after the wedding that the incident took place.'

'What was the time when you were returning?'

'I don't wear a watch but the big clock in Ghanta Ghar chimed ten times just as we reached the bus stand. Of course, we all know that it is always a little slow, so it could have been any time between ten to fifteen minutes past 10.' Urmila sat back, watching the scowl on Tim's face, wondering why he was annoyed.

Acharya knew the reason for the annoyance. Like the DSP, Tim wanted to believe that Gudyal was the murderer. It made everyone's job easy. This element of surprise had not been taken into consideration.

'So you were returning from a wedding,' Acharya prodded the woman in a gentle voice.

'It was a long walk, but that didn't worry us.' She smiled, recalling the evening. 'It is not often that we get an opportunity to wear heavy zari saris, or flaunt gold jewellery. Weddings are the only occasions—'

'Skip those details and tell us what happened later,' Acharya said, rolling his eyes.

'That evening, Laxmi was in high spirits.' Urmila wiped her eyes at the memory of her friend's untimely death. 'She was wearing her orange sari with zari embroidery. I love that sari and she didn't mind lending it to me sometimes—'

'What happened?' Tim hurried the woman.

Casting an exasperated look at him, she continued, 'The evening had been rather satisfying, what with the lavish meal, and a box of costly sweets given as a return gift. In fact, it was one of the most elaborate weddings we had attended in a long time. They gave each of the guests a kilogram of kaju barfi. Imagine!' The woman sighed at the memory of the sweets she had savoured for two full days.

'Skip the wedding details and tell us what happened at the bus stop.' Tim gestured impatiently.

Throwing a resentful look at him, Urmila continued. 'Chattering and laughing, the four of us walked past the bus stand, where a few people were huddled in the cold, waiting for the last vehicle to Almora. It was quite cold, but we were so happy that we didn't feel—'

'What happened next?' Acharya goaded.

'As we passed the busy bus stand, Laxmi stepped on a loose stone and stumbled. The bright light of an approaching vehicle blinded her for a few seconds. For the last one year, her eyesight had been failing her. She had contracted cataracts, you see. The doctor had told her to get an operation done, but she was reluctant. You know how it is. None of us likes to go through a surgery if we can do without it.'

'So, Laxmi stumbled,' Tim interpolated.

'Yes, she stumbled. The municipality guys had been digging the ground to lay some pipes. They are always digging the road. We have complained so many times but did they hurry? No, sir.' She made an expression of annoyance. The woman refused to be hurried with the story.

'Go on, what happened after Laxmi stumbled?' Tim prodded.

'She clutched at a passing man to balance herself.'

'Did you see him?' the colonel asked.

'Just a fleeting look. But it was Laxmi who had a good look at the man.'

'Tell us what exactly happened. Don't leave out anything,' urged the colonel. This could be important. Laxmi had wanted to relate the details of her encounter to the police and she was killed.

'Can you recollect his face? Voice? Clothes? Anything?' Tim pushed. His mind raced as he realized the importance of the woman's statement.

The woman drew a deep breath and closed her eyes to recall the fateful evening. '"Watch where you are going." Those were his words,' said Urmila. 'His voice was an evil hiss, not like that of a normal person. He was furious because my friend caught his arm to avoid falling. No normal man would react that way. Would he?'

Tim's hand flew over the notepad, making quick notes of the woman's words.

'Laxmi apologized,' continued Urmila. Her eyes narrowed in concentration. 'He cursed and pulled his woollen monkey cap down the face.'

'Did you notice the colour of his cap, clothes or the kind of shoes he wore?' There was an unmistakable urgency in Tim's voice. He was desperate for some clue, for any clue that could lead him to the man.

'No, sa'ab, I did not notice those things. We were teasing Laxmi for colliding with the man.'

'All right, go on with your story,' Tim said, sagging his shoulders in disappointment.

'Minutes later, he clambered into a Sumo, which was waiting for passengers. The SUV drove away. He was not a local, Laxmi told me. The next morning, Dabral's body was found in a van and my friend rushed to my house to share her misgivings. She was sure that the stranger she had bumped into was a suspicious character. "Mark my words," my friend said, "he is the murderer." In fact, Laxmi said she was coming here to share the information with the police.'

Acharya let out a frustrated sigh. Tim knew that the colonel hadn't stopped blaming himself for the carelessness that led to the woman's murder. He could feel the same thought running through his mind. If only they had heard her out …

Resolutely, the colonel turned his attention to the jabbering woman. 'You have to find that man,' she was saying tearfully. 'He has killed my friend.'

'Why do you say that?' Tim asked.

Urmila threw him a disdainful look before answering. 'Isn't it evident? Laxmi recognized the man and she was coming to tell you about her suspicions so he killed her.'

Exchanging a mortified look with the colonel, Tim cleared his throat and said, 'Don't you worry. We will catch him as soon as you give us a description.'

'I am sure the driver or the other passengers, who shared the journey with the man, can give you a better description than me. They must have had a good look at him. That man got into Kallu's Sumo and it was the last trip,' she informed helpfully. 'He is the only driver who risks his neck by driving his vehicle late in the evening on the treacherous road to Almora.'

The local women are quite something, thought Acharya. No wilting lilies, they were a hardy lot with agile minds. 'We will check with Kallu immediately,' he assured the woman.

'I want you to be on the alert and report any suspicious activity you observe near your house,' Tim cautioned the woman, walking her to the door. 'You have given us very important information. If you remember anything, anything at all, come and share with us. Just remember that no information is insignificant.'

The woman nodded gravely.

'Be watchful!' Tim warned.

He didn't want Urmila to meet the same fate as Laxmi. 'Do you think Urmila's guess is correct?' Tim asked the colonel. 'Could Laxmi have been killed because she recognized the murderer?'

'It is quite possible,' the colonel replied. 'In any case, it is a lead worth following.'

Tim summoned a constable.

Narayan trotted into the room after a few minutes. He had recently joined the police force and, unlike Shirt Pant, had proved himself to be an incompetent fellow. He was not someone Tim wanted to handle the matter.

'Yes, sir,' he said, raising his brows enquiringly. 'You called?'

Urmila had barely walked a few metres from the police station, her mind working furiously over the incidents of that evening, when she recalled something. She rushed back to Tim's office.

'Sa'ab, I just remembered. That man was wearing a white pyjama-kurta, a black woollen jacket and had a shawl around his shoulders. He looked like a neta.'

'That's fantastic, Urmila,' Acharya encouraged the woman. 'See, how the mind works. It begins recalling details the moment you begin concentrating on an event. Switch your mind to that evening when you go to bed tonight. I am sure you will remember a lot more by the morning.'

'He was wearing glasses,' she added, coming up with another nugget.

'Well done,' Tim cheered. 'I am sure you can come up with more details by tomorrow.'

Pleased with her feat, the woman walked out of the police station, her mind grappling to recreate the evening.

'I want you to go to the bus stand and find Kallu, the driver. Bring him here, as soon as you can,' Tim ordered Constable Narayan, who stood waiting at the threshold of the room. He was not particularly fond of the chap. Although Sharad was a smart-ass, he could be relied upon to do a good job. The same could not be said for Narayan, who displayed superiority because he could speak a smattering of English. A procrastinator, the chap was absolutely unreliable.

'He may not be available, sir,' said Narayan, reluctant to go all the way to the bus stand. 'That fellow is always on the move. He is in a hurry to make money because he wants to marry next month.'

'I don't want to hear any excuse,' Tim roared. 'Go and wait at the bus stand and grab him as soon as he returns from his trip to Almora. Wait at the bus stand till evening, if required.'

'Yes, sir.'

'Where is Sharad?'

'He is writing a report.'

'Send him here on your way out,' Tim barked. 'And don't return without Kallu.'

Chastised, Narayan trotted away glumly. He knew his boss was in a bad mood. Things were not moving the way they should have. Two murders in a span of a few days were unacceptable to the bigwigs. There was pressure from the top and the juniors, as usual, became the scapegoats for the DSP. *We are the ultimate sufferers*, grumbled the constable.

Sharad Pant entered the room and stood waiting for orders. Tim, who was busily typing on his laptop, didn't bother to look up. After waiting for a couple of minutes, the constable cleared his throat and asked, 'You wanted me, sir?'

'Yes, Sharad, I want you to keep a watch on Urmila Thapliyal's house. Let me know if you find any suspicious characters loitering around the place and, for heaven's sake, don't be too obvious about it.'

'Don't worry, sir, I will be as unobtrusive as an ant. Not a soul will know about my presence.' The constable was at his bragging best. It was another matter that he was more like an elephant than an ant.

Acharya chuckled.

Just my luck! cursed Tim. *I have to choose between the lazy bum and the show-off.* It was a difficult choice indeed. 'What are you waiting for?' he snapped at Sharad, who was hanging around hopefully. 'Not now, Sharad, we will speak about that matter after the murderer is caught.'

Tim knew that the constable had been waiting for an opportunity to discuss his promotion. In a softer voice, he added, 'I have a lot on my mind, you understand? We will discuss your promotion at an appropriate time.'

'Yes, sir,' replied the hapless chap, wondering how the boss could have guessed what he wanted to discuss.

'I thought Shirt Pant was inefficient till Narayan came along. That guy is nothing but brawn,' Tim grumbled. 'Not just that, he is the laziest person in town.'

'All these months you complained about being short-staffed and now you are complaining that the new guy is no good,' teased Acharya. 'You are a difficult person to please.'

'Let me tell you, life is no bed of roses. It is a tough one with the two jokers doing their own thing and Bulldog breathing down my neck.'

'Never mind, this too shall pass. I am confident we will crack the two cases before long. I have to make a move now. Laila will kill me if I don't report back for lunch.'

Like the bridge partners, Tim knew all about the colonel's love story. Laila's elopement and Acharya's defiance against his family to marry his sweetheart were common knowledge among the Rhodo Cottage regulars.

The colonel hauled himself to his feet and picked up his walking stick. 'Let me know what Kallu has to say about the stranger,' he said.

Leaving Tim to continue with the work, he limped out of the police station.

19

It was 2 in the afternoon when Narayan brought a protesting Kallu to the police station.

The usually well-dressed driver now looked scruffy. He must have been dragged willy-nilly to the police station, Tim guessed. No one in Ramsar took the chance of resisting the hefty police constable. But then, Kallu was hard-pressed to earn some more money so he could marry his sweetheart. The cheerful and hard-working fellow had been running additional trips to Almora since the last three months. A reckless driver, he could be found whizzing back and forth in his ramshackle SUV embellished with baubles and pictures of film stars.

'Sa'ab, I have done nothing wrong,' the man protested, shrugging off Narayan's restraining hand from his shoulder. 'This guy dragged me here, without a reason. I had to refuse six passengers waiting for a trip to Almora.'

'We have no interest in keeping you for more than a few minutes. We want to ask you a few questions. You can leave as soon as you have answered them. It is all up to you,' Tim tried to soothe the driver.

'Can the questions not wait for a couple of hours?' Kallu looked hopefully at the officer. 'I can come back after the last trip or early morning tomorrow.'

'No, the questions can't wait. There have been two murders in town and the police feel that you may have seen the murderer.'

'I have seen the murderer?' Kallu laughed loudly at the suggestion. 'How could I have seen him? If I had, wouldn't I have marched him straight to the police station? Everyone in Ramsar knows that I never break the law and don't tolerate anyone who breaks it.'

'This is serious, Kallu. Your cooperation can help in preventing yet another killing. We have information that shows the suspect took a ride in your Sumo a few days back.'

'So many people travel by my Sumo every day. How do you expect me to remember each and every person who travels with me?'

'This chap took the last trip to Almora on Sunday night. He was wearing a monkey cap, white kurta-pyjama, a black jacket and had a shawl wrapped around him.'

'A lot many people dress that way during the winter. You mentioned that it was the last trip, so it must have been freezing,' Kallu said, baring his mouth in a wide grin with stained teeth. He had no intention of getting caught in police procedures.

'Don't try to dodge the question. This man looked like an outsider, we were told. You couldn't have mistaken him for a local. In fact, you know everyone in town,' Tim rebuked the driver. 'Think back and tell us where you dropped the guy.'

'Sir, if you permit, I can prod his memory,' Narayan butted into the conversation. 'All I have to do is put him in the lock-up for a night. By tomorrow, he will recall everything about the passenger.'

Casting a cautious look at the constable, Kallu sidled away from him. 'You wouldn't dare,' he challenged.

'Try me,' retorted an aggressive Narayan.

'Enough!' Tim's voice rose sharply above the altercation. 'There is no need for rough methods. I am sure Kallu is a man with a conscience. He will do his best to help the police.'

Despite all efforts to retain his patience, Tim found himself wanting to slap the chap. Frustration was taking a toll on his temper. It was hours since he had eaten anything. His head was throbbing, and all he wanted was to go to Pia's Peaberry for sandwiches and coffee. That would have to wait till he finished grilling Kallu. He was struck with an idea to get the chap talking.

'You can go and sit outside till you remember everything,' said Tim, picking up the keys to his vehicle. 'Narayan, keep him here till I return. That will prod his memory.'

'Sa'ab, I remember the person,' Kallu shouted as Narayan herded him towards the door. He knew that an hour meant several hundred rupees and he couldn't afford to lose passengers. 'I will tell you whatever I can remember,' he grovelled. 'Please don't detain me.'

'I have no intention of detaining you if you cooperate.' Drawing a deep breath, Tim pushed his body back into the chair. *Why does it take threats to get information out of a person? Why does they come clean in the first place?* He wished the man would spill the truth, so he could get on with his lunch.

'He must be a neta, I remember thinking so when he got into the Sumo,' began Kallu. 'The man insisted on sitting in the co-driver's seat. He didn't want to sit near smelly people, he said. Such an arrogant man! I had a good look at him when he said that. The monkey cap covered his face, but I noticed the hooded eyes, straight and long nose, dimpled chin and thin lips. He was wearing big glasses with a red square frame. After we reached Almora, he took off his glasses. Sa'ab, I noticed his hands when he took out the wallet to pay his fare. The wallet had a lot of currency notes.'

'You seem to remember a lot about the money in the passenger's wallet,' Narayan commented.

'It took him a few minutes to settle the fare because he wasn't carrying change. The night fare to Almora is Rs 450, but he had nothing smaller than 500-rupee notes in his wallet. He rummaged in it for a while. That's when I noticed the photograph of a pretty girl in his wallet. He couldn't find smaller currency notes, so he paid Rs 500 and asked me to keep the change.'

'Good for you,' muttered the constable.

'Don't interrupt, Narayan,' said Tim sharply.

Kallu was a guy with good observation powers. He had been able to give quite a detailed description of the man. The only issue was that the description fitted many.

'He had rather large hands,' continued Kallu. He paused, trying to recall more. 'Also, he didn't have any bags with him.'

'You're quite observant,' Tim complimented the gloating man. 'I am sure you will recall a lot more after a while.'

'Don't put me in the lock-up, please, sa'ab,' begged the driver. 'I will be ruined.'

'No one is putting you in the lock-up. 'You will have to wait for some time while Narayan fetches a sketch artist.'

'How long will it take?' asked Kallu, his face falling at the thought of the lost hours.

'How long does it take for you to complete one round trip?' Tim asked.

The driver thought for a moment before replying, 'I can do it in three and a half hours if I go at good speed.'

'Don't break your neck and kill others,' warned Tim. 'Drive cautiously! Come back in three and a half hours and we will have the artist waiting for you. Don't be late.'

'Thank you, sa'ab, I will be back before that.'

Kallu hurried out of the room, happy to get back to work. Halfway down the corridor, he remembered something and returned to Tim's office. 'Sa'ab, the man didn't have bags but he was carrying a torch.'

'That's very helpful, Kallu.' Tim patted the man's shoulder before sending him on his way.

'Ask Shankar to report here in two hours,' Tim instructed Narayan. 'Tell him not to drink till he finishes the task. I don't want him to come here in a drunken state.'

'He must already be too drunk to do any drawing.' The constable sniggered. 'I will pass on your instructions, of course.'

Shankar, a brilliant artist with a drinking problem, had returned to Ramsar after struggling to make a career in the capital. Drunk by the day, the guy lived in near penury, surviving on the meals doled out by kindly neighbours. The little money he earned by doing odd jobs went to the hooch shop on the outskirts of town.

A chance encounter with the colonel at the annual fair, where he was sketching portraits, brought the artist some work. Recognizing the man's talent, Acharya recommended his work to a few friends, including Tim, who used his services occasionally.

Deciding to grab some sandwiches before the artist arrived at the police station, Tim directed his motorcycle towards Pia's Peaberry.

'Here comes the busiest man in Ramsar.' Pia greeted him with a smile.

It was long past lunchtime and the café was deserted.

'Is there any need for sarcasm?' Tim snapped, dragging out a chair. Frustration can give rise to the blackest of tempers, and he was no exception. 'Two unsolved murders are bound to keep the police busy.' He didn't mention that Bulldog was not making matters easy.

She had never seen him in such a foul mood. 'I am sorry, Tim. My day hasn't been very sunny either. It's not easy if your van is involved in a murder.'

'Did JBS speak to you again?' Tim appeared contrite. He knitted his brows and asked, 'Was he his usual obnoxious self?' *It must be tough on the girl to deal with murder,* he thought.

'Well, he dropped into the café the other day. While he didn't spell it out, his behaviour wasn't very congenial. In fact, his line of enquiry made me quite uncomfortable.'

'Though he is my boss, I don't mind saying that he is not the most intelligent of human beings. He can be insufferable and pig-headed while investigating a crime. Also, finding scapegoats is his favourite way of solving a case. Don't worry, the colonel is also working on the cases and I am confident that we will nab the culprit soon.'

'Thanks, Tim, for the comforting words.' She smiled at him. 'Did you have lunch? I am sure you didn't.'

'You are right, I didn't,' Tim confessed sheepishly. 'I am hungry enough to eat a horse.'

'I haven't eaten either. You are in luck. Gumma sent me her chicken pot pie. Let's have a quick bite together.'

'She sent you lunch?'

'She called me about an hour back, asking why I hadn't got back home for lunch. I was stuck at the café because there were two customers to attend to. Fifteen minutes later, I found the gardener arriving with the pot pie. Such are grandmothers.'

'I was destined to share your meal, I guess.'

'It would seem so.' Pia walked into the tiny kitchenette at the back of the café.

'Where is Meg?' Tim asked when she reappeared with a tray loaded with the pot pie, French fries and two mugs of coffee.

'Meg has an entrance test, so she won't be coming in for a couple of days.'

'Entrance test?'

'Didn't I tell you? Meg has applied for a hotel management course.'

'Which means you will have to hunt for an assistant if she gets admission.'

'It's going to be difficult, I know,' said Pia, heaping chicken pie on Tim's plate.

'This smells delicious. Don't mind me. I just can't wait,' he commented before attacking the food on his plate. 'Would you believe if I told you that this is the first time that I have tasted pot pie?' he said after a few spoons.

'Is that so?' Pia smiled. 'Did you know that the pot pie is believed it to have been invented by the Greeks? They called it *artocreas*. The Romans transformed the recipe by adding a top layer to the pastry shell, and the pot pie travelled to different lands with variations in the meat.'

'Interesting!' commented Tim, refilling his plate. 'You seem to know a lot about food. Frankly, I couldn't careless who invented it, as long as I get to eat delicious stuff. Please compliment your gumma and tell her I will drop by her house for pot pie one of these days.'

An hour later, his stomach sated and mood lighter, Tim drove back to his office.

Relieved to find the boss smiling, Narayan walked into Tim's office to report that the artist would be arriving at the appointed time.

Tim spread his long legs under the table, interlaced his fingers behind his head and leaned back on the chair, his brain processing the information provided by Urmila and Kallu. The lunch in Pia's company had brightened his mood. For the first time since the two murders, he felt happy and relaxed.

His ruminations were interrupted by the strident ringing of the phone.

'I just heard from my boss. He wanted to know if we have made any progress in solving the two murder cases in Ramsar. What should I tell him?' the DSP demanded without preamble.

'Sir, we hope to identify the culprit within a couple of days,' Tim replied, unwilling to let the senior's yelling ruin his mood.

'Words! That's all they are. Empty words! Do you think your words will pacify the SP?'

'There are fresh developments in the case and I am working on them, sir.'

'Don't try to hoodwink me, Tim. What fresh developments have you come across?'

Patiently, Tim narrated the facts that had emerged from Urmila's statement. He also informed Bulldog about the SUV driver's account.

'Based on Kallu's description, the sketch artist will create a likeness of the stranger. There is little doubt that the man stayed overnight in Almora.'

'I want you to scan and email me the sketch as soon as it is ready. Although it will be like looking for a pin in a haystack, we can try to find the man. Once we have the sketch, I can put a couple of men on the job. They can show the picture around the hotels and restaurants in Almora. Someone is bound to have seen this man,' said the DSP.

'Yes, sir.'

Bulldog was suddenly seized by doubts. He was convinced that Umesh Gudyal had committed both the murders and nothing less than a miracle could alter his belief. Sure that Tim was barking up the wrong tree, he remarked, 'What makes you think that the man seen by Laxmi is the murderer? Apart from the fact that he was seen leaving Ramsar on the night of the first murder, there is no evidence to show his involvement.' The DSP gave his opinion. 'Aren't we acting on flimsy reasoning? Laxmi suspected the man and she died before she could tell us anything. It is Urmila's assumption that her friend was killed by the same man. All this is too flimsy to investigate.'

Tim could visualize Bulldog sticking out his chin as he spoke. 'Sir, we have hit a roadblock. The only way forward is to examine every clue that crops up.'

'Where's the roadblock? It's as clear as day. I will give you twenty-four hours to find the killer, failing which you will arrest Gudyal,' the DSP issued an ultimatum.

'Sir, it is too little time. We won't even find the man we are looking for. Give us a few days, at least. I promise to find the murderer within a week.'

'Forty-eight hours and that's final.' The DSP ended the call.

'Damn!' Tim cursed. On one side was his boss, who was convinced that Gudyal had committed the two murders and was unwilling to investigate other angles. On the other hand was the colonel, who was sure that the hapless chap was being made a scapegoat.

20

Confident of his importance, Kallu swaggered into the police station at the appointed time. He had been driving since 5 in the morning and could afford to rest for an hour.

'Is the artist here?' he asked Narayan, checking the time on his phone. 'I have to go back within an hour.'

'Busy man, aren't you?' sniggered the constable.

'I have no argument with you, brother.' Kallu put up his hands in a gesture of peace. 'You don't have to be obnoxious.'

'Am I being obnoxious?' Narayan stood up and shook his fist threateningly. 'You better control your tongue or I will make you eat your words.'

'Don't threaten me. I am here to help the police. Also, I have a busier day than you.'

'How dare ...'

'What's going on?' Tim, who had stepped out of his office on hearing the commotion, demanded to know.

'He's threatening me, sa'ab,' Kallu complained. 'All I did was ask if the artist had arrived.'

'Sir, he called me obnoxious and—'

The constable's sentence was cut short by the artist's arrival. Wearing soiled clothes, his hair untrimmed, Shankar walked into the police station. A well-worn sling bag slung around his shoulder, his scruffy shoes caked with dirt, he looked more like a beggar than an artist.

'Take him to the outer room and open all the windows,' instructed Tim.

The outer room was a misnomer for the makeshift interrogation cell that the police used to extract confessions sometimes. The advantages of using the room were many. It was an airy room, slightly away from the main building and overlooked the ravine, which provided a pleasant view and privacy. With a large table, several chairs, ample light and fresh air, it also served as a conference room during the senior officers' visits.

Shankar's entry into the room fouled the air almost instantly.

'Good morning, sir,' he greeted the police officer.

'Morning is long past, Shankar. It's almost evening,' remarked Tim, wrinkling his nose at the nauseating smell emanating from the man. 'You have been drinking,' he accused.

'Just a tiny sip to keep my senses intact.' The man laughed. 'Narayan said you had some work for me.'

He must be just about thirty-five, thought Tim, *but he looks fifty*. Aloud he said, 'Yes, Shankar, I want you to sketch the face of a man from the description given by Kallu.'

'I will try.' That was Shankar's standard reply to all requests for a portrait. 'I can't guarantee its effectiveness.'

'That's fine. Do your best and leave the rest to us.' Asking Kallu to sit before the artist, Tim parked himself near the table.

'Okay, Kallu, what was the one thing about the man that stood out when you saw him?' the artist asked, ready to begin work.

'The eyes,' responded the driver eagerly. Kallu was sure it was a futile effort. How could the artist create the picture of a man he had never seen? But he was enjoying the importance of his words. 'When he removed the glasses, I noticed his eyes. They were hooded and close-set. They darted around suspiciously. Also, there were bags under his eyes. He looked tired, as though he hadn't slept for a couple of nights.'

'Go on,' instructed Shankar, sketching furiously. 'What kind of glasses was he wearing? Were they like any of these?' He displayed a few sketches of spectacle frames.

After careful deliberation, Kallu pointed at a full-rim rectangular pair of frames. 'His glasses were like these.'

'What about the eyebrows?'

Kallu closed his eyes and tried to remember. 'They were straight and half hidden by the upper rim of the spectacle frame.'

The artist then drew the glasses around the eyes he had drawn. 'Do you think his eyes inside the glasses looked like this?'

'Yes, they did. By God! How did you do that?' Kallu exclaimed. Based on his description, Shankar had managed a remarkable likeness of the man's eyes.

'All right, describe the shape of his face. Was it like any of these?'

Shankar displayed a few shapes—square, oval, round and pointed. Kallu went over the pictures one by one, hesitating, his finger pausing over the choices. Finally, he pointed at the square-shaped face. The artist then moved on to other prominent features like the nose, mouth, cheekbones, jawline, eyebrows, hair, wrinkles, smile and teeth. Literally every single feature on a person's face was addressed, including the symmetry of it.

Since more than half the face was covered by a monkey cap, Kallu had seen very little of it. He could not tell the kind of hair or mouth the stranger had, or any other details. Shankar continued sketching, irrespective of the loopholes in the description. Piece by piece, he drew each feature and fused them together to create the likeness of a man with a monkey cap covering the face.

In addition to drawing well, a police artist must also be a good listener, Tim had read somewhere. Shankar seemed to be the epitome of those virtues. Drunk or not, when it came to work, he made no compromises. No one could accuse him of being insincere to his profession.

The artist went on to sketch the hands and fingers as well as the rings worn by the man. The portrait was based on the descriptions given by the driver, who had seen the eyes, eyebrows, nose, the fingers, rings and hands. The focus was on the attire and the eyes.

It was a laborious and time-consuming process that required immense patience. Shankar had all the patience and time needed to complete the portrait. At the end of an hour, he displayed the fruit of his labour.

Kallu gasped. The sketch was as close to the man as could be possible without having met him. 'This is incredible,' he remarked.

'Point out the differences,' Shankar told the driver. 'It will help me refine the portrait.'

'I didn't see much of the face. You have accurately depicted the little I could see.'

'In that case, it is the best I can do.'

Tim studied the composite face drawn by Shankar. Although Kallu seemed satisfied with the portrait, he wasn't sure that the man could be traced.

'How did you do that?' the driver asked again.

'It works on a simple principle. You might not be able to fully describe your own mother to me, but you will know her features when you see them on someone else. All I had to do was show you different features and you could recollect the ones that fitted the man. When something looks familiar to a witness, I include it in the drawing. If it doesn't look right to him, I take it out. It is trial and error until it all comes together,' Shankar explained, gathering his paraphernalia and putting them back in the sling bag.

'You could start drawing classes for children,' suggested Narayan, who was equally impressed by the artist's prowess.

'Who will send their children to a drunkard?' The artist laughed.

'May I leave now?' asked Kallu. It was more than an hour since he had come to the police station and he was eager to get back to business.

'Yes, you can leave. If required, we will call you again. Just remember, not a word about this to anyone,' Tim warned.

Shankar was hanging back, hesitant to ask for payment. It was a tacit understanding. The police regulations didn't authorize Tim to employ the artist's services, and the procedure to obtain an approval was too cumbersome, so he paid the guy out of his own pocket. The artist was happy to settle for a modest amount and his sketch helped Tim's investigation. It was a satisfactory arrangement for everyone.

Paying off the artist, Tim scanned the portrait and mailed it to the DSP. After taking a few photocopies, he called the colonel.

'Shankar has made a composite of the suspect, and I am going to Urmila's house to show her the sketch. Would you like to be there?'

'You bet,' said Acharya. 'I wouldn't miss it for anything in the world.'

Smiling at his words, Tim took off for the woman's house.

When Tim reached Urmila's house, he found Shirt Pant strutting back and forth, speaking loudly on his phone. In the deserted street, the oaf stood out like a giraffe in a concrete jungle. To make things worse, he was yapping loudly on the phone. So engrossed was the constable in conversation that he missed Tim's arrival.

After parking his vehicle, Tim stole up on the constable and tapped him on the shoulder.

'Saala …' Shirt Pant, irate at being disturbed, turned around with an expletive. He cringed on seeing the officer. 'I am very sorry, sir,' he whimpered. 'I didn't see you arriving.'

'I asked you to keep a watch on the house and remain inconspicuous. With your shouting and strutting, you can be spotted from a mile.'

'Sorry, really very sorry, sir.'

'There's no point in being sorry now. The whole neighbourhood is aware that you are keeping a watch on the area. You are so not fit to carry out the task.'

'I made a mistake, sir. I will go and hide behind the bushes across the road.'

It was difficult for Tim to maintain a straight face. 'It's too late for that. Once you are spotted, no fool will make the mistake of coming to Urmila's house. I have another assignment for you.' Taking out a couple of photocopies from the folder, Tim handed them to Shirt Pant. 'I want you to take these and make enquiries. Go to all the hotels and restaurants. Speak to receptionists, waiters and other staff. Ask all the ruffians, bus drivers and vendors. Find out if anyone has seen this man. If so, when and where did they see him?'

'That's easy.' Shirt Pant was happy to be let off without a reprimand. 'I will bring you all the information about the chap.'

'If you make another blunder, I will not spare you,' Tim warned. The constable's overconfidence was his nemesis.

'I promise not to make a mistake.'

The colonel made an appearance as Shirt Pant scampered towards the market.

The two men crossed the street and rang the doorbell of Urmila's modest house. Like Laxmi, she was a widow and lived on her husband's pension. The outer walls had not seen paint for a long time. They were streaked by dripping water from a rusted gutter that ran along the edge of the roof.

She peeped cautiously from the window before answering the doorbell. Clearly surprised at their arrival, she darted a quick look around the street.

'Why did you take the trouble of coming here, sa'ab?' Urmila asked, flustered, as the two men entered the house. 'You could have called me to the police station.'

'It's no trouble,' Tim assured the woman.

Acharya's eyes ran around the sparsely furnished room. The inexpensive curtains fashioned out of thin material, a shabby divan covered with a bedsheet, a couple of straight-backed chairs and a folding dining table spoke of the prudent life led by the woman.

'How are you, Urmila?' asked the colonel, sitting down on one of the chairs.

'I am as fine as one can be after a friend's death,' she retorted, making it obvious that she had not got over Laxmi's murder. 'I am waiting for the culprit to be caught.'

'We are doing our best.'

'That's what the police always say.' Deep lines on either side of her mouth added to the unhappy look on her face. 'What brings you to my humble abode at this time of the evening?'

'We will take just a few minutes of your time. The police have got a drawing of the man you saw at the bus stand that night.' Tim held out the composite sketch of the suspect for her to examine. 'Take a look and tell us if he looked like this.'

Urmila held the portrait under the tube light and studied it for a long time.

Acharya watched narrowly as the woman tried to recall the face of the man she had briefly seen. 'Well, this seems a very good representation of the man, I must say,' she said at last. 'Where did you find this?'

'It was made by an artist, based on Kallu's description.'

'I think the drawing is very good,' she said, shaking her head in wonder. 'I didn't know an artist can make a picture based on description.'

'Thank you, Urmila. We hope to locate and question the man. Of course, we do not know if he had anything to do with the murders,' Tim was quick to point out. He had no intention of pronouncing the man's guilt without concrete evidence.

'Find him soon, sa'ab, before he escapes. He is the killer,' she said. 'He's the one Laxmi suspected.'

'He won't escape,' Tim assured the woman.

'She's pretty certain, isn't she?' commented Acharya as the two of them walked towards the vehicle.

'Urmila might be convinced about the man's guilt, but we will need evidence to arrest the chap.'

'First, we have to find him,' the colonel reminded Tim. 'It may not be easy to locate him.'

21

It took about twenty hours, several policemen and substantial burning of precious fuel to find a breakthrough. Although a couple of people claimed to have seen the man, no one could give positive information. It was a clerk, who also functioned as the front desk receptionist of Hotel Hillside, a seedy hotel in Almora, who finally provided a vital piece of information.

'Yes, I have seen this man,' he said, after scrutinizing the picture.

When asked the time of his arrival, the clerk said, 'He came late in the night and asked for the key to Room Number 5. It was past 11, so that drew my attention. Most guests return to the hotel by 10,' he explained. 'Room Number 5 had been allotted in the afternoon, but I had not seen the person since I was on the evening shift.'

'So you saw him only at 11.30 p.m.?' asked the constable from the Almora police station. Along with another colleague, he had been assigned the job of finding out about the stranger. 'Did you notice anything suspicious?'

'Now that you mention it, I found him a bit odd. He was not carrying any bags. All he carried was a torch. Tourists don't arrive without bags. Do they? We have to be careful, what with so many unpleasant incidents happening around us. If something goes wrong, you will haul me over the coals, won't you?'

The clerk looked at the constable for agreement.

'He was furious when I asked for proof of identity. The chap began abusing me for being discourteous and threatened to report to the management. I wasn't bothered. I was doing my duty by verifying his identity. But for the argument, I might not have remembered him He handed over his driving licence for verification and I handed him the key. Has he committed some crime?'

The cop ignored his query and demanded to know the name of the guest.

'Let me check the register,' said the clerk. Producing the hotel register, he went through the entries. 'Yes, here it is. He checked in under the name of Shubham Sharma.'

'I hope you verified his identity before registering,' said the constable. 'There are quite a few hotels which circumvent the procedures.'

'Our hotel may be modest but we never give rooms without verifying identity.' The clerk was offended at the constable's words.

'Don't try to pull a fast one. I know all about your hotel. Did you note down the details of the identity proof?'

'It's all here.' The clerk pointed at the entry against the guest's name. 'Details of his driving licence and address are in the register here.'

With that, he turned it towards the constable, who made a note of the information.

'Is the room occupied at the moment?'

'It's been quite a few days since the guest checked out. Rooms don't go vacant in our hotel. There have been two overnight stays since Sharma left.'

'Do you remember anything else about the guest?'

'He looked quite different from the photograph on the driving licence. The photograph on the licence was taken without glasses and he was wearing them when I saw him. One does look different with glasses, of course.'

'Where is the photocopy of the driving licence?'

The clerk shifted uneasily in his seat. 'You see, the photocopier was not working, so ...'

'So you didn't take a photocopy,' the constable finished the sentence for him. 'I am sure your photocopier must always be out of order. It costs money to take a photocopy. Right?'

The clerk grinned ingratiatingly.

'You know it is illegal to rent out rooms to a guest without keeping the photocopy of his identity proof. I can lock you up for the lapse.'

'It's not my fault, sir. I was not on duty. Had I been here at the time of his check-in, I would have run to the photocopying shop and paid the money out of my pocket. I am an honest man.'

'Of course you are an honest man. That is why you don't mind keeping the things forgotten by guests,' the constable reminded the clerk.

It had happened a few months back. A guest had forgotten his expensive wristwatch in the bathroom. Later, when he called the hotel, he was told that the wristwatch had not been found. The watch suddenly made an appearance after the person reported the matter to the police.

'I just remembered, sir.' The clerk hurriedly brought out a ballpoint pen from his drawer. 'The guest in Room Number 5 had forgotten this pen in the drawer. You can take it with you.'

'There you are. Had I not mentioned the incident about keeping back lost objects, you would have kept the pen in your pocket and gone about your business,' chastised the cop, putting the pen in a sealed bag. 'Do you realize it could be important and you can be hauled up for withholding evidence?'

'Has the man killed someone?' The clerk's eyes were shining with excitement. 'We have heard about the two murders in Ramsar.'

Realizing he had divulged more information than necessary, the constable tapped his stick on the clerk's desk. 'Don't go spreading rumours or you will find yourself dealing with me,' he warned. 'Not a word about this to anyone, you understand?'

Frightened, the clerk shrank behind his desk. 'My lips are sealed,' he promised.

When the matter was reported by the constable, and the ballpoint pen produced before the DSP, he displayed no sign of excitement. All he did was send the pen for fingerprints.

'Instruct my office to email the man's address to ASP Timothy at Ramsar,' he ordered the constable who had brought the information.

In Ramsar, though, the information was received with much excitement. Enthused by the breakthrough, Tim decided to drive up to the colonel's house and break the news in person. He knew that Acharya would be excited by the developments.

It was only after he had patted and paid enough attention to the frisky Bullet that Tim was granted entry into the charming bungalow. The Alsatian's bark was loud enough to wake the colonel, who was dozing in the veranda. It took nothing less than an earthquake to activate him during his post-lunch siesta. Ever since his retirement, the indefatigable man had begun taking his siesta seriously.

'Shut up, Bullet!' was all he said, before his head lolled on the chest once more.

Followed by the dog, Tim tiptoed around the garden but Laila was nowhere to be seen. This was the hour she usually spent in the garden, playing with Bullet or pruning the plants.

The Alsatian darted into a bush and brought out his ball. When Tim showed no signs of playing with the dog, it resumed barking.

'What is it, Bullet?' growled the master irritably. 'Why can't a man have some peace?'

'I am here to break the peace, Colonel,' Tim shouted from the garden.

'Tim? What brings you here at this hour? Don't you have anything else to do?'

'There's some exciting news for you.'

'Exciting news?' Tim's words drew Acharya to the garden. 'It better be important enough for you to disturb my siesta.'

'Of course it is. We have identified the man who took a ride in Kallu's SUV on the night of Dabral's murder.'

Tim went on to narrate the details. 'According to the hotel clerk, Shubham Sharma stayed in the hotel for a single night. He arrived at 2 in the afternoon and remained in the room till 6. Thereafter, he went out and returned only at 11.30 p.m. He checked out the next morning.

'I assume he arrived in Ramsar sometime in the evening. He was seen by Laxmi and her friend at 10 p.m. at the bus stand. After taking a ride in Kallu's SUV, he returned to the hotel, stayed the night and checked out the next morning. Interestingly, Dabral was murdered on the very evening Sharma visited Ramsar. All of this could be a coincidence, of course.'

'Whether it was a coincidence will only be known after we question Sharma. What brought him to Ramsar for just a few hours, the very evening of the murder? It is important to question the man before arresting Gudyal.' The colonel's tone was insistent.

'Bulldog feels otherwise. He feels we are misleading the murder investigation by delaying Gudyal's arrest.'

'Don't you think it is wrong to send a man to the gallows without examining the evidence that comes our way? I agree that there is a lot of evidence to frame Gudyal, yet it all seems too pat to be convincing.'

'I agree with you, Colonel. But my hands are tied. The law takes cognizance of evidence and gives no importance to hearsay. What Laxmi or Urmila have said is nothing more than perception and hearsay. Based on her intuition, Laxmi assumed that the stranger she saw at the bus stand had committed a crime, and Urmila is simply relaying her friend's concerns. How can we base a murder investigation on such flimsy factors?'

'You will be surprised to know that many murder cases have been solved by paying attention to hearsay. As for me, relying on sixth sense is an important factor.'

'It may be so, but the DSP has scant regard for sixth sense, or any sense for that matter. He wants hard evidence and there is enough of that to put Gudyal on trial,' Tim said, throwing up his hands.

'I would still pitch for an effort to track the stranger. You have the man's name, address and driving licence number. It will take just a visit to the address to disprove his involvement in the murders. Are you willing to put in that extra effort?' Acharya's eyes bore into his.

'It is impossible for me to get approval for the visit,' protested Tim. In his heart, he knew the wisdom of the colonel's words. 'Besides, the DSP has granted me forty-eight hours to arrest Gudyal …'

'Of which only twenty have passed. You still have more than twenty-four.'

'Well, what do you suggest?'

'Speak to JBS. Tell him to approve a day's leave. We will both travel to Delhi and find the man. I promise you will not regret the effort.'

They were still debating the issue when Laila arrived with coffee.

'You are an angel, Laila,' Tim exclaimed, rubbing his hands gleefully. 'Coffee is what I need to clear my mind.'

'It was meant to wake up my dear husband, not to clear your mind,' said Laila, smiling mischievously at the colonel. 'He can't focus on anything till he gets his cuppa.'

'I had been looking for you, so I could beg you for coffee,' Tim confessed. 'I expected you to be in the garden but you were not there.'

'You are likely to find me in the garden on most afternoons. But today has been quite hectic since I decided to clean up my wardrobe. I was too exhausted to tend to the garden, so I was resting upstairs.'

'Thanks for the coffee. I wouldn't have survived without it,' Tim said with a charming smile.

'Don't try to butter me up,' Laila warned. 'I am not preparing any snacks, even if you beg. For that, you can go to Pia's café.' Leaving the two men to their discussion, she disappeared inside the house.

'Speak to JBS,' Acharya goaded Tim after she left. 'If he doesn't agree to send you to Delhi, ask him for a day's leave.'

'You want me to speak to him just now?'

'Why not? There is no time like *now*.'

Tim was hesitant. 'I ...'

'Come on, Tim. What's the worst that can happen? He will refuse to grant you leave. We will find a way, don't worry.'

Tim said a silent prayer and called Bulldog. He rolled his eyes and put the phone on speaker as the DSP thundered, 'You will not go to Delhi on a fool's errand. That's an order. And the question of granting you leave does not arise.' He seemed to be on the verge of exploding when Tim asked for a day's leave.

'Damn you! There are two murder cases hanging in the balance and you want leave?'

'Sir …'

'You are not going to Delhi. That's it.'

'My visit is not connected with the investigation. I am going on a personal visit to Delhi.'

'Don't try to fool me, Tim. I am not willing to hear another word on this. You will arrest Gudyal and that's final.'

'I warned you about the outcome,' commented Tim after the call was over. 'I had not expected Bulldog to agree with my proposal.'

'It's all right, Tim. We tried, but it didn't work,' Acharya soothed the young man. He stared at the distant mountains thoughtfully for a few minutes, his mind churning up a plan to deal with the situation. 'Give me some time. I will come up with something,' he said at last.

'Well, it's time to get back to work. Let me know your plans.' Tim stretched his arms above his head wearily.

'Don't give up. I will have a plan by this evening,' the colonel called out as Tim made his way towards the gate.

The two murders had sapped Tim's energy. All he wanted was to find the culprit and go off on a vacation.

22

Dusk was falling, and the sky grew dark in the distance as Acharya made his way towards the doc's clinic. Mayfair Cottage, near the centre of the town, was a showpiece of modern construction and furnishing. Its name a misnomer, the double-storeyed structure housed the clinic on the ground floor while the upper floor was occupied by the doc.

All matchmaking efforts of the bridge partners having come to naught, the doc retained his bachelorhood. The clinic took up much of his time, dedicated as he was to his profession.

The doc was attending to a patient when the colonel reached the clinic. Another patient was waiting for the doctor's attention, so he waited for his turn.

'You can go in now, Colonel Sa'ab,' the helper announced when the doc had finished with the last patient.

Acharya pushed open the door leading to the consulting chamber and took his seat.

'What brings you here, Colonel? I hope everything is all right,' said Dr Rawat.

'Everything is fine, doc. I came here to bother you with a few questions.'

'Not something connected with the murders, I hope.'

'At this moment, I don't know if it has any connection with the murder,' the colonel said, producing the tube of ointment he had found in Laxmi's house. 'Can you tell me anything about this ointment?'

While the doc examined the tube, Acharya ran his eyes around the room. It had been a while since he had visited the clinic. He could see that the clinic had received a fresh coat of paint and boasted some accessories.

It was a cheerful room, furnished with a table, a swivel chair for the doctor and two straight-backed ones for visitors. There was a revolving metal stool for the patient and an examination bed along a wall.

The wall directly in front of the doctor's table was adorned with a bright painting of a snow-capped Himalayan range. It was a recent addition, as was the flower vase standing on the windowsill.

'This is a tube of hydrocortisone ointment used to treat skin conditions like eczema, dermatitis, allergies, rashes, insect bites, itching, poison ivy, etc. The medicine reduces swelling, itching and redness caused by these conditions.'

'Did you prescribe the ointment for Laxmi?'

'No. As far as I can remember, she was a healthy woman. I rarely had the opportunity of prescribing any medicine for her. In any case, most of the local women prefer to cure themselves with traditional medicine and consult me only if those do not bring relief.'

'I found this tube of ointment in her house. Can you recollect prescribing the ointment for anyone in the last one week or so?'

'I will have to consult my records. Seasonal allergies and rashes are quite common in these parts. Also, there are the cases of rashes breaking out and swelling caused by accidental contact with bichhu buti, which is the local name for stinging nettle.

It grows extensively on the hillside. Since the nettle has many health benefits, it is often used by the locals. Careless handling of the buti can cause skin rashes.'

'So it is possible that you prescribed the ointment to someone.'

'Like I mentioned, I can only tell after checking the records. Was it of any help—the information, I mean?'

'Yes, and no. I did not know that the ointment is used by quite a few locals. I had banked on finding out the person for whom the ointment was prescribed.'

'The best I can do is make a list of the patients for whom I prescribed the hydrocortisone ointment. Since you have asked for a record of one week, it shouldn't be difficult. I wouldn't have prescribed it to more than three-four patients.'

'The names of those three-four patients will be a big help.'

'Done! The list will be with you by tomorrow morning. Can you not give me any more details?' the doc asked. He was interested in knowing about the relevance of the ointment.

'It may be premature to share information,' replied Acharya. 'I am groping in the dark and working on a hunch. Give me forty-eight hours and you will know all the details.'

'Are you going to Rhodo Cottage for a game of cards this evening?' asked the doc, winding up for the day. 'Let's go up to my apartment. Girdhari can make us some tea while we chat.'

'Let me take a rain check on the offer, doc,' said Acharya. 'I am in a bit of a hurry now. As for Rhodo Cottage, I won't be there this evening.'

The colonel had no intention of wasting time over card games and banter. Seized with the desire to deliberate over the happenings of the last few days, he made his way towards the only spot that offered the privacy he needed at the moment.

The tiny isolated temple on the fringes of the forest near Ridge Road was his favourite spot for rumination. It was mostly deserted, save for an old priest who lived in an adjoining shanty.

His mind churning over the two murders, Acharya ambled along the snaking road flanked by pine and rhododendron trees. His breath came in uneven bursts as, aided by the walking stick, he walked up the incline. He needed to think clearly on the matter at hand and the walk energized his brain, the bracing wind doing its part.

As expected, there was no one at the temple. The priest was performing the evening aarti. Avoiding his eyes, the colonel walked to the rear of the temple and sat on the cemented steps. Darkness had fallen and the lights in the distance twinkled like fireflies in the dark. The sky was full of stars so brilliant that it hurt the eyes. A hundred voices whispered in the wind laden with the smell of the forest.

Taking a deep breath of the cool air, the colonel let his senses absorb the sight and the smells for a few minutes. The stress and fatigue of the day vanished, and he switched his mind to the details of the two cases.

Laxmi never forgot a face. She possessed extraordinary face-recognition ability. Just a fleeting glimpse of a face, and it remained etched in her memory. Not just that, the woman could give the time and place where she had seen a person.

The more he went over the statements they had recorded, the more he was convinced of Gudyal's innocence. The man called Shubham Sharma was the key to the mystery, he felt.

His mind was made up. He would travel to Delhi to untangle the twisted skeins of the plot. Once the decision was taken, the colonel made his way back to The Nook.

Back home, he called Tim. 'I have a plan,' he informed the police officer.

'I am reaching your place within the next fifteen minutes,' Tim responded eagerly. He rushed out, tripping over his words with excitement. All of a sudden, Tim could almost see the silver lining in the clouds.

'Will Laila be kind enough to include me in her dinner plans?' he asked hopefully. 'She does not have to cook anything special for me. Just rice and fish curry will do,' Tim added cheekily.

'Aren't you expecting too much, my boy?' Acharya chuckled. He was aware that Laila was fond of the boy. She liked pampering him. 'You are pushing on a dangerous path. Don't be surprised if you find me with a black eye.'

Laila was delighted when she heard that Tim was coming over for a discussion and dinner, but she pretended to be annoyed.

'I hate these impromptu invitations,' she grumbled.

'Correction, *meine liebste*!' Her husband smiled, wrapping his arms around Laila's waist. 'I didn't invite him. Your adopted son invited himself to dinner.'

Bullet was hovering around excitedly when Tim reached The Nook. The air was redolent with the smell of fish curry and the Alsatian loved fish as much as his master.

'So, what is the plan?' Tim asked as soon as the two of them had settled down in the tiny study.

'You will arrest Gudyal in the morning,' replied Acharya. Tim nearly fell off his chair.

'What are you saying?' he spluttered. 'All this while you were talking about going by one's conscience and professing Gudyal's innocence, and now you are asking me to arrest him?' Tim's voice went up by several notches, making Bullet growl. The dog had settled at Acharya's feet. It raised its head and stared suspiciously at the young man.

'You heard me, Tim. I want you to put the chap in the lock-up.'

'I am sure you have a valid reason for the change of mind,' Tim said conspiratorially. 'Tell me quick, what clever plan are you hatching? After harping on and on about Gudyal's innocence, won't putting him in the lock-up look like he is guilty, and prove JBS correct?'

'Calm down!'

'How can I remain calm when you give no reason for backtracking on your words?'

'It's quite simple. Gudyal's arrest will put the DSP's mind at rest and he might just grant you the desired leave. At the moment we have no option. Once we have met Shubham, Gudyal can be set free,' Acharya explained patiently.

The brilliance of the simple plan took Tim's breath away. It was a subterfuge to fool JBS. 'Hats off, Colonel.' He doffed an imaginary cap at Acharya. 'You are a crafty man. Not only will the trick deceive my boss, it will lull the actual criminal into thinking he has hoodwinked the police.'

'Let's go down for dinner before Laila changes her mind,' suggested the host. 'Later, we will list and analyse the facts that have emerged in the last few days.'

'Do you think the plan will work?' Tim looked doubtfully at the cheerful sleuth. The man's unflappable attitude never stopped surprising him. The only sign of the colonel's stress levels was a slight aggravation in his limp, he had observed.

'Que sera, sera … Whatever will be, will be … The future's not ours to see … Que sera, sera …' the colonel, in response to Tim's question, trilled in his unmelodious voice.

23

The very next morning, Ramsar's denizens were greeted with the news of Gudyal's arrest.

'Who could have imagined that the rascal had killed not one but two innocent people?' The wise ones nodded.

'I never liked the chap,' said a gossip. 'There's something loathsome about him.'

'Very true!' agreed another. 'He comes across as a violent person.'

'I am not surprised to learn that he has murdered two people,' added another voice. 'The shifty-eyed fellow has always behaved rudely with everyone.'

Umesh Gudyal was a much-disliked person, and most people avoided him. There were many who did not mince their words while expressing their dislike for the arrested man.

The town heaved a sigh of relief. Worried that the peaceful town had turned into an unsafe one, the locals had been waiting for the police to find the murderer. Now that the culprit had been arrested, they could carry on with their lives.

Gudyal's reaction came as a surprise. He neither ranted nor protested. The stoic manner in which he accepted the arrest took Tim aback.

'He seemed resigned to fate,' he told the colonel when the latter visited the police station.

'Does he have a choice? The poor sod must have realized the futility of resisting the arrest.'

The DSP, however, was not surprised at the man's reaction. 'Why would he protest or resist the arrest?' he remarked when informed of Gudyal's behaviour. 'He's guilty, and he knows it.'

'He is refusing to give a statement,' said Tim. 'He continues to repeat that he is innocent.'

'I am not surprised. Most murderers will continue to say that till they are hanged. You have to make him confess to the two killings. It will make our task easier,' Bulldog insisted.

'But, sir …'

'I don't care how you do it, but I want the man's confession. Give him the third degree, hang him upside down or starve him, do whatever it takes to extract a confession.'

Tim knew what the DSP wanted him to do.

The colonel, who was sitting across Tim, held up his hand in a placating manner. 'Play for time,' he mouthed silently.

Tim nodded his head and continued speaking. 'I don't think we will have to use force. I will allow him to languish in the lock-up for a day or two. I am sure he will come around,' he reassured his boss.

'You are too lenient,' barked the DSP. 'I will give you two days to make him confess, no more.'

'You are making a big mistake,' was all Umesh said when Acharya spoke to him. 'You are allowing the actual murderer to get away.'

The unfortunate fellow's mother, however, had a lot to say. She cried and shouted, cursed and blamed Tim for everything.

'My son is innocent,' she bawled. 'He had no enmity with Laxmi.'

'We have a lot of evidence against him,' Tim informed the wretched woman.

'It is not true. He has harmed no one.'

'He was seen coming out of Laxmi's house on the morning after her murder. We have a witness who will swear to the fact.'

'You have got it wrong. I agree my son went to Laxmi's house that morning. But he didn't murder her,' sobbed the distraught woman.

'Why did he go there?' Acharya asked. 'If he is innocent, why is he hiding the fact that he went to her house?'

'I don't understand why he went to her house in the first place.' Tim wanted to know. 'I don't see any reason for that. He's already confessed that there was no love lost between the two of them.'

'He didn't go there to kill her. He went because of me. I am asthmatic. The previous night, I had a severe attack of breathlessness and the medicine in my inhaler was over. Umesh knew that Laxmi was also an asthma patient, so he went to her house to borrow an inhaler from her.'

'Is that true?' Tim was incredulous.

'It is absolutely true. I won't start lying at this age. The asthma attack began at around 4.30 in the morning. I sat up on the bed, gasping for breath, but didn't want to disturb Umesh. I tried everything for relief, but the rasping continued. By 5.30, I was wheezing and coughing. It drew my son's attention, and he scolded me for not waking him up. He hunted around for a refill and when I told him that there were none in the house, he asked me if any of the neighbours could help. I told him that Laxmi would have an inhaler, so he rushed to her house. He found the door ajar and the woman dead.'

'What did he do when he found her dead?'

'He was shocked but, knowing my condition, he hunted around for her inhaler. A few minutes later, he returned with it and informed me of the woman's death. I was the one who told him to remain silent and not tell anyone that he had gone there.'

'Why did you do that?'

'Would you have believed his story?' countered the woman. 'You would have accused him of killing Laxmi.'

It was true, Acharya realized. No one would have believed his story. He had been on the police's radar since the first murder, and his early morning visit to Laxmi's house would have convinced the DSP of his guilt.

'Umesh should have told the truth, right in the beginning, irrespective of whether anyone believes or not. It is not wise to hide anything from the police,' Tim told the woman.

'He has to narrate the details of his movements truthfully,' insisted the colonel. 'No one will be able to help him otherwise.'

'Will you help him if he tells the truth?' The woman turned her tearful face towards the colonel.

'I will do my best to see that justice is served,' promised Acharya. 'But first he has to come clean. Your son has nothing to fear if he is not guilty.'

'Umesh does not trust the police,' she wailed. 'He says they will take the easiest way out and not bother with the truth.'

'You are his mother. Convince him,' the colonel said. 'He has nothing to fear if he is not guilty.' His tone was reassuring.

'May I meet him?' she asked.

'Yes, you can meet him for a while. We have to get some papers signed, so you can't spend more time with him. Come back in the evening,' Tim replied. He summoned a constable and sent the woman to meet her son. 'Poor woman! I feel sorry for her.' He shook his head ruefully.

'Maybe she is lying to save her son. Let's question Gudyal about his early morning visit to Laxmi's house.'

'I will summon him here after she leaves.'

Fifteen minutes later, Tim rang the bell on his table and instructed the constable to bring Gudyal.

Gudyal was in an uncooperative mood. 'There is no point in questioning me. I know that the police have already decided that I am guilty,' he said insolently. 'For your information, I will not make your job easier by signing a confession. You can do whatever you want.'

'Don't be stupid, Umesh,' said the colonel. 'We are trying to help you.'

'Why would you want to help me? You are with the police, aren't you?' Gudyal snarled.

'You are wrong. I am not with the police. I just help them in the investigations,' Acharya spoke calmly. 'I am on the side of the truth.'

'What's the truth, Colonel?' sneered the man. 'Truth, in your definition, is what you want to believe.'

'Why are you afraid to trust me?' the colonel asked. 'How can I help if you don't tell me everything?'

Acharya's words had no effect on Gudyal. He continued to sulk.

'Your mother said you had gone to Laxmi's house to fetch her inhaler. Is that true?' Tim asked.

'Does it matter why I went to her house? Will you believe me if I told you the truth?'

'Try me.'

'All right, for once I will trust you.' The dejected man sighed. 'My mother suffered a severe asthma attack late that night, but she didn't wake me up. It was only towards early morning, on hearing her rasp, that I learnt about the attack. She had run out of her medicine and we didn't know what to do. Mother told me that Laxmi had a similar medical problem, so I rushed to her place to borrow some medicine or an inhaler.

On reaching her house, I found the door was open. Thinking she was up early, I called out for her. There was no response. It was dark inside, so I lit a matchstick and found the light switch. The room looked as though it had been hit by a storm. The television had fallen and its screen was shattered. And then I saw her. She was lying on the couch. Her face pasty, she was absolutely still. The woman seemed dead.' Gudyal gulped nervously at the memory.

'Did you touch anything?'

'I hunted around for her inhaler and found it lying on the floor. Switching off the light, I rushed out of the house. Then I informed my mother. Worried that the police might think of me as the killer, she advised me to keep quiet. I must have dropped the pen as I leant to inspect the dead woman. That is the truth. Whether you believe me or not, the fact is that Laxmi was killed by someone else. I didn't kill her.'

'Have faith in the system. It will not let you down,' Tim advised. He called for the constable and Gudyal was taken back to the lock-up. 'Do you think he is telling the truth?' he asked Acharya.

'I think he is telling the truth. The more I think, the more I realize that Umesh Gudyal has been framed for a crime he didn't commit.'

'The fact is that he left his fingerprints all over Laxmi's front room.'

'He must have been flustered,' the colonel said, shaking his head. 'Just think of the situation. His mother lay wheezing and gasping for breath, so he had to get back to her with an inhaler. And then he found Laxmi dead. He must have gone through a harrowing time.'

'That may be so, but the law doesn't give credibility to such things. The fingerprints speak for themselves.'

'He didn't kill Laxmi,' declared the colonel. 'I am convinced about that.'

'But how do we prove it to the DSP?'

'The DSP has given you two days to extract a confession. I hope to resolve this case within those two days. Gudyal will walk free,' muttered the colonel, his jaw set resolutely.

'Amen!' Tim crossed himself.

'Now that the first part of our strategy is in place, it is time to roll out the second. Ask your boss for leave. Begin by asking for three days so he has the satisfaction of reducing it by a day or two. It never fails to work. The boss feels victorious and adopts a generous attitude. It's all about psychology.'

'You are so devious.'

The DSP was in a cheerful mood. The bosses were satisfied with the arrest and so was he. After accepting the felicitation for solving the two complicated murder cases, he took off for the day. Bulldog's wife had been complaining about his lack of attention, so he decided to give her a surprise by taking her out for a movie and a meal. Beaming happily, he drove home.

If she is nice, I could even buy her a sari, he thought. A good mood always made him benevolent. Imagining the delighted look on his wife's face, JBS rang the doorbell of his house.

Such was the state of his mind when Tim called. Almost immediately, the DSP's face creased in a grimace. He was fond of the young officer, but this was the wrong time to call.

'Yes, what do you want?' bellowed Bulldog, his podgy finger pressing the doorbell.

'Now that Gudyal has been arrested, I want to go on leave. Will you grant me three days' leave?' Tim came directly to the point. He would not plead, he had decided. If Bulldog didn't grant the leave, he would approach the higher-ups.

'Three days?' bellowed the DSP. 'Impossible. You have not yet got the scoundrel's confession and you want to go on leave for three days.'

'Sir, you wanted me to put Gudyal behind bars and I have done that. You have given me two days to get his confession. I will do that as soon as I return from leave.'

'I wanted you to arrest the chap, but I didn't say you can go on leave after you do that. It was not a precondition to granting leave.'

'But ...'

'You misunderstood.'

'Sir ...'

Bulldog's wife stood gaping at her husband. He was not the type of person to return early from the office. She wondered if he was unwell. Covering the mouthpiece of his phone, the DSP growled at her, 'Don't stare at me. Bring me a cup of tea and then change. We are going out for a movie and dinner.'

Sure that something was definitely wrong with her husband, JBS's wife scurried away to obey his orders. Amused at her reaction, he chuckled.

Tim, who was waiting for an answer, heard the boss chuckle and wondered if something was wrong with him.

'All right, I will grant you leave. But it won't be for three days,' Bulldog said.

'Why, sir? I have not taken leave in a long time.'

'That doesn't matter. Considering the current situation in Ramsar, I can grant only one day's leave.'

'Two?' Tim was smiling at the other end as the colonel winked at him.

The DSP's wife returned to the room and hovered around for his attention. She wanted to know if they could halt en route to pick up some groceries.

Wanting to cut short the call, Bulldog yielded to Tim's badgering. 'All right!' He sighed, wrapping his arm around his wife's ample waist. 'Remember, I want you to get Gudyal's confession as soon as you get back from your leave.'

In Ramsar, Shirt Pant, who was walking past Tim's office, was shocked to hear the jubilant hooting within. He shook his head.

'It just goes to show that the sanest of people can crack under stress,' he commented to no one in particular.

24

Delhi was basking in pleasant weather when Acharya and Tim alighted from the overnight train that had brought them to the capital. While on the train, assisted by the copious notes made by the diligent young man, the duo had meticulously gone over the events that had occurred in the past one week. They made a list of tasks that had to be carried out in the next twenty-four hours.

'We will need help in Delhi,' opined the colonel. 'You are on leave and have no authority to arrest or detain anyone. It might be worthwhile contacting your local colleagues for help. Remember, we have very little time.'

'I have already got in touch with my friend Sameer Malhotra. The two of us were together at the police academy. There was not much time to explain, but I informed him of our arrival. He won't hesitate to help us.'

'Hey! Where are you, asshole?' exclaimed Sameer when Tim called him from the New Delhi railway station.

'I am in your city, idiot,' returned the buddy. 'When are we meeting?'

'You are one helluva lucky bastard, taking off at whim while I am stuck at the desk on a holiday.'

'Who said I am here on holiday?' Tim retorted.

'I thought ...'

'Keep those thoughts to yourself. I am here on work.'

'You didn't tell me that,' Sameer accused. 'Well, what brings you to our glorious capital? First, tell me how long are you going to be here and where are you staying?'

The colonel smiled indulgently as the two pals sparred. It awakened memories of similar arguments with his army coursemates.

'Halt! Don't kill me with your questions. To reply to them in the same order: I am here for twenty-four hours, stretchable to thirty-six at most. Colonel Acharya is here with me and the two of us plan to stay at the Defence Services Officers' Institute, which has been booked by the colonel's friend.'

'The colonel is here too?' Sameer knew Acharya and his exploits.

'Yes, he is here with me.'

'So I have double the excuse to see you at the DSOI, Dhaula Kuan. The DSOI is not too far from the R.K. Puram police station, which happens to be my current place of posting.'

'So, when do we meet?'

'Just now,' replied the boisterous Sameer. 'It's a Sunday. I am going to the police station for about an hour. I can be there by the time you guys check in and freshen up.'

'Let's have lunch together,' Tim suggested as the cab wound its way through the thin early morning traffic.

* * *

'Food first,' said Sameer, tucking into the prawns. They were meeting at Spicy Duck, over kung pao chicken, king prawn fu yung, wok-tossed asparagus and Yunnan noodles. 'It would be blasphemous to discuss blood and violence while our table is loaded with delicious stuff. It is my favourite restaurant. Though the prices are on the steep side, the owner owes me a favour and bills me at a discounted rate. So I indulge myself on special occasions.'

'Perks of remaining a bachelor, I would say,' laughed Tim. 'You are not thinking of marriage, are you?'

'Nope! I am commitment-phobic. There is a girlfriend hovering on the fringe, hopefully, but I am not ready to tie the knot. Our profession is not conducive to marriage. We make bad husbands. Don't you think so, Colonel?' Sameer probed the kung pao for pieces of cashew nut.

'That goes for our profession too.' The colonel sighed and forked a piece of chicken into his mouth. He counted himself as a foodie, and Chinese food demanded his full attention. 'The list of my wife's complaints during my working days could run into dozens of miles.'

'I am ready for dessert.' Having ended the main course, Sameer rubbed his hands gleefully and summoned the waiter to order his favourite lemongrass crème brûlée. 'What about you, don't you want dessert?'

'Don't skip dessert, Colonel.' Tim winked at Acharya. 'Our large-hearted Delhi pal is paying for the meal.'

'Bastard!' Sameer sent a mock punch his way. 'Wait till I visit Ramsar.'

'You will be the loser, Sameer. Ramsar has no expensive restaurants.' The colonel chuckled. 'As for dessert, I will skip this once. Overeating makes me sleepy and I can't afford to waste time napping.'

'That was a bloody good meal, almost orgasmic.' Sameer wiped his mouth with the napkin and slumped in the chair. 'It is worth the empty wallet.'

'As long as it is your wallet.' Tim smirked. He had followed the colonel's example and eaten judiciously.

'Now that the stomachs are full, let's discuss business. You have not come all the way to empty my wallet, I am sure. So, what brings you guys here?'

'You are right, we are here on work.'

In brief, Tim narrated the events that had taken place in Ramsar in the past one week.

'Let me get this straight. You suspect the guy called Shubham Sharma so you are here to nab him,' Sameer said. 'Where do I come into the picture?'

'You are the one who's going to detain him,' Tim explained. 'I am here on leave and have no legal authority to question or detain anyone.'

'In short, you want to bring down the curtain on my career.'

'Not really! As soon as we can get some evidence or confession, I will pressure JBS to arrange for an arrest warrant. He has influential friends in this city.'

'You don't have any evidence against this Sharma character?' Sameer expressed shock. 'And you want me to detain the fellow? Forget it, man. It's highly irregular.'

'We are convinced of his guilt,' Acharya intervened. 'The guy is very clever. Finding evidence might be difficult. But a bit of pressure—physical or mental—might break him.'

'Let me put my cards on the table. My boss is an unethical bastard. He is in cahoots with local politicians. My goose is cooked if he gets to know of this,' Sameer confessed.

'How will he get to know?' Tim asked.

'This is Delhi, my friend. Here a guy can get away with several murders if he has the right connections. "Connections" is the key word. My boss has the right connections. Besides, he has spies everywhere. Nothing escapes his ears. I can't risk taking your man to the police station.'

'What do you suggest?'

'Let me think about the matter.'

'I am banking on you, pal. It will be impossible to catch the guy without your help.' Tim prodded his friend. 'We need a place to question the guy. The DSOI will not serve the purpose. Unless we question him in the right setting, the guy will not crack. We need the psychological pressure of a police station and uniforms for the right effect.'

'Why don't you guys go ahead and locate his address? In the meantime, I will think of something.' Sameer summoned the waiter and asked for the bill. 'I will call you as soon as I have something.'

'Thanks, pal, I will be waiting for your call.' Tim hugged his friend.

'I can drop you at the DSOI.'

'Thanks for the offer, but we aren't going back to the DSOI. We are planning to visit Nisha Dabral before we go hunting for Sharma.'

'Where does she stay? Do you have her address?'

'Yes, she stays in Saket.'

'Well, I can drop you part of the way, if you like,' Sameer offered.

'Don't bother,' said Acharya. He was a tad disappointed with Sameer's reluctance to put his weight behind them. 'We will take a cab.'

Hailing a cab, Tim gave directions to the driver and they drove towards Nisha's house. At 4 p.m. the road seemed to be teeming with vehicles. Delhiites were out in full force to enjoy a day of leisure.

'Sameer will come up with something,' he assured the anxious colonel. 'He always does. At the academy, he was known for formulating devious plans.'

It took them forty-five minutes to reach the upmarket colony in South Delhi and ten more to locate the house, only to find it locked.

'Now what? The lady is not home.' Tim cursed.

'Don't lose heart,' consoled Acharya. 'It gives us an opportunity to speak to the neighbours. Who knows what we may learn while speaking to them! Let's knock on the nearest door.'

It was one of those typical housing societies of flats constructed by the Delhi Development Authority under the self-financing scheme. Owning such a flat in an upmarket area like Saket was a middle-class family's ambition. It required deep pockets and loads of luck.

The Dabrals lived on the second floor. There were four flats on each floor. Two other flats on the floor were locked, so the colonel rang the doorbell of the flat across Nisha's apartment.

The hefty lady who answered the neighbour's doorbell eyed them suspiciously. From within came the sounds of dialogue from a Bollywood movie that must have been showing on TV. 'Yes?' she demanded rudely, her large body blocking the entrance.

'Sorry to disturb you,' began the colonel politely. 'We came to meet Mrs Dabral, but the door is locked. Do you have any idea where she has gone?'

'She doesn't keep me informed about her comings and goings, nor do I care. Who are you?' she said, eyeing them curiously.

'We are Deepak Dabral's friends,' replied Tim. 'We heard he is no more, so we came to express our condolences.'

'Yes, we also heard that he was killed at some place near Almora.' Her inquisitiveness seemed to thaw her behaviour. 'Someone said he was having an affair with a woman there and got killed by the jealous husband.'

'Really! We didn't know about that.'

'Not that I blame him. With a wife like her, why shouldn't a man stray?'

Tim and Acharya exchanged an amused glance. Fortunately for them, the woman loved gossiping.

'Who is it, Sarita?' came the voice of a man from inside the apartment.

'There are a couple of people looking for Mrs Dabral,' she replied.

Minutes later, a bespectacled man, clad in shorts and a T-shirt, joined the woman at the door. 'Are you the police?' he asked belligerently.

Tim hesitated. There was no point in telling the truth.

'I am Colonel Arjun Acharya, a friend of Deepak Dabral. And this is Timothy Thapa. We came here to convey our condolences to Mrs Dabral,' Acharya stepped forward and introduced himself. 'She is not at home—'

'So what do you expect us to do?' the man asked in a gruff voice. Pulling his wife inside, he banged the door shut.

'What an obnoxious man!' Tim exclaimed. 'Obviously they were not on friendly terms with the Dabrals.'

'Let's try another flat on the first floor,' Acharya said, going down the steps.

'Do you think …' Tim tried to object, but the colonel had already pressed the buzzer of an apartment on the first floor.

This time the door was opened by a teenager. She looked enquiringly at the two men.

'We were looking for Nisha Dabral,' the colonel began.

'She lives on the second floor.' Saying that, the girl banged the door on his face.

Tim laughed. 'We are not getting anywhere, Colonel. Let's go,' he said. 'This block of apartments seems populated with rude people.'

'Let's try one last time before giving up.'

Acharya pretended to mumble a prayer before ringing the doorbell of the flat across.

They got lucky this time.

'You are looking for Nisha?' asked the middle-aged lady who opened the door. 'I doubt anyone will be able to help you.'

'Why do you say that?' Tim asked curiously.

'They are not very popular here,' the lady replied.

'We were hoping someone could tell us when she is likely to return home,' said the colonel. 'We have come a long way, you see.'

'Would you like to come in?' she invited.

'Thank you.' Relieved at having struck a spot of luck, Acharya walked into a tastefully decorated room with Tim in tow.

25

'The Dabrals were an odd couple,' began the lady after the two men had settled on a couch. 'Deepak, bless his soul, was an unsociable man. In any case, he remained away from home for long periods of time. Being his friends, you must already be aware of his nature. His wife, Nisha, is a smart cookie. I wonder what attracted the man to her. When the husband would go sailing for a long time, she kept herself entertained by gallivanting around town.'

'Gallivanting?' Acharya raised an eyebrow enquiringly.

'What else would you say when a woman is never home?'

'You mean she is out gallivanting right now?'

'No doubt about that. From her behaviour, no one can say that her husband was murdered barely a week back. The hussy is out every evening with her boyfriend.'

'Boyfriend?' The story was becoming quite bizarre.

'I am not a nosy woman but no one can ignore what goes on under their nose.' She lowered her voice conspiratorially and said, 'That man is her constant companion. I have found him staying the night at her place on many occasions, when the husband went seafaring. In fact, Deepak's absence was a blessing for the two lovers. But then, who can blame her? She is a bright young woman. In our times, we made do with whatever destiny thrust on us.' She sighed. 'It's no longer so. Young women don't want to have anything to do with a dull husband. They hunt for excitement.'

Tim was aghast. Never in his wildest dreams had he pictured Nisha as a promiscuous woman. 'Can you tell us anything about her boyfriend? I mean, where he lives and what he does?' he asked.

'I don't know where he lives or what he does.' The lady shook her head. 'All I can tell you is that the chap is smart enough to turn any woman's head and drives an expensive car. Don't ask me about the brand because I won't be able to help you there. I met him once on the staircase and found him utterly charming.'

'Do you have her office address?' asked Acharya. 'I don't think it is worth waiting for her to return. We will try to meet her at work tomorrow.'

'All I know is that she works for an advertising company. Let me ask my son. He may have the name of her company and its location. Rishi, come here, beta,' she hollered.

Rishi turned out to be a skinny young man with an inquisitive look in his spectacled eyes. Clad in shorts and a T-shirt proclaiming him as the most handsome dude in town, the youngster studied the two visitors closely.

'Can you help these gentlemen? They want to know Nisha's office address.'

'Are you her friends?' Rishi asked, his eyes glinting through the spectacles. 'You look like detectives.'

'We are friends,' replied Acharya, surprised at the young man's perception. 'I am a retired colonel, and this is Tim.'

'Just checking! We don't want to create trouble for Nisha. She is a nice lady.' The lad continued to eye them with suspicion.

'Rishi reads too many detective books,' his mother said. She seemed embarrassed by the son's attitude. 'He sees detectives, police and murderers in every stranger.'

'That's all right.' The colonel smiled. 'I was the same at his age.'

'We were shocked to hear of Deepak Dabral's death. He was a friend. All we want is to express our condolences for her husband's death,' said Tim. 'Since Nisha is not at home and no one knows her whereabouts, we will try to meet her at work. It would be nice if you could help us with the address.'

The youngster stared doubtfully at them for a few moments before replying, 'Well, all I can tell you is that Nisha works for Sphere Advertising Pvt. Ltd. The office is in Nehru Place. Don't ask me about the address because I am not sure about it.' A moment later, he said, 'I have her office number, if you care for it.'

'Thank you for the information, Rishi. The office number will be very helpful,' said the colonel.

Rishi took out his phone and scrolled through the numbers. 'Here it is,' he exclaimed. 'If you give me your number, I can text it to you.'

'Don't bother, I will feed it in my phone,' replied Tim. He had no intention of sharing his number with the inquisitive fellow. 'Just read it out to me.'

Once the number had been saved, they thanked the lady and took her leave.

'Don't tell Nisha that I told you about her boyfriend,' she called out as they stepped out of the door.

'We won't tell her anything,' promised Acharya.

'What next?' Tim asked as they walked out of the building. 'We seem to draw a blank everywhere.'

'Cheer up, Tim. The day has been quite fruitful. We have learnt a lot about Nisha Dabral. Now, let's hunt for Shubham Sharma.'

'Sameer has not called yet. Even if we were to locate Sharma, where do we take him for questioning?'

'We begin by questioning him at his place and follow it up with further questioning at the police station, once your friend comes up with a plan. Just for your information, while in Kashmir, I did a good job of interrogating suspected terrorists.'

Tim knew all about the colonel's exploits in the Kashmir Valley and respected the officer's proficiency in handling difficult situations.

'According to the address on Sharma's driving licence, the guy lives in a DDA apartment in Janakpuri.' Tim looked up the address noted in his pad and followed it up with an internet search. 'We shouldn't have a problem finding the address, I think.'

'Let's grab a quick cup of tea and then we can book a cab to take us to Janakpuri,' suggested the colonel, eyeing the tiny café across the road.

With traffic congestion forcing the cab to crawl, the drive to Janakpuri took longer than expected. Once there, they asked for directions from a man waiting at the bus stand. His limp now pronounced because of fatigue and stress, Acharya's gait was slow as he approached the block of apartments pointed out by a helpful resident of the area. The layout of the housing society was not too different from the one they had visited in Saket.

The door was opened by a young man wearing a pair of frayed jeans and a soiled T-shirt. In his arms was a restless toddler. He looked nothing like the portrait in Tim's pocket.

'Shubham Sharma?' asked the colonel.

'You have the wrong flat. There's no one by that name here,' replied the young man.

'We have been given this address,' insisted Tim, checking Sharma's address once again. 'You can see for yourself.' He held out the piece of paper in his hand.

The man checked the address and nodded his head. 'The address is correct, but I live here with my wife and parents and my name is Tarun Tyagi. There is no Shubham Sharma here.'

Tim exchanged a glance with the colonel. 'That's strange,' remarked Acharya. 'We have been told that Shubham lives here. The two of us have come from a distance. Can you help us find him?'

'I moved here about two years back. Shubham Sharma might have been staying here before I came,' said the young man, keen to help the men standing at his door. 'You could ask one of the older residents in the block. They might be able to help you.'

'Thank you, Tarun.' The colonel shook his hand. 'We will check with the neighbours.'

Tim was disappointed. The elusive Sharma weighed on his mind. 'It doesn't seem to be our lucky day. Which of the doors should we knock on now?'

Acharya walked away from the block of apartments as fast as his feet could move, unaffected by the situation.

'Where are you going?'

'Can you see the park across the road? I am going there,' he said, pointing with his walking stick.

The park was teeming with young parents pushing children on swings, frolicking teenagers, jogging youngsters, romantic couples and ambling aged ones. The dozen benches lined along a path were mostly occupied by old people or young lovers.

'You are not planning to jog around the park, I hope,' Tim sneered. He was feeling frustrated. The trip to Delhi was turning out to be a futile one

'Don't be nasty. You are feeling dejected, I know. It's not time to give up yet. I am looking for a bench to sit down and rest my legs.'

Contrite, Tim turned solicitously towards his companion. 'You must be exhausted. Why don't we call it a day? We could go back to the DSOI for dinner and rest.'

Ignoring his suggestion, Acharya hurried towards a bench and plonked himself next to an old man, who gave him a welcoming smile.

'Sit down, Tim,' he said, shifting to make space on the bench.

The old man was watching the antics of an amorous couple on the adjoining bench. 'Bloody voyeur,' muttered Tim.

'Nice place,' the colonel remarked to no one in particular.

'Did you say something?' asked the man, fixing his eyes on Acharya. 'I haven't seen you here before.'

'I am Colonel Acharya. I am visiting a nephew who lives here. You must have been coming to the park for a long time.'

'Yes, a long time.' The spry old man sighed. Happy to find a listener, he continued, 'I began coming here after my retirement, eighteen years ago. Since then, I have not missed a single evening. In fact, I wait eagerly for the sun to set. My wife, God bless her soul, made her final journey five years back. It is a lonely existence for me now. There is not much an old person can do.'

'True.' The colonel nodded.

'As long as I was working, there was no time to sit in a park. The moment I retired, time began weighing heavily on me. If you take a walk along the park, you will find 90 per cent of the benches occupied by old people like me. Sometimes, I spend time chatting with a retiree but most days I like to sit alone and do some pranayama or meditate. And if I am not in the mood for those, I listen to the chatter of the birds and watch people.'

'You must know everyone who comes to this park. How long have you been staying in this area?'

'It's been a very long time. These apartments had just been constructed when I moved here with my family. Which block is your nephew staying in?'

'He is in A4.' The colonel mentioned the block they had just visited.

'A4? I know everyone in that block. What's the name of your nephew?'

'Tyagi. Tarun Tyagi.' Acharya's glib lie made Tim chortle.

'Tyagi! Oh, I know the senior Tyagi. We often walk together in the morning.' The conversation was moving towards unknown territory and Tim wondered if the colonel would be able to field too many questions from the old man. 'They shifted here just two years back.'

'Yes, Tarun was telling me that someone called Shubham Sharma lived in that flat before they rented it.'

'Shubham Sharma? Yes, I know that charming young scoundrel. An incorrigible flirt.' The old man chuckled. He directed a piercing look at the colonel. 'How do you know him?'

And just like that, Acharya struck gold. He winked surreptitiously at Tim.

'It's a small world. Imagine my surprise when I learnt that Shubham Sharma stayed here. I happen to know his father.' Acharya treaded on slippery ground. 'The boy, of course, is the black sheep of the family.'

'I agree. No wonder the father has cut off all relations with him. Youngsters are a strange breed. They have scant respect for their parents or elders.' The septuagenarian was delighted with his captive audience. It was not frequently that he found a good listener. Most old men he met liked to talk instead of listen to others.

'How did you learn about the father-and-son spat?' Tim interjected.

'Everyone in the block knows about the incident. The chap's father was here on a visit. That night, Shubham returned home drunk to the gills. It was a normal routine for him, but the father didn't know. There were loud arguments and slanging matches till the father stomped out of the house, vowing to sever all ties.'

'How long did Shubham stay in the flat?'

'He stayed for over a year, I think.'

'Do you know where he lives now? His mother is very upset. The father had a heart attack recently, and she cannot contact the son. When they learnt I was visiting Janakpuri, they told me to convey the message to Shubham.'

'I don't know his address.' The old man shook his head. 'In fact, I don't think anyone in the block has his address. The braggart didn't have too many friends here. Just imagine, parents don't know the whereabouts of their son. What's the world coming to, I wonder.'

'His mother will be disappointed,' said Acharya.

They seemed to have reached a dead end as far as Shubham Sharma was concerned. Tracing the guy looked impossible without police help.

The man thought for a while. 'Wait! There is someone who can help,' he exclaimed suddenly. 'Radhika! That's the person you should contact. She stays on the third floor of the same block and dated him for a while. Their relationship ended abruptly, when she learnt he was two-timing her. She might know where he works.'

'Thank you, sir.' The colonel got up and shook the man's hand. 'You don't know what a big help you have been. It is the question of someone's life and death.'

'One should help wherever possible. That's always been my policy.' The old man smiled smugly. 'Don't thank me yet. Meet Radhika and find out the chap's office address. I hope the rogue is still working there. A rolling stone rarely gathers moss.'

Waving cheerfully at the helpful man, they made their way across to the block once again.

Radhika turned out to be an uncommunicative young woman. Apart from spouting expletives, she was unwilling to speak about her ex-boyfriend.

'We just want his office address,' appealed the colonel. 'We have come a long way to locate him. As you must be aware, his family had severed all ties with Shubham. His father suffered a heart attack and the doctors have given him very little time. He hopes to reconcile with the son before dying.'

Acharya used the emotional angle to extract information. Tim marvelled at his capacity to invent stories at the drop of a hat.

The woman appeared to consider the matter. 'All right, I will give you his office address,' she said, succumbing to the colonel's emotional appeal. 'It is 1320, thirteenth floor, Ansal Tower, Nehru Place. Don't mention my name, though. I am done with that rascal.'

'Thank you, Radhika. You have been an immense help.'

'I hope he hasn't changed his job,' she said. 'Relationship or job, he can't stick to one for too long.'

Armed with Shubham Sharma's office address, they called for a cab.

'What a day!' remarked Acharya, sinking tiredly into the seat.

'That took some ingenuity!' Tim complimented. 'I had given up, but you didn't.'

'I am a big follower of King Bruce's philosophy. If at first you don't succeed, try again. The problem with your generation is that you have not implemented the wisdom of the past. Impatience is not a virtue.'

The cab driver zigzagged through the thick evening traffic as though there were ants in his pants. An hour later, reaching their destination, the colonel heaved a sigh of relief.

They had barely reached their room when Sameer called.

'Did you find a solution to our problem?' Tim asked excitedly.

'Relax, buddy! I promised to find a way, didn't I? Do you remember Roxy from our academy?'

'You mean Rakesh Pandey? The brash idiot who managed to get himself on the wrong side of every instructor?'

'Yes, the very chap. He is heading the police station in Khajoori Khas.'

'Khajoori Khas? The name sounds rather khas. Where's the damn place?'

'You've never heard of the place, I guess.' Sameer chuckled. 'It is a godforsaken place and Roxy is there on punishment posting. The guy managed to rankle a lot of people with his adamant and uncompromising attitude.'

'Poor sod. He was always a difficult guy. Anyway, what has his posting got to do with us?'

'Can't you guess? I have spoken to him about your case and he is willing to let you use his office for interrogating your man. Roxy can't resist getting involved in thrilling cases. Your story appealed to his sense of adventure. Khajoori Khas, with its terrible location, doesn't attract the attention of the bigwigs, so it should suit your purpose.'

'That's fantastic!' Tim exclaimed. 'Thanks, chum.'

'I hope you have located the chap.'

'No, we haven't found him yet. We have managed to get his office address. We hope to find him tomorrow.'

'Let me know when you find him. I will lend you a police vehicle and a constable to take you to Khajoori Khas. Roxy is a whiz at extracting confessions. With a few kicks from him, your guy will be singing in no time.'

'Thanks, pal. Send me Roxy's phone number. I want to speak to the bastard.'

'On second thoughts, I will send you the vehicle and a constable as soon as you reach Nehru Place. Just share his office address. The traffic is unpredictable. I don't want you standing on the road with your suspect.'

'That will be fantastic. I owe you a big one, Sameer. Come to Ramsar and I will make it up to you. I am texting the address.'

'You bet! I will be there for my next holiday to extract my pound of flesh. All the best and keep me informed.' Saying this, Sameer disconnected the call.

Dinner was a relaxed affair, now that things seemed to be falling into place. They ordered drinks at the bar and Tim entertained the colonel with stories of Roxy's faux pas at the police academy.

'Everything is tied up.' Acharya heaved a sigh of relief. 'Hopefully, it won't be too difficult to locate Shubham Sharma,' he said as they parted for the night.

26

It was 10 a.m. and Nehru Place was teeming with people. It was business as usual as the mass of humanity dressed in smart-casuals walked resolutely towards various buildings in the massive complex.

Their excitement palpable, the colonel and Tim stood near Ansal Tower, planning their move. True to his word, Sameer had sent a constable and a police vehicle to Nehru Place. Having informed Tim about his location, the constable stood waiting near the parking lot.

'I feel we should split the tasks,' suggested Acharya. 'I will go hunting for Nisha while you look for Shubham Sharma. We could converge at a designated point after finishing the tasks. That will help us save time.'

'Do you want to go after Nisha or Shubham?'

'You should go to Ansal Tower and buttonhole Shubham Sharma since you are a police officer. If required, you can take the constable's help. Since I have no authority to question or detain the chap, I will hunt for Nisha.'

'Fair enough,' agreed Tim. 'How will you go looking for Nisha? All you know is that she is working for a company called Sphere Advertising Pvt. Ltd, which is located in Nehru Place.

This is a vast place with thousands of offices,' he said but his tone was apprehensive.

'I will find out. Give me half an hour.'

'Half an hour? Aren't you being overconfident? This is a beehive, Colonel.' The colonel was one of the most optimistic guys he had met. *But optimism without realistic limits is of no use, Tim mused.*

'You go ahead and take the lift to the thirteenth floor and find your chap. I will see you sooner than you expect.' Waving cheerfully, the colonel walked into a shop to enquire about the location of Sphere Advertising.

Shaking his head at the foolhardiness of his friend, Tim joined the queue of office-goers and visitors waiting for the elevator.

A few minutes later, he found himself staring at a large signboard on the right side of the swivel door. Engraved on a brass plaque were the words 'Sphere Advertising Pvt. Ltd'. He stood transfixed, a flurry of thoughts rushing through his befuddled mind.

His fingers trembling with excitement, he dialled Acharya. 'Seek no further, Colonel. Come right up,' he said.

'Why? Is the guy giving you a tough time?'

'I have yet to speak to him.'

'In that case, why do you want me there?'

'You ask too many questions. Trust me, this is where you should be.' Tim couldn't help but chuckle.

'All right! I will be with you in a few minutes.'

Tim was waiting at the entrance when Acharya rushed there. 'Will you—'

'Shhhh! Not so loud,' admonished Tim, pointing at the signboard. 'Isn't this the address you are seeking?'

'Bloody hell!' blurted the colonel. 'This is the weirdest of coincidences.'

'I agree! This is totally unexpected. So, what do you think?'

'I think it explains a lot of things, Tim. There is more to the matter than meets the eye. It is murkier than we initially assumed.'

'Look at the brighter side. You don't have to go hunting all around Nehru Place for Nisha. She is right here, since the two of them work in the same office. We can question them together.'

'Don't even think of it,' warned the colonel. 'Clearly the two of them are involved in shenanigans. Questioning them together would give them the strength to face us. We have to catch them by surprise.'

'What do you suggest we do?'

'Let me go in first. I will ask for Nisha and take her to some café close by. While she is out of the way, you can corner Shubham Sharma. Give me a call when you start for Khajoori Khas. I will think of the next step once you are on your way. Don't allow him to make any calls. In fact, seize his phone. Get rough if he resists. That way, they will have no opportunity to warn each other.'

It sounded like a plan that made sense. 'The scoundrel will not follow me like a lamb. I might need help to take the chap with me.'

'Call the constable and post him outside the entrance. That done, you will have no trouble summoning him for help,' suggested Acharya. 'In any case, try to keep it pleasant. Think of some excuse to take him down to the police vehicle. We don't want to create a racket and draw too many eyeballs.'

'All right, I will loiter outside till I see you walking away with Nisha. After the two of you take the elevator, I will go inside and ask for Shubham Sharma.'

'Wish me luck.' The colonel winked, pushing open the frosted swivel door. Minutes later, Tim watched him walking jauntily towards the receptionist, who was busy attending a call. She pushed a piece of paper and a pen for him to write the name of the person he wanted to meet.

'Please wait while I inform Nisha,' she said, cupping her hand over the mouthpiece.

He sat down on the vinyl couch and picked up a newspaper. Opening it to cover his face, Acharya peeped from a corner of the newspaper. He did not want Shubham Sharma to spot him sitting there. A few minutes passed. Then he saw Nisha striding towards the receptionist, and the girl pointed towards him.

Her heels clicking smartly on the marbled floor, Nisha walked over to the colonel.

'You wanted to meet me?' she asked.

'Good morning, Nisha.' Acharya lowered the newspaper and smiled at her.

'Colonel Acharya! What an unexpected pleasure!' she exclaimed, taken aback by his sudden appearance. It didn't take her long to regain her composure, though. A false smile lighting up her face, she asked, 'What brings you here?'

'I was passing Nehru Place, and thought it's a good opportunity to update you about the case. You must be eager to see the culprit behind bars, I guess,' Acharya said and got to his feet.

'That's very nice of you. In fact, I was thinking of calling you for an update. I want the culprit to rot in hell, and the sooner the better.'

She waited for the colonel to speak.

'It is a little awkward discussing this in your office. The matter is confidential and I don't want your colleagues to eavesdrop.' Acharya looked suspiciously around the place. 'Why don't we grab a cup of coffee? Let's go somewhere we can speak freely.'

'Yes, of course.' She was at her charming best. 'It's stupid of me. I should have offered you coffee.'

'No, no, it is perfectly understandable.' He was keen to get away from the office before Sharma spotted him. 'My sudden appearance at your place of work must have come as a shock to you.' He turned to the woman and said in an urgent manner. 'I don't have much time, Nisha. Can we go down?'

'Give me a minute to inform the reception and fetch my purse, then we can go,' she said, sashaying towards the receptionist. 'I will be back in thirty minutes,' she told the girl before joining Acharya near the door.

The colonel spotted Tim standing behind a pillar as they made their way towards the bank of elevators. From the corner of his eye, he spotted a constable hovering around the entrance, and a satisfied smile lit up his face.

They walked down the block for about 500 metres, and Nisha led him into a coffee bar. It appeared to be a popular place, crowded with office-goers and college students. He saw young executives in formal attire, as well as teenagers dressed in jeans and T-shirts. It was a couple of minutes before they could find a vacant table.

'This place is always crowded because it offers the best coffee in this area,' she remarked, pushing the menu towards Acharya. 'Did you have breakfast? They have excellent burgers in case you want something to eat.'

'I don't mind one. What about you?'

'I will settle for coffee and a chicken sandwich,' she said, poring over the menu. 'The crispy chicken burger is quite good. Would you like to have one?'

'That sounds good.'

'I will fetch the coffee and burger,' Nisha said as she got up. 'Would you like a serving of fries to go with them?'

'I will help you,' the colonel offered.

'We will lose the table if both of us leave it. Why don't you guard it with your life while I fetch the stuff?'

While he waited, the colonel resisted the temptation to call Tim. He wondered if things were going smoothly at the young man's end.

Ten minutes later, the coffee, sandwich and burger in front of them, Nisha raised the topic of her husband's murder. 'Have you arrested the culprit?' she asked.

'You will be happy to know that Umesh Gudyal has been arrested for the murder,' informed Acharya. He sipped the coffee and smacked his lips appreciatively.

Her eyes sparkled at the news. 'I knew he was the one. The only regret I have is that I couldn't see him behind bars.'

His mouth full of the burger, the colonel nodded his head in agreement. He could sense the woman's excitement.

While the colonel was enjoying coffee and a burger with Nisha, Tim was suffering tense moments at Sphere Advertising's office. A couple of minutes back, he had asked for Shubham Sharma and now, hidden behind a newspaper, he sat waiting for the chap to emerge from one of the cubicles in the hall.

It was a few minutes before Tim heard a familiar voice. 'You asked for me?' Shubham addressed the person behind the newspaper.

Lowering the newspaper, Tim stared gobsmacked at the person standing before him. It was the man who had introduced himself as Sudhir Sabharwal—the man whom they knew as Nisha's brother.

The crook looked equally shocked to see Tim at his office. 'What are you doing here?' he croaked. His eyes darted around and he looked for an avenue to escape.

Tim's mind raced as it tried to process the information. *If this man is Sudhir Sabharwal, who is Shubham Sharma? Are they the same person?*

'Hello, Shubham, or should I address you as Sudhir Sabharwal?'

A hunted look appeared in the man's eyes and he began backing towards the door. Tim was immediately on his feet. He grabbed the fellow and pushed him on to the couch. 'Don't make a fuss,' he hissed. 'Don't compel me to use force. I have a couple of policemen standing outside to help me rough you up. All I have to do is call out for help. Come quietly with us and there will be no trouble. You wouldn't want the entire office to know about your misdeeds, I gather.'

Sensing trouble, the constable moved closer and waited for an order. The receptionist's fingers hesitated over the phone as she toyed with the idea of calling security. Shubham Sharma wasn't one of her favourite people, and she didn't mind him being roughed up a bit. The arrogant chap needed to be taken down by a peg or two.

'Are you arresting me?' Sharma asked.

'Not at the moment. I just want to ask a few questions.'

'Get an arrest warrant and I will come with you.'

'Don't be under any illusions. This is neither a request nor a friendly visit. I am a police officer investigating a double murder and you are a suspect. If you act tough, you will find us acting tougher. I will be forced to use handcuffs if you do not cooperate,' Tim warned. 'Do you want me to do that?'

Shubham dithered. He had no intention of ruining his reputation at the workplace. Being led out of the office in handcuffs would cause no end to his humiliation. Not just his office, the entire building would see him in handcuffs. 'This is my office, and I am supposed to be working. I am not free to leave at my whim and fancy.'

'I understand that. Why don't you call your boss and I will explain the situation to him,' said Tim, confident that the rascal would not want that. The threat worked.

'How long will it take for you to finish questioning?' Sharma changed tack.

'It could take anywhere from an hour to a day, depending on your cooperation.'

'Let me inform the receptionist.'

He walked towards the receptionist, who was throwing anxious looks at Tim and the constable. *Something is amiss.* The girl glanced at Tim, who, unwilling to take a chance, accompanied his quarry to the reception.

'I will be away for an hour.' Shubham feigned nonchalance and winked at her. He was relieved that none of his colleagues were anywhere near the reception.

'What shall I tell the boss?' asked the girl, her eyes troubled. 'He will want to know where you have gone.'

Why are the visitor and constable looking for Shubham? Her mind was in a tizzy. *Should I inform security? But if Shubham is not resisting, there is no point in creating trouble.*

'Tell him that I have to attend to a personal matter. I will speak to him later.'

They filed out of the office, leaving the flabbergasted receptionist staring.

Tim called the colonel as they walked towards the parking lot. 'We are on our way,' he informed. 'Do you want me to send back the vehicle and an escort?'

'That won't be necessary,' came Acharya's confident reply. 'Just send me the location of Khajoori Khas police station and I will reach there. Good luck!'

'Thanks,' said Tim. Aided by the constable, he hustled Shubham into the waiting vehicle.

He made one last call, and the driver took off for Khajoori Khas.

'Where are we going?' asked the captive as they raced towards the destination.

No one replied.

It was going to be a long day.

27

At the café, Acharya sat back in his chair and studied the woman sitting across the table. There was a discernible change in her mental state as she sipped her coffee. From an alert stance, Nisha had gone into a relaxed mode after hearing about Gudyal's arrest. He knew she was dying to share the good news with her accomplice.

'By the way, Tim is also here,' said the colonel, picking up a fry from her plate.

'Really! What brings him to Delhi?' Her eyes were alert once again. The tension was back in her posture. The sudden arrival of Acharya and the ASP disturbed her.

'He is here to arrest a murder suspect.'

'That's interesting.' She pretended to be absorbed in sipping the coffee, but her mind was racing. The colonel had not revealed the reason for his presence in her office. She decided to find out why the two men had travelled all the way to Delhi. 'Has there been another murder? It is impossible to associate serene Ramsar with bloodshed and gory happenings.'

'You are right. Things are changing. However, we are determined to stem the rot.'

She remained quiet, her mind straying to Ramsar.

'Who is Shubham Sharma?' the colonel sprang the question and watched her reaction.

Taken aback by the sudden question, she countered the question with her own. 'How do you know him?'

'I will tell you after you have replied to my question.'

'He is a colleague,' she snapped. 'In any case, why are you asking me about Shubham Sharma?'

'Does your relationship extend beyond that of a colleague?' Acharya toyed with a spoon on the table.

'Colonel, you are crossing the limits of decency,' she rebuked. 'I presumed you to be a gentleman.'

'I have a reason for asking you the question. Please answer.'

'The answer is the same. Shubham Sharma is a colleague,' Nisha repeated sternly. 'One more question of this sort and I will walk out of this place,' she threatened.

'I was just wondering to what lengths a colleague would go in order to kill someone for your sake.'

Acharya's statement had rattled the woman. 'What are you trying to imply? I do not like your insinuation.'

'It's not an insinuation, Nisha. The police know about your affair.'

'I don't have to listen to you.' She stood up and made a move towards the exit.

'I have some bad news for you,' the colonel called out. 'It is in your interest to hear the latest.'

'Bad news?' She stopped.

'Shubham Sharma has been arrested by Tim.'

'Shubham arrested?' For a moment, her mind refused to register the statement. Then she retraced her steps to the table and stood before the colonel. 'Why?'

'He has been arrested for his involvement in your husband's murder. They are at the police station at the moment.'

Nisha sank into the chair and remained silent for a minute.

'That's not true,' she said. 'You are joking, right?'

'I am absolutely serious.'

Nisha's dull eyes were appraising Acharya. 'Where has he been taken?'

'The call I received a few minutes back was from Tim. He informed me that Shubham has signed a written statement in which he holds you responsible for Deepak Dabral's murder. According to him, you are the one who plotted and killed Dabral.'

'Nonsense! I had nothing to do with Deepak's murder. I refuse to sit here and listen to this nonsense.' She stood up.

'Don't you want to speak to Shubham?'

For a couple of moments, she stood undecided. 'Of course I will speak to him. I don't believe one word of what you are saying,' she declared defiantly.

Her fingers unsteady, Nisha punched a button on her phone. She tried two more times before turning accusingly towards Acharya, her composure visibly shattered. The woman was agitated. 'What's going on? His phone is switched off. I can't reach him.'

'Is that unexpected? The police must have taken away his phone. You can request Tim to let you speak to the guy. Here, use my phone,' Acharya offered. Punching in Tim's number, he handed over his phone to her.

'Why have you arrested Shubham?' Nisha demanded as soon as Tim responded to the call.

'Don't worry, he will be home soon. Shubham Sharma has given a statement declaring his innocence, so we are letting him go. By the way, he has put the entire blame on you. According to him, you plotted your husband's murder,' Tim's voice rode the distance. The colonel and he had already discussed the strategy and he played the role.

Nisha paled. Grabbing a chair to support her trembling legs, she flopped down. 'This can't be true,' she mumbled. 'He would n't let me down.'

'There is no saying what a person will do when the noose tightens around his neck,' said the colonel.

'I don't believe it. The two of you are playing a trick on me.' A sudden determination came over the woman. 'I am going.'

Acharya caught up with her as she rushed blindly out of the café.

'Do you want to meet him?' he asked. 'I can help you, if you want.'

'No.'

'You could convince him to withdraw the statement,' prodded the colonel, trying to match his steps with her. He would have liked her to accompany him to Khajoori Khas so they could have the two culprits contradicting each other. 'Speaking in person is always more effective than speaking on the phone. I am on my way there. Join me, in case you change your mind.'

He began walking away. *Will she, or won't she?* It was a gamble.

Torn with indecision, she stood hesitating for a few minutes. And then Acharya heard her heels tapping away from him. He turned and watched as Nisha walked back towards her office. Shrugging nonchalantly, the colonel took a cab to Khajoori Khas.

* * *

At Khajoori Khas police station, Shubham Sharma was led into what seemed like a storeroom full of broken furniture, piles of old files and all kinds of junk. It gave a dank smell as well. A low-watt bulb lit the peeling walls festooned with spiderwebs.

Sharma was pushed into a broken chair by the constable who had accompanied them from Nehru Place. Tim stood nearby, sending text messages from his phone. Minutes later, they were joined by a mean-looking police officer. He felt trapped.

Distraught, Shubham faced the police officer. 'You have no right to detain me,' he protested. 'I want to speak to a lawyer.'

'Listen, smartass!' Roxy waved a baton under his nose. 'This is Khajoori Khas and I am the officer in charge, so my order runs here. I decide when and to whom you may speak.'

'Why don't you give a statement and we will let you walk away,' cajoled Tim, adopting the good-cop act. 'All I want to know is why you went to Ramsar.'

'I have never been to Ramsar,' Sharma shouted. He felt the walls closing in on him.

'You made several appearances at the Ramsar police station, masquerading as Nisha's brother and calling yourself Sudhir Sabharwal. Do you need a little prodding to remind you of that?' Tim threatened. 'Then you stayed at Hotel Hillside, Almora, as Shubham Sharma and presented your driving licence as proof of identity.'

A look of determination came upon the man's face. He would not succumb to pressure, he decided.

'I don't know anything,' he said. 'I did not go to Almora.'

'We have several methods to nudge a person's memory. You seem to require some prodding.' Roxy laughed and started to walk aggressively towards Shubham.

'We should give him some time to think,' Tim suggested, trying to restrain the menacing officer.

'Yes, I think that is a good idea. Mr Sharma can refresh his memory while we grab some food and drinks,' said Roxy.

Shubham looked around fearfully. He had spotted rats scurrying around the room. He was scared of them. A desperate look crept into his eyes and he shouted, 'You can't keep me here and make me confess to a crime I haven't committed.'

'In that case, you are welcome to be my guest for as long as you want.' Roxy sniggered. 'We are a hospitable lot.'

They left him alone in the tiny, suffocating room. He was cold and thirsty. Exhausted and anxious, Shubham knew he was doomed. The police officer was right. He could remain here forever, without anyone learning of his whereabouts.

He cradled his head in his arms and began sobbing softly as the sound of the footsteps of his interrogators died down the corridor.

It was past noon when the colonel reached the police station. He found Tim and Roxy in a buoyant mood as they reminisced about the good old days at the academy.

'There you are, Colonel,' Tim greeted. 'Meet my friend Rakesh Pandey, popularly known as Roxy. He is one of the last few honest officers remaining in the country.'

'You flatter me, Timmy boy,' Roxy muttered, delighted at his friend's words. Pumping Acharya's hand, he said, 'Hello, Colonel, Tim has been telling me about your exploits in the army and in Ramsar.'

'You know, Colonel, Roxy aced several competitions while at the academy. Javelin, discus—you name it and he has won them all.' Tim continued praising his friend.

'What a rollicking time we had!' Roxy reminisced. 'We were a troublesome threesome, Timmy, Sam and I. They called us the Three Musketeers.'

'Hearing about your exploits brings back memories of my days at the academy,' said Acharya. 'Nothing can beat those times.'

'Oh! Those good old days.' Tim sighed. 'I would give anything to get them back.'

'So would I, but life does not stop nor can you rewind time. We have to get back to the business at hand. What is the latest on Shubham Sharma? Have you been able to get a statement out of the guy?'

'Not yet, but Roxy is a tough chap. No one gets an upper hand with him. Did you have any success with Nisha?'

'That woman is a hard nut to crack. It took her just a few minutes to overcome her shock after hearing of Shubham's arrest. She refused to succumb to my suggestion of meeting him. The woman is too sharp to be trapped.' Acharya spread out his hands in a gesture of helplessness. 'However, there's still hope. I am sure we will make headway with Shubham. All we need is a statement from him.'

Two phones rang simultaneously. While Acharya received a call from the doc in Ramsar, Tim received one from his friend at the forensic laboratory. Both of them stepped out of the room to take their calls.

'You wanted to know the names of the patients for whom I had prescribed hydrocortisone ointment,' said the doc. 'I am sorry for the delay. There were a few emergencies, and I had to travel to Almora for medicines.'

'That's all right. Do you have the names?' The colonel was impatient to know if his guess was right.

'Yes, in the last week, I prescribed hydrocortisone ointment for three patients. Bhagirathi and Nara Bahadur both reported skin rashes. They were suffering from a seasonal allergic condition. There is one more name on my list.'

'Is it anyone I know?'

'Sudhir Sabharwal visited me with complaints of severe itching on his hand and I prescribed the ointment for him.'

'Did he give any reason for the severe itching?' Acharya's voice had risen with excitement.

'He gave some stupid excuse, but I think it was caused due to contact with bichhu buti. I have seen enough such cases in Ramsar not to be deceived.'

'Are you sure, doc?'

'I don't make mistakes about such matters,' retorted the doc.

'Thank you, doctor. You have given us a big leg up.'

The colonel rushed inside excitedly. 'We've got a break,' he declared to no one in particular. 'Do you remember the tube we found in Laxmi's house?' he asked Tim.

'Yes, I do.'

'It must have fallen from Sabharwal's pocket. Dr Rawat called to confirm that he had prescribed hydrocortisone ointment for the guy.'

'I have some news too. The information could make our task simpler,' said Tim.

'What's the news?'

'I just got a call from my friend at the forensic laboratory. One of the hair samples submitted by us match the ones found in the van and on Laxmi's person.' Tim's eyes were shining with excitement.

'Don't tell me they match those of Sabharwal?'

'Yes, they do. The guy does not have a leg to stand on.'

'Let's see what he has to say about these pieces of evidence,' suggested Roxy, his fingers beating an impatient tattoo on the table. He had been listening to the entire conversation with interest. 'What a bloody scoundrel! My hands are itching to give him a few whacks if he doesn't cooperate.'

'Let's grab a quick lunch before dealing with the rogue,' Tim suggested. 'It may take longer to break the guy than we assume.'

'Good idea!' seconded Roxy. 'I haven't had breakfast this morning. There is a dhaba close by. It is nothing more than a shack with a few spindly chairs and a couple of charpoys but the food is pretty decent.'

'Sounds good,' said Acharya.

Fifteen minutes later, they sat down to a delicious repast of simple fare at the dhaba, which was a stone's throw away from the police station. The lunch was as good as promised.

'I think we should check on Shubham Sharma. It's been a couple of hours since we brought him here.' Tim got to his feet. Seated in Roxy's office, the three men were enjoying a smoke after the heavy lunch.

'What's the hurry?' Roxy remarked. He blew a ring of smoke. 'Let the man stew in his own juices for a while. Keeping them in suspense is the best way to cow them. I have seen it work on the toughest of hoodlums.'

'How long do you propose to keep him in suspense?' asked the colonel. He was not in favour of using crude methods to break down suspects. 'We can't keep him overnight.'

'Who says that? We can keep him for two nights, if required. There's no point in letting him go without achieving the aim, is there? You want him to give a statement and I think we should hold him till he gives one,' Roxy proposed. 'Why are you worried, Colonel? I have broken stronger fellows than Shubham Sharma.'

'So what do you suggest?' Tim asked his friend.

'It's almost 3 now. Let's go to my place. My wife is away, so you won't have to be decorous. You can relax for a while and freshen up. We could play a few games of cards and have tea. My Jeeves is good at making kadak chai. We will visit Sharma around 6. I am confident that he will be willing to toe the line.'

It seemed a good idea, so the three of them clambered into Roxy's car. At 6, refreshed and in high spirits, they returned to the police station.

28

The sun sank lower in the sky and daylight ebbed away. The room, with its solitary low-watt bulb, began humming with the buzz of mosquitoes and the clucking of house lizards. Shubham's spirits fell to a new low as the darkening sky diminished his hopes of an early release.

It had taken just two hours for Shubham to realize that he could be detained forever within the confines of the peeling walls unless he decided to cooperate with the police. His angry outbursts interspersed by bouts of crying remained buried within the room in the basement of the police station. He harboured no illusions about the local police. Roxy terrified him.

'Get me out of here, please,' desperate for a lungful of fresh air, he begged, his voice rising with each word. 'Help me, please.'

No one heard him. No one cared.

Throat parched, he continued to whimper.

Swatting the bloodthirsty mosquitoes, he paced the room. They had taken away his phone, and he had no way of knowing the time, but he guessed it to be close to 6.30 p.m.

Then he heard footsteps. The unmistakable sound of a walking stick tapping down the steps reached his ears. The colonel had arrived.

They were coming for him.

His mind was made up by the time the three men reappeared in the dingy storeroom. He would make one last effort before giving in. Squaring his shoulders, he sat down and faced his interrogators.

'How are you, Sharma?' asked Acharya.

Shubham Sharma felt his hopes rising. From the interactions he had in Ramsar, he had realized that the colonel was a decent man. He would not let Roxy torture him. Acharya's arrival renewed his hopes. *I will not succumb to threats*, he decided.

'It is illegal to detain a man without an arrest warrant,' Sharma raised his voice. 'You have nothing against me. No evidence and no arrest warrant. I was brought here by force, and that's called kidnapping. Even police officers are not allowed to kidnap, I know.'

'You were kidnapped by a police officer and brought here in a police vehicle. Right? Why don't you report the matter?' Roxy jabbed him in the chest with his forefinger.

'I can do that only after you release me. By the way, how long do you intend to hold me here?' The impudence was back in Shubham's behaviour. He was sure of the colonel's support. 'You can't expect to get away with this. I will approach the higher authorities with my complaint.'

'By all means, approach the higher authorities. Do you want the police commissioner's office address and phone number? I could help you with the information. Or do you want to approach the chief minister? I could give you the phone number.'

'I have committed no crime and you have no evidence of wrongdoing. Holding and harassing an innocent citizen is a crime too.' Sharma continued his protest.

'This is going to stretch into a long session,' declared Roxy. He walked to the door and hollered for the constable. Just as Sharma was wondering if he would order the hefty cop to beat the daylights out of him, Roxy asked the chap to fetch three chairs.

The chairs were brought and the three men settled comfortably before continuing the interrogation.

'A tube of hydrocortisone ointment was found at the scene of the crime and Dr Rawat has confirmed that he had prescribed the medicine for you,' the colonel said.

There was silence for a couple of minutes as Sharma digested the information. The trapdoor had begun closing.

'That proves nothing. How can you connect me with a tube of ointment found at the scene of the crime? There must be dozens of people using hydrocortisone ointment. Yes, I had gone to the doc for consultation and he prescribed the ointment, but I neither visited Laxmi's house nor dropped the tube there,' Sharma blustered unconvincingly.

'That is a valid argument. There are a lot of people who use hydrocortisone ointment,' endorsed the colonel. 'But your fingerprints will certainly not be found on their tubes. I will be happy if you could tell me how your fingerprints happened to land on that tube?'

Shubham's eyes darted wildly around the room as his brain struggled to come up with an explanation. *Darn! The tube must have fallen out of my pocket when I took out the nylon rope.* 'It … it …proves n-nothing,' he stammered incoherently. 'I dropped the tube somewhere. Someone must have picked it up …'

'… and dropped it in Laxmi's house,' Acharya finished the sentence for him. 'There's also the possibility that the tube of ointment walked to her house to say hello.'

'That's the most ridiculous excuse I have ever heard.' Tim snorted. 'Even if we were to ignore the fingerprints on the tube, there is enough evidence to incriminate you in the two murders.'

'What evidence did you come upon now?' Sharma sniggered.

'For your information, I received a call from the forensic laboratory a while ago. Your hair sample matches the strands found in the van in which Dabral's body was found. It also matches the ones found on Laxmi's person. Not just that, your DNA also matches the tissues found under her nails.'

'You really do amuse me. Where and when did you find a sample of my hair?' Sharma was sure Tim was bluffing.

'I got them from the barber at the cremation ground. You went to the extent of getting your hair cut by a barber during the cremation, just to prove you were a close relation of Dabral. In fact, I collected hair samples of Nisha as well. We sent both the samples for forensic investigation.'

Aware that a DNA match spelt doom, Shubham paled at Tim's words. His head throbbed and he felt faint. The evidence against him was stacking up. He realized the folly of his actions. *I should have been more careful.* Desperate, he wondered if there was some way to bargain for a lesser punishment.

'By the way, Nisha has accused you of murdering her husband,' Acharya informed the hapless man, extinguishing his last flicker of hope. 'She has also been arrested and has given a statement to that effect.'

'Bloody bitch! She is lying,' Sharma raged. 'I didn't want to kill Deepak. It was all Nisha's idea. She plotted, planned and goaded me into committing the crime. I won't allow her to get away with lies.'

'Be reasonable, Sharma. While the police have ample proof to send you to the gallows, they have no evidence against her,' said the colonel.

'From what you have said, it is evident that Nisha is a very cunning woman. She has planned well. Unfortunately, it is impossible for us to convict her without proof.'

'You can't let her get away with the murder,' Sharma said with a shocked expression on his face. 'If I am hanged, she must hang too. I might be the hands that killed, but she was the brain behind the murder.'

'There is a way to convict her,' Tim said. 'But for that, the police will require a signed statement from you.'

'I will give you a signed statement.' Now that he was convinced of his conviction, Sharma was unwilling to allow his accomplice to get away.

Roxy pushed a sheaf of papers and a pen towards Shubham. 'Put down the entire sequence of events in detail,' he ordered.

'May I have a glass of water?' requested the wretched chap, his lips trembling with emotion. Feeling light-headed and dizzy, he gulped down the water brought by a constable.

Roxy, alerted by the ashen look on the young man's face, spoke in a low voice to the constable. A few minutes later, the policeman reappeared with tea and some biscuits.

'We are not entirely heartless, as you can see,' said Roxy, noting the thankful look in Shubham's eyes. 'All we wanted was your cooperation. Had you agreed to help, there would not have been any need to detain you.'

A few minutes later, his hands shaking, the young man began writing.

'Why did you kill the poor woman?' asked the colonel after Shubham handed over his statement. He could not get over the guilt of not preventing the woman's death. 'Laxmi had done you no harm.'

Shubham shook his head regretfully. 'I had no intention of killing the woman. It was not a part of our plan, but I panicked when she visited the police station. She had spotted me in disguise and suspected my involvement in the crime. Nisha felt it would be dangerous to let the woman live.'

'Don't you regret committing two murders in cold blood?'

'It's too late for regrets.' Shubham drew a deep breath. 'However, I am satisfied that Nisha won't get away.'

The determined look on the young man's face convinced his interrogators that the last hurdle in their path had been cleared. With a signed statement from Shubham, Nisha Dabral's arrest would pose no difficulty.

The colonel's strategy of playing one against the other had worked wonderfully. Satisfied, the trio trooped into Roxy's office to consider the next course of action.

'I think it is time to speak to the DSP,' suggested the colonel as they sipped the strong and sugary ginger-flavoured tea supplied by the dhaba. 'Considering the evidence, he should have no objection to sending arrest warrants for Shubham and Nisha.'

'He will have a seizure when he realizes that Gudyal will walk free.' Tim chortled. 'JBS does not take kindly to being proved wrong. Besides, he has given statements to the press and boasted of arresting the perpetrator of the twin murders. He will have to eat his words.'

The colonel was aware of the DSP's fondness for bragging. He loved hogging publicity and had no compunction about robbing others of the credit.

'I am sure he won't be very happy to hear the news, but we can't afford not to inform him about the events that unfolded in the last twenty-four hours.'

Tim was clearly reluctant to carry out the task. 'Would you do the honour of speaking to JBS?' he asked Acharya. 'I am on leave, remember?'

'Definitely not. Come on, Tim, he is your boss and you are officially bound to report the matter to him. Anyway, I am sure he would have received the forensic reports by now. That alone should be sufficient to get him thinking.'

Reluctantly, Tim punched the boss's number on his phone.

'Hello, Tim. Are you back from leave?' Bulldog lobbed the question.

'I am in Delhi, sir.'

'Well, what do you want now?' growled the DSP. 'Hope you don't want to extend your leave, because I will not grant you a single day's extension.'

'I want you to arrange for arrest warrants for Shubham Sharma and Nisha Dabral. We will also require a police escort for taking the two back to the police headquarters in Almora.'

'Who the hell is Shubham Sharma and why should I send you an arrest warrant?'

The DSP was behaving in his usual blustering manner. Slow on the uptake, he would require a long explanation before agreeing about the warrants.

Drawing a deep breath, Tim explained, 'Shubham Sharma has murdered Deepak Dabral and Laxmi Badola. Nisha Dabral is an accomplice in the crime.'

'Are you insane? How can this Sharma chap be the murderer? Gudyal is the killer and he is in the lock-up.'

It was obvious that JBS had not seen the forensic reports. Realizing it was going to take a very detailed explanation, Tim flopped on a chair and began speaking. Fifteen minutes and a dozen questions later, the DSP was caught up with the happenings. The facts put him in a worse mood. It was going to be embarrassing for him to explain the events to the commissioner. Also, the police would have to admit the gaffe to the press. Gudyal might issue his own statements to the newspaper after being released from the lock-up. The thought of having to backtrack on his statements upset JBS more than anything else.

'I will be damned!' he cursed.

'The colonel is with me. In fact, he was convinced that Gudyal was being framed. He is the one who insisted we journey to Delhi to investigate the matter.'

JBS brooded for a few minutes, trying to swallow his pride. It was so unfair. Each time he thought he had cracked a case, the colonel proved him wrong. He managed to find the culprit, and walk away with all the glory. Shaking off the negative thoughts, he tried to concentrate on Tim's words.

'We have put Shubham Sharma in the lock-up at Khajoori Khas police station. Since the detention is unofficial, keeping him here could prove difficult. I would request you to see that the arrest warrants are faxed as soon as possible.'

'Wait for my call,' instructed the DSP.

To his credit, once he had got over the initial reaction, JBS responded with remarkable swiftness. Within the next twenty-four hours, arrest warrants had been faxed to Roxy's office and a couple of policemen, along with a woman constable, had been despatched to escort Shubham and Nisha to Almora.

'Keeping in mind that the accused may try to escape, they will have to be kept under close watch throughout the journey,' JBS instructed over the phone. 'By the way, I am treating your Delhi visit as an official trip. So you will be entitled to the allowances and reimbursements.'

'Thank you, sir,' said Tim, surprised by Bulldog's change of heart.

There was a momentary pause as JBS struggled with his ego. 'Let me speak to the colonel,' he said after a couple of heartbeats.

Winking at Acharya, Tim handed over the phone to him.

'Congratulations are in order, I guess. You have done it once again. I hate to admit it, but you have proved me wrong. I will exact revenge, one of these days.' The DSP cackled on the phone.

Acharya knew how difficult it must have been for JBS to swallow his pride and admit his blunder.

'We all make mistakes,' he said soothingly. 'My list of errors is long, JBS. One of these days, I will share it with you. Justice must be served, and that is all that matters. The wrong man should not hang.'

29

The last vestiges of the setting sun disappeared behind the mountains and the sky was filled with a beautiful medley of colours, punctuated with the occasional glitter of the evening star.

For Tim and the colonel, it had been an exhausting day, packed with action. Right from the arrival of the policemen and policewoman in Delhi sent by the DSP, to Nisha's dramatic arrest, followed by the long journey to Almora, each step had been a challenging one. The journey was anything but easy. Nisha tried to make one last attempt at fleeing. Shubham insisted on seeing a doctor for an imaginary palpitation of his heart.

It was only after Nisha and Shubham had been handed over to the police headquarters that Tim and Acharya heaved a sigh of relief. They set Gudyal free, and the news of his release spread like wildfire through the town. It evoked endless debates and discussion about police ineptness and the injustice meted out to Gudyal. The once-unpopular chap became an object of public sympathy.

For the first time since their arrival in Ramsar, the mother and son found themselves as the centre of attention. A group of people, some curious to hear the inside story and some out of compassion, came calling on the duo. And, for the first time, they were received with warmth.

The next day saw considerable excitement in the spacious living room of Rhodo Cottage, where a gaggle of people sat waiting for the denouement. It was time to hear the full story and the colonel, a skilful raconteur, was about to narrate it. Acharya stood smiling at the centre, with the others seated around him.

A lot had happened in the last one week. The two consecutive murders had shattered the peace of Ramsar and given sleepless nights to many people. Now that the real culprits had been arrested, the town heaved a collective sigh of relief. Once again, the colonel, with his uncanny ability to sniff out the perpetrator, had led Tim to the right place.

Prominent among those gathered at Rhodo Cottage were Pia and Violet, both of them relieved after the arrests. They had decided to invest in a new van.

Umesh Gudyal and his mother sat at the back, waiting to hear the story. The woman had brought a box of sweets to celebrate her son's release.

JBS had taken care to seat himself in the front, so he could seek clarification for the doubts that crowded his mind. The colonel was in no hurry to divulge anything. He liked the tension and drama that filled the room as his audience waited with bated breath.

The Bhandaris were also present at the gathering. Dabral's murder had taken place on the evening of the party thrown by them. Besides, they had hosted Nisha Dabral in their guest room and sympathized with her. The news of her complicity in the murder had come as a shock to the family.

'Ladies and gentlemen.' Acharya cleared his throat and ran his eyes around the room. 'It has been a trying time for everyone. I know that there has been insecurity among the townsfolk ever since the two murders.'

The DSP wished he would stop beating around the bush. It was getting late and he had to get back to Almora.

'I am sure everyone is dying to hear the story, Colonel,' he growled. 'Please trim the frills and get to the point.'

'A little wait will do you no harm, JBS,' Acharya chided the fidgeting officer. 'Tim and I toiled hard to unravel the mystery. The least you can do is hear me out till the end.'

Sensing several eyes on him, the DSP shifted embarrassedly in his seat. He hated the patronizing manner in which the colonel was treating him.

Turning to the audience, the colonel began. 'I will deal with the two murders in the sequence they were committed. The first one was committed during the party held at Bhandari Villa. The victim was a guest, a stranger to Ramsar with no connection to the town. The body was found in Violet's van, which had been pushed down the gorge. The man had been hit with a rolling pin that belonged to Pia, Violet's granddaughter. What baffled me was the fact that the van was in neutral gear. No one parks a car in neutral gear, nor did Pia. I checked with her about the gear and she confirmed having put it in gear along with the handbrake. Yet a car cannot be rolled when in gear, so the killer must have put it in neutral before pushing it down the ravine. Pia couldn't have killed Dabral since she was at the coffee counter throughout the evening. When she came out at the end of the party, accompanied by her assistant, the van was missing. I have no shame in admitting that the case mystified me.

'As usual, the list of suspects was headed by Nisha Dabral, the young wife of the victim. She had a rock-solid alibi. The lady hadn't left the party for a moment, neither did any of the guests who attended the party. Dabral had been seen leaving the venue at around 8.40 that evening, to keep his appointment with Umesh, who, we later found, is Dabral's cousin. The two of them had exchanged angry words over their uncle Ratan Negi's property.

'It got me thinking. Then Laxmi reported having seen Dabral and Umesh arguing. Her statement gained strength when Nisha and her brother handed us a note in which Umesh had asked Dabral to meet him at 9 p.m. at Negi Mansion. The motive, opportunity and means fitted the assumption that Umesh had killed his cousin. All evidence pointed to his guilt. But something troubled my mind. It was a little too pat.'

Acharya paused for his words to sink into the brains that were busy processing the information.

'Now, let's come to the next murder. This time, the victim was Laxmi Badola, a harmless albeit nosy woman. It was her nosiness that killed her. She had nothing to do with Deepak Dabral. The only thing that tied her to the first murder was a statement that she had seen the victim arguing with Umesh. It didn't make sense. If Umesh had committed the first murder, why would he kill Laxmi after she had shared the information with the police? Laxmi's murder proved the innocence of Umesh Gudyal.'

'How could Laxmi's murder prove Gudyal's innocence?' asked the DSP, perplexed at Acharya's statement.

'It is simple. If Gudyal had to kill Laxmi, he would have done so before she came to the police station to report his argument with the victim. There was no point in killing her after she had shared the information with us,' explained the colonel.

Although the DSP grunted to express his doubt about the inference, several heads in the audience nodded in agreement with the explanation.

'Ladies and gentlemen, it is important to pay attention to the incidents that took place on the day of the second murder. On the morning before her murder, Laxmi rushed to the police station to report the sighting of a suspicious stranger, but we were too busy to hear her statement. The poor woman was asked to return the next day. She went back and was murdered the same night. That raised my antennae. Why would the poor woman be murdered unless she had seen or heard something?

'It was clear that her death had something to do with the second visit, when she went back without having the opportunity to share her information with the police. Someone wanted to stop her before she went back to the police station the next day.'

Acharya took a sip of the lukewarm tea sitting on a side table near him.

'Laxmi Badola's murder was as puzzling as the earlier one. Though we found enough evidence that led to Umesh Gudyal, there were many disquieting factors.' He resumed the narration. 'We found a cigarette butt in a flowering pot near the front door of Laxmi's house. It was a brand Umesh smokes. An expensive pen that belonged to him was found near the victim's body. That convinced me of Umesh's innocence. He is a fairly intelligent man and no intelligent killer leaves so many traces. The cigarette butt was a dead giveaway. Why would Umesh leave a cigarette butt outside the victim's door, especially when he lived across her house? It was clear that the evidence had been planted at the crime scene with the sole intention of misleading the investigation. The killer was trying to implicate Gudyal and his effort succeeded to a certain extent. At least one person was convinced of Gudyal's culpability.'

Aware the colonel was mocking him, the DSP fidgeted in his chair. 'Bloody asshole,' he muttered under his breath.

'What led you to suspect the real culprits?' Violet asked.

'It took me a couple of days to fit the pieces of the puzzle. I was uneasy about Sudhir Sabharwal's sudden appearance in Ramsar. Although he professed to be Nisha's brother, their behaviour was not that of siblings. Eyes often give people away. I had noticed the way they looked at each other when they suspected no one was looking at them. The angry rashes on Sudhir's hands, along with constant itching, aroused my curiosity. It niggled at my mind. While at Laxmi's house, I found a tube of hydrocortisone ointment under the couch. When I asked the doc about the ointment, he told me that the ointment is prescribed for skin rashes, itching and allergies.

'A tiny statement made by him caught my attention. The locals are often prescribed the medicine to cure the rashes caused by the bichhu buti found in the hills of Ramsar, he said. As we all know, the buti has therapeutic uses and is used by locals as a natural diuretic and laxative. It is also used as a dish because it is highly nutritious.

'I went around the area where the van was found and discovered that it was teeming with stinging nettle. The tiniest bit of carelessness could lead to contact with it. While the locals would handle the buti carefully to avoid contact, an outsider was not likely to know about the irritation and rashes cause by contact. That was the first mistake made by Dabral's killer.'

There was absolute silence in the room as Acharya's audience listened to the story. There were many unasked questions, but no one wanted to break the spell.

'When Urmila, Laxmi's best friend and confidante, came to the police station to meet us, I was convinced about the killer being an outsider. She told us about the incident in which Laxmi had collided with a stranger, who got into Kallu's SUV. For some reason, the man aroused Laxmi's suspicions. We asked Kallu to describe the passenger and based on the description, an artist sketched a portrait of the man. When the portrait was shown around Almora, the manager of a hotel identified him as Shubham Sharma, who stayed at the hotel for one night. He also produced the details of the driving licence submitted by Sharma as identity proof.'

There was a gasp of surprise at the introduction of an ominous character.

'It added to the confusion in our minds. Who was Shubham Sharma? Did he have anything to do with Dabral's murder? What was he doing in Ramsar? While my mind was riddled with these questions, I knew that his presence in Ramsar on the night of the murder could be a mere coincidence. I wanted to investigate the man before ruling out his involvement in the crime. With that aim in mind, I decided to travel to the address provided in the driving licence.

'In the meantime, on the DSP's insistence, Tim had arrested Umesh Gudyal. Although I was convinced of his innocence, it was essential to lull the murderer into a sense of security. Tim accompanied me on my journey to the capital. In Delhi, we stumbled upon a string of disjointed information. Shubham Sharma, whom we were tracking, had changed his address. The only address we could find was the one of his office. Nisha was also unavailable at home, but we learnt a few things about her and managed to get her office address too. It was a lot of legwork.'

Acharya paused once more to study the effect of his words. He wanted the audience to realize the effort that had gone into the two arrests. Satisfied with the reactions that ranged from an appreciative nod to a quizzical look, he resumed his spiel.

'To our surprise, Shubham and Nisha worked in the same office. By now, we had discovered a link between the two. Shubham was Nisha's boyfriend. More surprise was in store for us. We learnt that the man we knew as Sudhir Sabharwal was, in fact, Shubham Sharma. He had masqueraded as her brother and given a false name in Ramsar. It was clear that we had to take the guy for questioning, but there was a major hurdle in our path. Tim had taken leave to visit Delhi. He had no authority to arrest or detain anyone. He sought the help of his academy batchmates and they helped with a venue and vehicle.

'It took a bit of effort to get our hands on Shubham Sharma and call his bluff. While we were questioning the slimy guy,

I got a call from the doc confirming that he had prescribed hydrocortisone ointment for Sudhir Sabharwal. At the same time, Tim received a call from the forensic laboratory informing him that the strand of hair found in the van as well on Laxmi's person matched Shubham's hair sample.'

'Where did you find his hair sample?' asked JBS suspiciously.

'Tim was enterprising enough to obtain it from the barber who had chopped Sudhir Sabharwal's hair at the crematorium,' informed the colonel. 'When we confronted Shubham with the information, he broke down and admitted to have acted on Nisha's behest. He also obliged us with a written statement, which implicated Nisha.'

'The point is, why did they kill two people?' Pia wanted to know. 'If it was for love, there are easier ways than killing. Nisha could have divorced her husband and married Shubham.'

'It's not so simple. Lust and lucre caused Dabral's murder. Not only had the man amassed a lot of wealth and property, the shipping company that employed him had bought a hefty life insurance for him. Being the sole beneficiary of the insurance and wealth, the husband's death would make her a very rich woman. By removing Dabral from the path, Shubham Sharma could marry her, and become rich too.'

'I feel sorry for Laxmi. The poor woman had no reason to be killed,' commented the judge.

'So do I. She became a liability for the killer because she had spotted him.' Acharya shook his head regretfully.

'Why did the two lovers decide on Ramsar as the venue for the crime? They could have killed Dabral in Delhi,' said Umesh Gudyal, who could not get over his horrific experience. 'Then Laxmi wouldn't have died.'

'Nisha and Shubham had murder on their mind, but they were waiting for the right opportunity. Dabral had two things on his mind while angling for an invitation to Bhandari's wedding party. He wanted to discuss the property matters with Umesh and check out the place too. Little did he know that he was receiving an invitation to die. For Nisha, it was the perfect setting to carry out the crime. Shubham travelled to Almora, disguised himself and came to Ramsar a little after 8 p.m. and checked out the cars parked along the ridge. Fortune favoured his plan. Pia had not only parked her van at the edge of the ridge, she had carelessly left the door of the van unlocked. It suited the killer's purpose. While looking for a weapon, he found the heavy rolling pin in the van's back seat. Armed with that, he waited for Dabral to emerge from Bhandari Villa.

'Nisha had already informed Shubham about the meeting at 9 p.m. He intercepted Dabral on the pretext of having brought a fresh note from Umesh. Not only did he halt the victim, he also suggested they walk to the street light so he could read the note. It was while Dabral was bent over the piece of paper, trying to read the matter in the street light, that Shubham hit him with the rolling pin. He was then dragged and put in the driver's seat of the van, which was in neutral gear and pushed down the ravine. Unfortunately, the van didn't go down all the way. Its downward journey was blocked by a large boulder.'

A collective gasp went through the listeners as they visualized the gruesome murder.

'That was when Shubham panicked. Using a torch to light his path, he hazarded a descent down the slope to check if the victim was dead. That was a big mistake. He tripped and fell near a bush of stinging nettle. After confirming that Dabral was dead, he went back to the bus station and travelled to Almora for the night. The next day, he was back as Sudhir Sabharwal, Nisha's brother. The second mistake he made was to go to Dr Rawat for a prescription. His brush with the stinging nettle had caused angry rashes and welts along with severe itching. The fingerprints found on the tube of hydrocortisone ointment found near Laxmi's body gave him away. Laxmi was a brave woman. She fought tooth and nail to save her life. A DNA test of the tissues found under the victim's nails also matched those of the murderer.'

'Didn't he stay at Hotel Misty Meadows as Sudhir Sabharwal? How did he prove his identity there?' Bulldog shot another question, hoping to faze the colonel.

'That stumped me initially,' admitted Acharya. 'In fact, I studied the copy of the Aadhar Card he had submitted as proof of identity. I asked him about it during the interrogation. Shubham confessed that he had a colleague called Sudhir Sabharwal. He managed to get a copy of the Aadhar Card from the colleague's personal file. The rest was simple. He scanned the card. Using a software, he affixed his own picture above the original one and printed a copy. The tampered photocopy was the one he gave at Misty Meadows.'

'So he produced two different identity proofs at the two hotels, one in Almora and the other in Ramsar?' Laila interrupted the colonel.

'Yes, he submitted the fake Aadhar Card at Hotel Misty Meadows, and flashed the genuine driving licence at the Almora hotel,' Acharya explained.

'You have to hand it to him. The guy is smart. It must have been tough to nail him,' said JBS grudgingly. 'How did you manage to extract a confession?'

'The long detention at Khajoori Khas police station and the pile of evidence had done the trick, but it was the fear of having to spend the night in the company of rats that broke him down. The man has murophobia. Credit for his confession should go to the pack of rodents who scurried around the room where he had been locked. Not only did he give a signed confession, he narrated the entire sequence of events, which was recorded by Tim on his phone.'

An appreciative murmur went through the crowd.

'Can you take us through the second murder?' suggested Violet, who had been quiet so far.

'Nisha and Shubham were present at the police station when Laxmi rushed there to tell us about the stranger she had seen at the bus stand. When the two heard of this, they panicked and decided that the woman had to die. That very night, Shubham strangled the poor woman. In his pocket he was carrying a packet of cigarettes of Umesh's favourite brand. The plan to implicate Umesh had been hatched right at the outset. On his way out of the victim's house, the killer dropped a cigarette butt in the potted plant just outside the door.'

'What about my pen? How did that land up there?' Umesh wanted to know.

'It must have fallen out of your pocket when you went to Laxmi's house to borrow the inhaler for your mother. You mentioned bending down to check her breathing, remember?' Acharya looked at the young man, who nodded sheepishly. 'You panicked on finding her dead and rushed out blindly.'

'All is well that ends well,' muttered the young man, who had almost been convicted for murders he didn't commit. Her eyes brimming with tears, Umesh's mother clasped his hand firmly in her hands.

While everyone seemed to be satisfied with the colonel's explanation, the DSP was not happy with the explanations. 'Why did Shubham use the rolling pin when he could have used the heavy torch he was carrying?'

'He may not have been confident that the torch was heavy enough to kill a person,' responded the colonel. 'Besides, the rolling pin could not be traced back to him. It would divert the police's mind.'

'I don't understand why he was carrying a torch in the first place.' Bulldog continued to look unconvinced.

'The exact reason can only be given by the man concerned.' Acharya threw a disarming smile at the doubting Thomas. 'I think he used the back alleys to avoid detection and knew that the torch would come in handy while picking his path through the dark lanes. All of us know that there are street lights only on the main roads and power cuts are not infrequent. The last thing he wanted was to be lost in the lanes of Ramsar.'

'The guy seems to be an astute planner,' remarked Tim. 'His moves had been very well planned.'

'That's right, Tim,' the colonel agreed. 'He had an accomplice in Nisha, and we all know that the two are intelligent young people. They almost succeeded in pulling off the stunt.'

'But they had not expected to cross swords with the colonel,' quipped the professor. 'Thanks to his sleuthing skills, no one gets away with murder in this town.'

'That's a very magnanimous statement, Professor. Let's hope I can keep your faith in my ability. However, I wish to point out that the credit for solving this case lies with Tim. I was just assisting him.' Acharya passed off all credit to the young man.

'Bravo!' shouted the judge. The bridge gang echoed his words.

'It is all because of Tim's efforts. He is a champion, one of a kind.' Acharya's words were directed towards the DSP, who never lost an opportunity to harass the young officer. 'He truly deserves your appreciation and applause.'

The crowd got to their feet, and the room resounded with a round of applause. The colonel lapped up the accolades with great relish. A tad embarrassed by the attention, Tim smiled self-consciously. His eyes were fixed on Pia, who was looking tenderly at him. Violet Williams blew him a kiss, and he reddened.

30

'You have another feather in your hat, Colonel,' Bulldog remarked, shaking hands with Acharya. 'I envy you.'

'Actually, I should be the one envying you, JBS,' remarked the colonel. He was in a magnanimous mood. 'You did a commendable job by arranging the arrest warrants. Your swift action saved the situation.'

The physical and mental stress of the past few days had taken a toll on the colonel. Now that the excitement had ebbed, all he wanted was to sleep undisturbed.

'Ladies and gentlemen, I request all of you to join us for a celebratory cup of tea,' announced the judge just as the colonel was preparing to leave. 'Kindly proceed towards the dining table.'

'Hear, hear,' applauded his friends.

'Friends, I would like to make an announcement too,' said Violet, her eyes sweeping around the room. 'I request you to join us for a party on Saturday. It's my granddaughter's birthday and I want everyone to share our happiness. Although the birthday falls on Thursday, we have planned the party for Saturday, so everyone is able to attend. I will be sending out the cards, of course.'

Surprised at the announcement, Pia rolled her eyes. 'Gumma!' she hissed.

'It is good that the killers have been arrested before Pia's birthday. We can let our hair down and let the good times flow,' declared the colonel.

'To Pia's health!' said the professor, raising his glass of water.

'Cheers!' some more voices joined him.

All paths led to Elm Cottage the next Saturday. The bungalow wore a festive look, with lights and streamers decorating the lawn and the hall. Soft music floated in the air as the guests walked into the house. The mood, ambience—everything—was just right.

It was an eclectic guest list, with several neighbours and eminent people. A few waiters attired in smart uniforms floated around the room, their trays laden with drinks and snacks. Tim, smart in his casuals, sauntered in with the colonel and Laila. Together they raised a toast to Pia's health.

'I hope we will be raising another toast soon,' Claire whispered into Violet's ear.

'At a wedding,' added the irrepressible grandmother.

Watching Tim and Pia, who were speaking in hushed voices, their heads close together, Claire raised her wine goblet and declared, 'Cheers to a happy ending!'

'Happy ending!' echoed the guests.

Acknowledgements

Writing another book in a series puts pressure on an author. Not only does the book have to be better than the previous ones, maintaining the continuity requires a conscious effort. It needs fine tuning, teamwork and tenacity. Finally, my manuscript has been completed, polished and is ready to go to press, and it's time to thank the people who helped me put it together.

There are so many people who have contributed to my growth as a writer. They have inspired me to continue on this rocky journey of writing.

I am grateful to my mother, who instilled the love for written word in me. To her goes the credit for whatever I am today.

To my father, I owe my fortitude, a trait I have inherited from him. It has enabled me to face the many challenging situations and curveballs thrown by life.

To my sisters who are my strongest allies, and friends, who continue to cheer my attempts.

A big thank you to Udayan Mitra for spotting potential in this series, and to the fabulous Swati Daftuar, who supported me all the way.

To Bidisha Srivastava and Shatarupa Ghoshal, the wonderful editors who helped me polish the manuscript.

To Gavin Morris for the beautiful cover.

As always, I am thankful to my husband, Ajoy, for the support and encouragement. I couldn't have done it without you.

Finally, a big round of thanks to my readers. They continue to inspire and motivate me with their love, support and feedback.

About the Author

Tanushree Podder worked in the corporate sector for eight long years before she quit the rat race to write.

A well-known travel writer and novelist, she is passionate about travelling and writing. Climate change and environment are of special interest to her. Tanushree enjoys writing in different genres. This has led to historical, crime and military books.

She has written eleven novels. Among her books are *Nurjahan's Daughter, Boots Belts Berets, On the Double, Escape from Harem, A Closetful of Skeletons, Before You Breathe, No Margin for Error, Decoding the Feronia Files, The Teenage Diary of Laxmibai, The Girls in Green and Spooky Stories.*

Two of her books, *Boots Belts Berets* and *The Girls in Green,* will soon be adapted into web series.

Tanushree lives with her husband in Pune.

The small and peaceful hill town of Ramsar wakes up to mysterious break-ins on two consecutive days. While the first one takes place at the local doctor's clinic, the second is at the residence of the town's latest and most affluent resident—Shekhar Sharma.

Inexplicably, nothing has been stolen in either case. The mysterious incidents confounded the police as well as Ramsar's residents.

And before one mystery can be solved, another turns up, with a death of a stranger whom no one can identify.

And so begins a game of cat-and-mouse between the criminal and the town's resident amateur sleuth, Colonel Arjun H. Acharya.

Who is intent on wreaking havoc in Ramsar? And can Colonel Acharya find out the truth before time runs out?

.